A Book Sense Children's Pick
A Junior Library Premier Selection

"Fast-paced and suspenseful. . . . There's a lot to like in this science-fiction adventure."
—*Kirkus*

"Will keep many a reader up nights for 'just one more chapter.'"
—*VOYA*

"With subtlety, Carman delivers a strong message. A fluid and compelling fantasy and mystery." —*Publishers Weekly*

"Readers will be caught up in the accessible, sci-fi premise, extended with evocative illustrations. Meaty points about privilege and ecological responsibility will provoke thought."
—*Booklist*

"This is a lively and absorbing adventure. . . . There is plenty of danger and mystery, too, for young adventurers who will eagerly follow Edgar in his quest to save his world."
—*The Bulletin*

"A fast-action story with heart-stopping moments throughout. Readers will be riveted." —*KidsReads.com*

...ARMAN

THE DARK PLANET

THE THIRD BOOK OF ATHERTON

LITTLE, BROWN AND COMPANY
New York   Boston

For Skip, fellow traveler

Little, Brown and Company

Hachette Book Group
237 Park Avenue, New York, NY 10017
Visit our website at www.lb-kids.com

Little, Brown and Company is a division of Hachette Book Group, Inc.
The Little, Brown name and logo are trademarks of Hachette Book Group, Inc.

First Paperback Edition: June 2010
First published in hardcover in May 2009 by Little, Brown and Company

Library of Congress Cataloging-in-Publication Data

Carman, Patrick.
The dark planet / by Patrick Carman.—1st ed.
p. cm.—(Atherton ; bk. 3)
Summary: After the destruction of the planet Atherton, Edgar must journey to a dark and damaged world named Earth in order to find the secrets of his civilization's past.
ISBN 978-0-316-16675-1
[1. Science fiction.]   I. Title.
PZ7.C21694Dar 2009
[Fic]—dc22   2008014196

10 9 8 7 6 5 4 3

RRD-C

Printed in the United States of America

TABLE OF
CONTENTS

THE WORLD OF ATHERTON viii

THE KEY CHARACTERS OF ATHERTON xi

PART 1: THE DOCKING STATION

PROLOGUE: The Silo 5

CHAPTER 1: Over the Edge 13

CHAPTER 2: The Dark Planet 21

CHAPTER 3: Edgar's Secret Revealed 31

CHAPTER 4: Down the Longest Shard 42

CHAPTER 5: Across the Burning Bridge of Stone 54

CHAPTER 6: A Leap of Faith 64

CHAPTER 7: 4200 72

CHAPTER 8: The Docking Station 84

CHAPTER 9: The Raven 93

PART 2: THE SILO

CHAPTER 10: The Forsaken Wood 111

CHAPTER 11: The Key to Mulciber 122

CHAPTER 12: Spikers 130

CHAPTER 13: Into the Silo 141

CHAPTER 14: The Way of the Yards 154

CHAPTER 15: Powder Blocking 165

CHAPTER 16: The Centurion. 181

CHAPTER 17: L-I-F-T-B-5 191

CHAPTER 18: The Vine Room 207

CHAPTER 19: The Widest River. .221

CHAPTER 20: The Passageway of Lies 231

CHAPTER 21: Dr. Harding's Laboratory 246

CHAPTER 22: Hope 257

CHAPTER 23: On Gossamer's Wings. 267

CHAPTER 24: The Yards. 280

CHAPTER 25: Dr. Harding Returns. 297

CHAPTER 26: A Spiker on the Beach 306

CHAPTER 27: The Chill of Winter 318

CHAPTER 28: The Story of Atherton Finds Its End. 334

THE WORLD OF
ATHERTON

If you read The House of Power *or* Rivers of Fire *but it's been a while since you turned the last page, you might benefit from this brief reintroduction to the story and the characters of Atherton. If, on the other hand, you know nothing of the climbing boy Edgar, the mad scientist Dr. Maximus Harding, or the collapse and inversion of the three levels of Atherton, then this introduction will be helpful reading. See you on the inside!*

●

Atherton is a made world, forged by the mind of a madman. It is inhabited by volunteers from the Dark Planet, a future Earth ravaged by pollution and overpopulation. Every inhabitant of Atherton has undergone a kind of memory retraining, leaving them under the assumption that Atherton is the only world that's ever been, the only place they've ever known.

Atherton was originally created on three circular levels, each one smaller than the level below it. The lowest level — the Flatlands — was a vast, barren, and largely unknown place. The middle level was known as Tabletop and contained most of Atherton's people, all of whom were poor laborers charged with maintaining the groves of fig trees or herds of livestock (sheep and rabbits) that provided all means of sustenance. At the top, the lush and beautiful Highlands were inhabited by the ruling class, who controlled the sole source of water.

The Flatlands, Tabletop, and the Highlands were all separated by treacherous cliffs that established almost complete separation between the lands. But that distance exists no more.

By the time the third book of Atherton begins, the world of Atherton has undergone a complete transformation: The Highlands descended until no cliffs remained and the ruling class was forced to come face-to-face with the people of Tabletop. Soon after, the joined lands of Tabletop and the Highlands collapsed as well, until they became level with the Flatlands. The world was, quite literally, flat. The images below, drawn by Dr. Maximus Harding, will help you better understand what happened to Atherton in *The House of Power*.

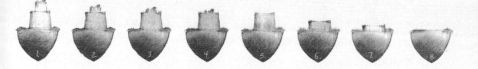

As Atherton changed, people from all three levels were forced to confront one another, choose sides, and ultimately decide whether they would stand together or apart against a mounting threat that arose from the Flatlands. Though many lives were lost, most chose wisely. For the transformation was not yet over: The center of their new world was sinking, and the source of water, whose origin was under the House of Power, rose until the entire center of Atherton was flooded. It turned into a vast lake, teeming with life for all of the survivors.

After the flood came peace. It was all part of the plan of the man who created this complex satellite world, Dr. Maximus Harding, who perished in the flooding of Atherton. But his plan did not end with the redemption of this refuge from the Dark Planet.

The Dark Planet will reveal the whole truth of the matter.

THE KEY CHARACTERS OF
ATHERTON

Dr. Maximus Harding

The creator of Atherton, Dr. Maximus Harding, was a mysterious man of science who drifted into madness over a period of years. Dr. Harding created not only the fantastic world of Atherton, but also the remarkable boy, Edgar. As one might imagine, Dr. Maximus Harding had a severe Dr. Frankenstein complex. When Edgar was hidden away against Dr. Harding's will, the scientist fell into deep madness and despair. It was then that Dr. Harding's alter ego, the cruel and treacherous Lord Phineus, came into being. Lord Phineus ruled over all Atherton for a time, but in the changing world the truth emerged and Dr. Harding was restored in the end. He died in the cataclysmic flood, leaving Edgar, his most precious creation, to find his own way in the world.

EDGAR

A young orphan and gifted climber who lived in the fig grove on Tabletop, scaling the cliffs of Atherton in secret. In his search for answers to Atherton's destiny, he became the only person on Atherton to have climbed above to the Highlands or below to the Flatlands. Through a series of events, Edgar discovers his true identity: He is the penultimate creation of Dr. Maximus Harding, the maker of Atherton.

SAMUEL

A boy formerly of the Highlands, he had lived within the House of Power under the watchful eye of Lord Phineus until he escaped in search of his new friend, Edgar, who appeared mysteriously one night from the land below.

ISABEL

A wily, bright girl of the grove and longtime friend of Edgar's who can use a sling with great skill. Samuel met Isabel in his search for Edgar, and together they embarked on a quest that trapped them under the House of Power during the great flood of Atherton. Their harrowing escape led them through the fiery center of Atherton — known as the Inferno — where Isabel nearly lost her life.

DR. LUTHER MEAD KINCAID

An old man of science, presumed at one time to be Edgar's father, but later discovered to be a mentoring figure to Dr. Maximus Harding. Dr. Kincaid has lost control of the world he helped build and now hopes to somehow reconnect with the Dark Planet, where Atherton was first envisioned.

Vincent

A protector of people on Atherton, he is charged with watching over Dr. Kincaid. He is the only other adult on Atherton who knows the complex history of Atherton and its mad maker, Dr. Maximus Harding.

Maude

A feisty woman from the Village of Rabbits, one of the three villages on Tabletop. She previously helped Edgar escape Sir Emerik and becomes one of a handful of leaders of the free world along with Horace and Wallace.

PART
ONE

THE DOCKING STATION

I go now beyond the forest and the field,
Where winter lay exhausted on a distant shore.
I will find you on the untouched paths of the sea.

Dr. Maximus Harding
Into Hidden Realms

PROLOGUE
THE SILO

It was the middle of the night when Red Eye and Socket came into the barracks and started walking between two long rows of beds. The bottoms of their boots were metal and so was the cold floor they stood on. Every step they took was like a deep and clanging word of warning. But it was their voices — like angry dogs that had been woken in the middle of the night — that woke the children.

"Don't . . . you . . . move!"

"One of you's out of bed!"

The voices cracked and echoed through the Silo, bouncing off steel walls and rusting rivets.

The rows of beds were as old as the Silo itself, and all the girls who slept in them awoke at once. The springs of thirty metal mattress frames jumped to life and made a sound like an orchestra preparing for a concert. Though, to be fair, none of the children in barracks number three had ever heard a violin or a flute or an oboe. There was no place for beautiful music in the strange world of the Silo.

"Stay put!" barked Red Eye. "No moving from those beds!"

"Or get the *bender!*" added Socket. The word slithered out of his mouth as a long and raspy whisper. He knew there was nothing children in the Silo feared more than a swat from the metal whip.

Each of the children became perfectly still, and the springs in the beds beneath them echoed into a chilling silence.

The lights were left off, which made the presence of these men at the foot of the beds all the more frightening. They carried the most dimly lit lanterns one could imagine in their left hands and thin, metallic rods in the other. *Benders.* All of the children had felt the sting of a bender for one cruel reason or another. They'd seen the long, thin bruise it left behind.

Red Eye and Socket reached over their backs and let go of their weapons. With a whirl, then a *clang*, the benders were gone. They seemed to have been devoured by a hidden, hungry eater of metal.

"Don't you move!" repeated Socket.

The two men each lifted the end of a bed to check its weight. When they were satisfied each bed was heavy enough to contain a child, they ceremoniously let the bed drop back to the floor with a teeth-rattling *bang!* — followed by a shocked yelp from the child within.

"We know one of you's out of your bed," seethed Red Eye. "We saw you!"

Bang! Bang! Two more beds were dropped. Someone let out a shriek.

In the silence that followed there arose a new voice. It was the small voice of a girl who, only a few moments ago, had opened the door to the barracks, wandered out into the long hallway, and let herself be seen by Red Eye and Socket. She spoke softly, but with great purpose.

"You didn't see me."

The voice came from above Red Eye and Socket, and then *bang! bang!* The two men dropped the bed rails they were holding and reached over their shoulders. The benders reappeared with the sound of snapping metal.

Red Eye and Socket stared into the darkness, holding their dim lanterns high, Socket tapping his bender anxiously against the metal toe of his boot. Red Eye swung his back and forth in the air overhead.

"We see you!" he cried. "Come down from there!"

But the girl who'd gotten out of bed had other plans. Her name was Aggie and she knew Red Eye and Socket wouldn't turn the lights on. In fact, if they could have it their way, the Silo would have no lights at all, because lights hurt their eyes. And this was what Aggie wanted.

To hurt them like they'd hurt her best friend, Teagan, a few hours before.

"You don't see me," repeated Aggie.

And they didn't. Aggie was crawling through the spiderweb of rusted steel girders that ran all through the ceiling of the barracks. And she was fast! Too fast for Red Eye and Socket.

The two men had an idea of what was about to happen, though they could hardly believe it was possible.

"Don't you do it!" cried Red Eye. He began fumbling in his pockets, searching for something.

Aggie hung from a beam by the door, holding steady above a certain white knob sticking out from a slick metal wall. The white knob that was for Red Eye and Socket only.

Aggie glanced down at the two rows of beds and saw that all the heads were covered with blankets as she'd instructed. Satisfied that everyone was safe, she let go of the beam. As Aggie fell she pulled her goggles down over her eyes from where they'd rested on her forehead. When she was within reach of the white knob, she grabbed it and pulled. The room was filled with the buzzing sound of fluorescent tubes.

And something else as well — light! A raging flood of light.

Red Eye and Socket screamed and fell to the floor. It felt to them as if someone had lifted their eyelids and dropped a burning circle of lit fuses inside. The feeling intensified even after they closed their eyes and searched their pockets.

By the time the two men had found their goggles and put them on, Aggie was already back in bed, eyes closed as she lay still under a thin blanket. Her goggles dangled from the bedpost.

"You're all wicked little creatures!" howled Socket.

"All of you!" cried Red Eye. They twisted their necks uncontrollably as if the effort might shake the sting from their eyes.

With the goggles safely attached, Red Eye and Socket saw the world as it had been before: dim and shadowy. Their eyes continued to burn and itch with a growing intensity. They knew from past experience that their damaged eyes would sizzle with nauseating pain into the morning. The headaches and the heat behind their eyes would follow. It was going to be a long, sleepless night for both of them.

"We'll be back before your shift!" screeched Red Eye, cringing from the growing agony behind his goggles. "You'd best give up your own for punishment. Give her up or you'll all get the bender! Every last one of you!"

"Stupid buzz cuts! Stupid little monsters!" yelled Socket.

The two men made for the door and Socket hastily turned off the light. Everything was dark again but for the soft glow of the lanterns. Teagan pulled the blanket down just enough to watch the shadows of Red Eye and Socket as they removed their goggles and scratched violently at their eyes, fouling the air with their angry cursing.

"You'll pay for this, you will!"

"All of you!"

Aggie felt the terrifying shaking of their steps as they moved off. When she was sure Red Eye and Socket were gone she got up on one shoulder and looked out over the thirty beds. She removed a thin nightcap and held it in her hand. *Stupid buzz cuts!* The cruel words rang in her ears as she felt along the prickly half inch of hair that remained on her head.

"Is everyone all right?" asked Aggie. "Kate? Ash? Teagan?"

Everyone assured Aggie they were all right. No one had been harmed.

"I'll tell them it was me in the morning," said Aggie. "They'll calm down a little by then."

No one protested. All the girls in barracks number three were glad to see Red Eye and Socket get some of their own medicine, but they also knew what it felt like to be hit with a bender.

Aggie put her nightcap back on and lay down, staring up into the darkness. There was a long silence, then a whisper from beside her.

"I hate this place," said Teagan. She was in the bed next to Aggie's, rubbing a long, thin bruise on her arm.

"I know," said Aggie. "I hate it, too."

They heard a faraway sound of something heavy slamming into the ground, followed by the muffled cry of an angry creature wailing outside. As hazardous as life was inside the Silo, it was even more treacherous in the forsaken wood.

"At least we're not out there."

Aggie nodded just a little. She pulled the itchy woolen cover up close to her face.

The pounding came again, closer now.

"What's going to happen to us?" asked Teagan.

Aggie turned to her best friend and wished she could see Teagan's blue eyes. But it was pitch-black in barracks number three.

"I don't know," she answered.

Aggie thought about the morning and the long, thin bruises it would bring. She thought about the many levels of the Silo in which she was held prisoner. She imagined the broken world outside and the curls of blond hair that had once hung about her shoulders. But mostly she thought of her birthday.

She had a secret on this particular night that she had chosen not to tell anyone.

In the morning she would be eleven years old.

4017 days.

A very bad thing to be in the perilous world of the Silo.

CHAPTER

1

OVER THE EDGE

"What's taking him so long?"

Isabel hated to admit it but she was worried about Edgar, and in the past this had always been a bad sign. She had a knack for knowing when Edgar was in terrible danger.

He's climbed to the Highlands and back again.

He's been inside Atherton and lived to tell about it.

He almost never falls.

This last thought turned out to be a bad one, because it reminded Isabel that even Edgar wasn't totally invincible. He'd fallen — just the one time — but all the same, he'd let his fingers slip and it had nearly killed him.

"We should have tried harder to discourage him," said her friend Samuel.

"It was only a matter of time," Isabel told him. "At least he let us tie him to a rock."

Isabel and Samuel were lying down on the ground a few feet away from the far edge of Atherton. Dr. Kincaid and Vincent, and all of the other adults, had forbidden them to go all the way out there by themselves. But Edgar had convinced Isabel and Samuel to come with him, so here they were. Only Edgar wasn't there anymore. He'd kicked his feet over the edge, turned over, and climbed down the curved side of Atherton.

A rope made from the twisted bark of the first-year fig trees ran between Isabel and Samuel. It was tied around a boulder that sat heavy and immovable twenty feet back.

"At least he's got the moonlight," said Samuel. "It will help."

"I don't know why he insists on doing this," said Isabel. She knew Samuel would understand her frustration. "With the lake in the middle, Atherton is *flat*. Why can't he accept it? I realize it's a lot for Edgar to get used to, but I don't understand why we can't convince him that Atherton's not made for climbing anymore."

Isabel touched the rope to see if she could feel Edgar's weight on the other end. She could not.

"I didn't believe he'd go through with it. I'm beginning to wonder if he's lost his mind."

"You do know why he's down there, don't you?" asked Samuel. The mere thought of Edgar hanging on to the bottom of Atherton made Samuel feel like throwing up. He was the least likely of the three to take risks that might get him killed.

"Because he loves to climb," Isabel replied, "and it's the only place left on Atherton where he can do it."

Samuel had been thinking a lot about this very topic.

"I think that's only part of the answer."

"He climbs for the thrill of it," said Isabel. "There's something in the climbing that makes him feel more . . . I don't know . . . alive. He tells me that all the time."

Isabel had moved forward and was now even closer to the edge than Samuel. Her head peeked out over the rim of the world. Samuel had made a point of holding back a few feet, but now he moved forward on his elbows, careful not to rise up too far into the watery current of gravity. He came alongside Isabel and glanced down.

Gazing over the edge, Samuel marveled at what he could see in the soft grey light. He'd seen it before when they'd come to look at night, but every time it surprised him. A distant orange light, the source of which he could not see, cutting through long chasms of stone on the bottom of Atherton.

"I think Edgar climbs for another reason," said Samuel, regaining his voice as he held the rope running between them.

"Why else would he do it?"

"I remember the first time I met Edgar," answered Samuel. "He had climbed all the way up to the Highlands before it collapsed. I thought he used magic to trick me into believing he'd done the impossible. But later — when he came back a second time — I stopped wondering *how* he could climb so high, and began asking myself *why* he had done it."

"And you've been thinking about it ever since?" asked Isabel.

Samuel nodded. "It's too dangerous to do it just because it's thrilling or even just because he loves doing it. I think something else drives him. Maybe Edgar began climbing as a means to an end. What if it was only ever about finding things, never about the climbing itself? What if he was always searching for something?"

Samuel took a deep breath and looked out into the stars.

"What if he's still searching for something?"

Isabel shook her head and sighed. "I just wish he'd find safer places to search for whatever it is he's looking for."

Isabel thought of how she, Samuel, and Edgar had become totally inseparable after the fall of Atherton. As the world had gone from three levels high to three levels deep, it seemed to have tried to destroy them with falling rocks, fierce quakes, and a billion gallons of rising water. Somehow the three of them had not only survived, they'd each played an important role in the evolution of Atherton.

But Edgar had never stopped feeling restless.

The rope between them moved ever so slightly and Isabel leaned out, craning her neck down in search of Edgar in the darkness below. For a while she'd been able to see him clearly, but he was too far away now.

She noticed that the rope seemed to lie differently than it had when he'd started. Gravity pulled everything in toward the bottom of Atherton, so the rope didn't exactly hang straight down. It curved inward with a big looping shape. She could not see its end.

"Edgar?" said Isabel. She couldn't yell his name too loudly. The village was only a half-hour walk away and voices carried something fierce on Atherton. What if someone were out looking for them? She said his name once more, a little louder, and then she scampered away from the edge and began hauling in the rope. It was much lighter than it should have been. The rope was a hundred feet long and as it piled up beside her she grew more and more afraid.

"Keep pulling!" said Samuel, still lying at the edge of Atherton. "I don't see him!"

Soon the end of the rope came over the edge with a soft snapping sound. There was no one tied to the other end.

Edgar was gone.

●

The rocky terrain of Atherton's outer shell was a perfect place for Edgar to regain his confidence. Giant rocks and fissures provided plenty of hand- and footholds. And the surface was bursting with sharp edges and protruding masses of grey and brown stone. The gravity on Atherton pushed against his back so his legs and arms didn't dangle out into the air. And yet, if he'd let go altogether, he felt certain he would freefall until he smacked into something hard. The thought of crashing into the bottom of Atherton made Edgar extra cautious as he continued down the curved side of the strange world he lived on.

One thing had made the going slow and tedious: the rope tied around his midsection, which had bothered him from the start. It kept getting in his way, wrapping around an arm or a leg and forcing him to rethink his position. And what was worse, the rope kept snagging on sharp rocks and jerking him to a stop as he descended. He actually felt unsafe with it tied around him.

He didn't want to scare Isabel and Samuel, so at first he'd

managed to untie the rope and put it between his teeth. But it kept snagging, pulling his head back, and soon he'd decided to let go of it altogether. He opened his mouth and let the rope swing lazily against the rocks.

"It hangs almost like someone's holding on," Edgar said aloud. "Maybe they'll think I'm still attached to it."

He looked down at the vast space left to be explored.

"Just a little farther . . ."

Samuel had only been half right when he'd guessed about what drove Edgar to climb. It was true Edgar had first begun climbing so long ago because he'd had a distant memory of something hidden in the stone walls above him and he wanted to find it. But somewhere along the way the climbing became something more.

There was something amazing about holding on to Atherton itself, like he was truly *part* of Atherton. Whenever he reached the top or the bottom of a climb he felt sadness at having to let go. It was like cutting himself away from the world.

Tonight Edgar wanted to go far enough to see where the orange light came from. There were two men Edgar had asked about this: Dr. Kincaid, the often secretive old man of science, and Vincent, Dr. Kincaid's protector and companion. Both men had lived in the Flatlands long before Atherton's violent collapse. They'd had years and years near the edge without anyone else around.

When he asked the two men about the light, they responded with what seemed to Edgar like rehearsed shrugs. Either they didn't know where the light came from or they wouldn't tell.

The light glowed brighter as Edgar traveled down a certain

fissure, but he couldn't guess how much farther it would be to its source. It looked like it might be a long way.

Edgar had come to where the sides of Atherton curved more sharply toward the bottom. It would be tougher going from here on out with a far greater chance of losing his grip. Still, Edgar decided to go a little bit farther, because Samuel had been partly right, too. Edgar *was* searching for something — he was always searching — and he had a deep feeling that climbing would bring him to something more. His heart told him that Dr. Harding, the maker of Atherton and so much more, had left him something else. He remembered the voice of Dr. Maximus Harding:

I made you, Edgar. Just as I made Atherton.

Edgar held this thought firmly in his mind as he felt his aching hands and forearms. Maybe he'd pushed hard enough on his first attempt at scaling these new, unknown places.

I don't want them to worry, Edgar reasoned to himself. He touched the side of Atherton with what one might describe as affection. "I won't be gone long," he said aloud. "You'll see me again."

He started back toward the flat surface of Atherton, racing up the side with alarming speed and skill. Edgar wanted to return in the light of day so that he could see the surface and better make his way to the very bottom. His fingers tingled with excitement at the thought of spending an entire day exploring this hidden world, a world only he could see.

This place is mine and mine alone, he thought.

When Edgar came to where he thought he should see the rope hanging and did not find it, he climbed faster. They had discovered him missing. Edgar felt terrible that Isabel and Samuel might think he'd fallen or been trapped below.

As he neared the top he glanced up and saw the silhouettes of two small heads — but a moment later they were gone.

By the time he had finally pulled up his head and shoulders and looked over the top edge of Atherton, Samuel and Isabel had moved back by the rock, their arms folded over their chests. And what was worse, the old, stooped figure of Dr. Kincaid stood with them — and he did not appear the least bit happy.

Edgar scrambled the rest of the way back onto Atherton and walked toward the three figures in the dark. "It's not as hard as I thought it would be," he began, hoping to head off questions before they started. "And I didn't go very far. Honestly — it was easy."

"We were worried about you," said Isabel. "I mean *really* worried. How could you leave the rope like that?"

Edgar wanted them all to understand that he felt safer when he was climbing than almost any other time. "You don't need to worry about me. At least not when I'm hanging on to a rock wall."

"Not very different from walking, right?" asked Samuel. He was closer to the truth than he might have imagined. As he and Isabel came toward Edgar they all smiled at one another at last.

That is, until they saw that Dr. Kincaid had turned away and begun the journey back home without them. There was a grave tone in his voice when he uttered the only words he would say on the long walk.

"All of you come with me. I have something to show you."

CHAPTER

2

THE DARK PLANET

There was a fire burning at the entrance to the cave Dr. Kincaid lived in. Soft light drifted into the opening that led inside, but Dr. Kincaid's closest companion was nowhere to be found.

"Where's Vincent?" asked Isabel. "He wouldn't just leave a fire burning like that, would he?"

Dr. Kincaid ignored her question. The long walk in the middle of the night had made the bottoms of his old feet ache. He slumped heavily on a wooden bench and waved his walking stick in the direction of a row of low, fat boulders on the other side of the fire.

"Sit down — all of you."

Edgar, Samuel, and Isabel did as they were told, wondering just how much trouble they were in.

"Vincent likes to scout at night," said Dr. Kincaid, returning to Isabel's question now that the pressure was off his feet. "He's been going out later and longer, but he'll return before dawn."

The old man breathed a deep sigh and looked at the glowing embers. He laid the walking stick across his lap and tapped it slowly. Lately he'd been carrying the walking stick everywhere he went and, as far as Edgar could tell, Dr. Kincaid never let it out of his sight. He seemed to have gone from merely old to ancient in the space of a year. His hair was whiter than it had once been. His big ears flopped more freely and his eyes drooped heavily over a long nose. He was nearing the grave, and what remained of him was in rapid decay.

But when Dr. Kincaid finally spoke, his voice sounded as crisp and strong as it ever had in its nearly ninety years.

"I might have known you'd do something like this. I suppose I should have expected it. But for some reason the idea of you climbing off the edge of the world — I guess I tried to avoid thinking about it."

Dr. Kincaid fumbled around in his mind for the right words. He began pulling on one of his ears as he looked at Edgar.

"I thought your searching was over."

Edgar raised his eyes from the fire. When the two locked eyes, Dr. Kincaid knew.

"But you haven't stopped searching, have you? You know we haven't come to the very end just yet." The way Dr. Kincaid spoke was almost spooky, like he was unearthing thoughts he wasn't sure should be out in the open.

"What's that supposed to mean?" asked Isabel.

Edgar touched her hand and discovered she was trembling. In the stillness before the fire Edgar ran the words over in his mind. *You know we haven't come to the very end just yet.*

"Tell us what you mean," Samuel said. "Where is the very end?"

Dr. Kincaid thought about how he should answer. He always struggled with communicating clearly.

"Far away, down there." Dr. Kincaid turned the bottom of his walking stick toward the ground and tapped it twice on the dirt. "The Dark Planet turns darker still."

Something about those words broke Edgar's heart. *The Dark Planet turns darker still.* He was speaking of the place where Dr. Harding had made not only Atherton, but made Edgar as well. The planet far away in the distance that looked so grey and bleak.

"Minute by minute, hour by hour, the Dark Planet is dying," continued Dr. Kincaid. "Somewhere in the backs of your minds you all know this."

"That sounds terrible," said Isabel.

Dr. Kincaid felt like a failure as he thought about his past.

"In a way, this is completely my fault."

"What's your fault, Dr. Kincaid?" asked Samuel.

Dr. Kincaid seemed on the verge of revealing a dreadful mistake he couldn't quite bring himself to confess. "I convinced everyone I could control him, even after he became more and more secretive," said Dr. Kincaid.

"You mean Dr. Harding," said Edgar.

"I still thought I could trust him, even after he made you."

This stung Edgar somewhere deep inside. The thought of being made was always confusing for Edgar, because he had no idea what having been made by a mad scientist meant. *How* had he been made? What was he, really, if not a normal child of normal parents?

Sensing he'd said something that might hurt the boy, Dr. Kincaid tried to be clearer.

"Don't misunderstand what I'm saying, Edgar. Once you were here, I was very happy he'd made you, but that doesn't change the fact that he knew it was wrong. He was encouraged to make a great many things. But making human beings was strictly forbidden. It was a line we were never supposed to cross."

Dr. Kincaid smiled then, thinking of something he could say that might encourage the boy.

"You were the only one, did you know that? He never made anyone else."

"You hid me, didn't you?" asked Edgar.

"Yes, we hid you," said Dr. Kincaid. "The commander couldn't know. *No one* could know. The whole project would have been in jeopardy. We had to keep you a secret. And that proved very difficult. There was so much work to do, and Dr. Harding had no idea how to raise a child. He was always, in so many ways, a child himself. He wanted you, so he made you, but he didn't think about what it would mean, how it could compromise everything. So I helped him take care of you."

Isabel and Samuel looked at Edgar. They couldn't believe what they were hearing. It all sounded so unimaginable: a boy not born but made, like Atherton had been made.

"There were some very close calls near the end. Dr. Harding was — well, he was having a lot of problems keeping track of everything. He became angry at times. His behavior could be hard to predict. At some point he decided he wanted to show you to the world. You were his greatest creation, greater by far than even Atherton — that's what he used to say."

"I agree," said Isabel.

"Me, too," said Samuel.

"And Atherton was the perfect place to hide me," said Edgar. "From anyone who might find out. Even from my own father."

"Dr. Harding was not your father," said Dr. Kincaid. "He was your maker. There's a big difference."

"It doesn't seem different to me," said Edgar, wanting more than anything to be normal like everyone else.

"I'm sorry, Edgar, but you're wrong about that. I don't want to scare you or hurt you, but you must understand — I brought you to Atherton and hid you from Dr. Harding precisely *because* you were made. Dr. Harding never would have hurt you, but Dr. Harding was of very limited power on the Dark Planet."

"But he was the greatest scientist who ever lived!" said Isabel. "He must have had power to burn."

Dr. Kincaid looked at Isabel with a sort of sad smile. "Being smart doesn't make you powerful, young lady," he said. "Ambition and greed, those will make you powerful. And there were plenty of both at Station Seven."

"What's Station Seven?" asked Edgar.

"So many questions," said Dr. Kincaid. He held up his walking stick as if to say enough was enough and he would talk about what he pleased whether they liked it or not.

"Dr. Harding crossed a line that was not to be crossed when he made you. There were people I couldn't protect you from, people who would have had other plans for you if they'd found out. So you see, it does matter that you were made in a special sort of way. It matters very much."

"I still don't see why it makes any difference. So what if I don't have a mother? I had a father." Edgar pointed to a wicked scrape on his arm he'd gotten while climbing. "I bleed just like everyone else. I've got skin and bones and a brain. Who cares how I got here?"

Dr. Kincaid's mind was scrambled with conflicting ideas. The next part was very hard for him to say, but the truth was the truth and the boy was old enough to know for himself.

"Sometimes a maker *unmakes*. Things are taken apart and examined, remade, changed, tinkered with. *Resurrected*. It's what scientists do, Edgar. And there were plenty of scientists at Station Seven who would have done just that if they'd discovered you."

Edgar was appalled. And that word — "resurrected" — what did that mean? Had he died and come back to life, is that what it meant? Had he been broken down into pieces and put back together again? It couldn't really be true. "I don't want to talk about this anymore," said Edgar.

Dr. Kincaid quickly changed course.

"We couldn't reveal your existence, Edgar. Atherton was assumed by many — most, actually — to be a catastrophic waste of time and resources. There was great excitement at first. Isn't there always at the start of something new and promising? But after decades of work and trillions of dollars with no end in sight, nearly everyone stopped believing. The Dark Planet was dying and the satellite world of Atherton was nothing but a fantastic idea that would never amount to anything useful."

Dr. Kincaid's shoulders slumped noticeably, as if the weight of tremendous pressures Edgar knew nothing about had settled over him all at once.

"But I never stopped believing in the power of Dr. Harding and the making of Atherton," said Dr. Kincaid. "Even after all the mistakes — and there have been many, to be sure — a hope still remains."

Dr. Kincaid grew more animated as he came to the heart of the matter. "I am sure of one thing."

With a groan he stood and edged closer to the fire. His watery eyes sparkled in the light of the flames. "There is a way to discover the true reason why Dr. Harding made Atherton. And for you, Edgar, to find out all you could ever want to know about your maker. Your *father,* if that's what you choose to believe."

"Tell us! Tell us what you know!" said Isabel.

Then Dr. Harding said something that almost surprised himself at the sound of it, something he had long given up all hope of achieving.

"We could reconnect."

Samuel was the first to understand what Dr. Kincaid meant. He'd been thinking about it already without saying it out loud.

"You mean with the Dark Planet? Reconnect with them, so they know where we are."

"But how would we do that?" asked Edgar. "What does that even mean?"

Dr. Kincaid turned more animated still and began pacing back and forth.

"There was once a way to do it — to actually *go* to the Dark Planet — but that way was cut off."

Dr. Kincaid glanced toward the entrance to the cave. Hidden inside was a locked, round door, and behind the door lay a secret place. The children had known it was there but were under no circumstances allowed to enter.

"*Inside* Atherton. That's where the path used to be."

Edgar still had his hand on Isabel's and he felt it shudder. Isabel had journeyed through the inside of Atherton with Samuel at her side and nearly lost her life.

"Deep inside Atherton — deeper than any of you have ever dared to go — there used to be a path, a tunnel if you will. In its place is a pile of rubble no man or beast could break through."

"And at the end of the tunnel?" asked Edgar.

"The docking station," said Dr. Kincaid. The words had no meaning for Edgar, but he felt the power they held over Dr. Kincaid. "I have long been certain we could never go there again. But tonight has made me think differently."

"What do you mean, differently?" asked Samuel. For once Isabel seemed unable to open her mouth. She was holding Edgar's hand tighter, because she knew what Dr. Kincaid was getting at.

"I know what he means," said Isabel. "He means to send Edgar by another way."

The words stabbed Dr. Kincaid. Did he really mean to put Edgar in great danger in order to have a chance at reconnecting with the Dark Planet? It went against everything he believed, and yet, knowing Edgar could climb as he did, Dr. Kincaid couldn't help but imagine the unimaginable.

"It's all right," said Edgar, standing and moving toward Dr. Kincaid. "The truth is, none of you can stop me. So long as there are places on Atherton where I can climb, I can't even stop myself. So if I'm going to climb down there anyway — and trust me, I am — I might as well be of some use."

"But do we *want* to reconnect?" asked Samuel. "What if they come here? What if they destroy Atherton like they destroyed the Dark Planet?"

It was an excellent question and a real concern. It hung in the air for a good long time before Isabel broke the silence.

"Are there children on the Dark Planet?"

Dr. Kincaid didn't hesitate when he answered.

"There are many, many children."

Isabel, Samuel, and Edgar glanced at one another. They all seemed to be thinking the same thing.

"It's up to you, Edgar," said Isabel. More than anyone else it was she who would worry. "I think you're probably right. No one can stop you from climbing, not even your closest friends. And if you won't listen to reason, then let's at least make the risks you'll take worthwhile. Maybe there's something down there, something that can help."

Samuel nodded but didn't speak. He wished more than ever that he, too, could climb so that he could see the docking station for himself. He longed for adventure of the kind Edgar would have.

Dr. Kincaid sensed there would be no better time to reveal a little more about what Edgar was planning to undertake. "We need to talk with Vincent. There are things down there Edgar will need to avoid."

"What kind of things?" said Isabel.

Dr. Kincaid wouldn't answer. He simply smiled with a renewed spirit and departed into the night to search for Vincent.

As his figure turned to shadow he called back, "To bed with all of you! Come back at the crack of dawn for a plate of Black and Green and the beginning of what we must do!"

And then he was gone.

Isabel, Samuel, and Edgar were left to wonder what sorts of creatures might be hiding on the underside of Atherton.

CHAPTER

3

EDGAR'S SECRET REVEALED

Morning came stark and glaring through Isabel's window at the crack of dawn. She bolted from her bed and peered around the corner of her tiny room.

"I was beginning to wonder when you'd wake," said Isabel's mother. Isabel turned with a start and saw her mother looking through an open window.

"You scared me," said Isabel. She tried to run her fingers through her long, tangled hair without much success. "Where's father?"

"He's already out in the second-year grove tying up the remaining rows, but he'll be back for breakfast."

Isabel's mother held up a basket. Inside Isabel could see ripe, juicy figs and a loaf of bread. Not long ago fresh figs were rare indeed and bread hadn't even been known among the people of the grove. How quickly they'd all become accustomed to such extravagance.

"I want to stay, but I can't," said Isabel. Even she couldn't resist tearing a piece of the bread loose and fetching one of the many figs. "Dr. Kincaid wants to see us this morning about something. Edgar and Samuel are going to be there, too."

"Your father expects all of you in the new field by mid-morning," said her mother. "Don't be late."

Isabel smiled and nodded as her mother handed over the basket of food.

Her mother stepped aside and Isabel darted past, taking a bite out of the fresh fig and the piece of bread.

"Clean your teeth along the way. And don't come back for dinner if you haven't washed up."

Isabel half trotted, half walked down a line of first-year trees as she finished the fig and bread. The first-year trees were barely taller than she was, but they ran in long lines all the way down to the edge of the lake. She stopped at one of the trees and snapped a little twig off, something she would never have done to a first-year when mean Mr. Ratikan was running the grove. But the lake seemed to feed the trees like never before. They were vibrant and healthy and didn't mind being picked at now and then.

She used the twig to scrub her teeth, working it into the corners and along the sides. When she was finished she put the twig in her mouth and chewed on it. The twig turned a little soft and Isabel could feel her teeth growing squeaky-clean as the bark lifted bits of bread and fig. She spit out the twig and ran for Dr. Kincaid's cave.

As Isabel came nearer the water's edge she could see way out into the middle. It was the bluest water one could imagine, bright and sparkling, teeming with new life. Cleaners, once dangerous creatures that roamed on land devouring everything in their paths, now lived in the great blue lake at the center of Atherton. Some of them were getting big — really big — but those stayed very deep in the lake and didn't taste very good, or so she was told.

Isabel glanced down the shoreline and saw the herds of sheep on a long, grassy plain. She made her way toward Dr. Kincaid's unusual home and ascended the path between the cluster of giant, egg-shaped rocks until she reached the opening of the cave. In place of the fire was a table set for five. Edgar, Samuel, Dr. Kincaid, and Vincent were waiting for her to take her place at it.

"I told them to wait," said Samuel. He was struggling to speak through a big, sloppy mouthful of Black and Green. "But they wouldn't listen."

"He took the first bite!" said Edgar, who had also just taken an enormous chunk of black meat slathered in green pudding.

Vincent stood and pulled out Isabel's chair. His long, thinning hair was pulled back in a tail. His nose had been broken and had healed wide and flat against his face. "An excellent hunt last night. Please, join us. And by all means, take as much as you like. There's plenty more inside if we run out."

Isabel sat and filled her plate with fresh Cleaner from the lake. It wasn't much to look at, but Black and Green was everyone's favorite food. Better than rabbits or sheep or bread. Even better than figs.

Dr. Kincaid took his walking stick and twisted its top hard and fast. With a click, the end of the stick popped free.

Edgar felt a sudden pang, remembering how the sculpture of Mead's Head had operated in much the same way within the House of Power. He looked toward the lake and wondered how far below the surface Mead's Head now lay, and how many Cleaners were swarming around it.

"Are you absolutely sure about this?" asked Vincent. His eyes spoke volumes as he stared at Dr. Kincaid. *This is a foolish idea. It won't work. There is still time to change your mind.*

"Of course I'm sure," said Dr. Kincaid. "And besides, it's already decided."

He stole a glance at Edgar and the boy looked up. He was slurping down a handful of green pudding and only nodded with excitement. He appeared to be trying to bulk up for a long journey.

"Ahhhh, here we are then," said Dr. Kincaid.

He had removed a piece of rolled-up paper from the inside of the walking stick.

"You're full of surprises," said Edgar.

"Is it a map?" asked Samuel. "Does it lead inside Atherton?"

There had long been a dispute between Samuel, Edgar, and Dr. Kincaid about going back inside. The way was locked, though, and the boys didn't know the combination. Samuel was overwhelmed with curiosity about the inside and wanted to show it to Edgar. It was the one place in the world he knew better than Edgar, and he knew his friend would love it inside.

"It's dangerous," Isabel said warily, "and there's nothing

much to see, anyway." Things hadn't gone well for her on the long trip across the inside of Atherton. She had no interest in seeing firebugs and cave eels and rivers of fire. And the Nubian! "Why would anyone want to go back in there with those giant winged creatures with razor-sharp beaks ready to snap you up? No, thank you."

"It's not so bad," said Samuel. He knew Isabel's fear was warranted, but he couldn't help wanting to go. He would do it against his father's wishes and those of Dr. Kincaid and Vincent, if only he could find the combination. "You want to go there, don't you, Edgar?"

Edgar had stopped eating, and wiping his face with his hands, he pondered the idea before answering.

"I'd rather go to the Dark Planet."

"You don't want to do that, Edgar," said Vincent. He looked at Dr. Kincaid in disbelief. "You didn't tell him he could *go* there, did you?"

"Of course not! Only to the docking station. That was all I said."

And so it was that everyone at the table had conflicting ideas about the inside of Atherton, the bottom of Atherton, and the world outside of Atherton. Vincent, knowing Dr. Kincaid's wishes, sought to find common ground among the five.

"All of you must understand something very important. We're only hoping to reconnect with the Dark Planet, not go there. If the docking station can be reached from the outside — and that has yet to be proven" — Vincent shot Dr. Kincaid a glance before continuing — "our hope is that it can be used to contact the Dark Planet. What happens after that is anyone's guess, but one thing is certain: No one from Atherton is going to fly off into space anytime soon."

"Then why are we doing it at all?" asked Isabel. "Why risk it?"

"Because Dr. Kincaid believes . . ." started Vincent. But he couldn't bring himself to lay the whole burden on the old scientist. "We *both* believe that connecting is the important thing. Letting them know we're still alive is the first in a chain of important events. Nothing else can happen until they hear a voice from Atherton."

Edgar swallowed a last big bite of food and washed it down with a gulp of cold water.

"I'm full," said Edgar, whose mind seemed to have gone somewhere else. "I don't need to eat again for a couple of days if it comes to that. When can I leave?"

Dr. Kincaid loved Edgar's spirit of adventure. He couldn't help smiling while he chastened the boy.

"Don't get ahead of yourself, Edgar. There's a lot we have to consider."

Vincent removed the plates and food and unrolled the paper from Dr. Kincaid's walking stick. He placed rocks at each corner and everyone huddled close, looking at a three-dimensional map of one side of the bottom of Atherton. Edgar could see the top edge — the Flatlands — and everything that lay hidden below, all the way down to the bottom. It was a view of Atherton from space, which was a new idea for Edgar.

"Who made this?" asked Samuel. It was a marvelous rendering of the world in which he lived from a viewpoint he'd

FIRE

¡DANGER

DESCEND to HERE

DOCKING STATION
EXIT

EXTINCTION

INVERSION
VIEW

CAUTION
Precarious
Point

THE LONGEST SHARD

only been able to imagine. It made him see the place differently than he'd ever seen it before.

"Dr. Harding drew this a long time ago," said Dr. Kincaid. "Before anyone was brought here, back when the world of Atherton was a much lonelier place."

He looked at the two boys and the girl.

"In the beginning it was only Dr. Harding, Vincent, and me. Can you imagine? The whole world of Atherton and only the three of us. It was so quiet then."

Dr. Kincaid was thinking of a time when the three men had walked together along the rim of the Highlands, like walking in a new and empty Eden. He remembered having the distinct feeling that it was devoid of not just people, but of a soul as well.

"You were saying?" said Vincent, rousing Dr. Kincaid back to reality.

"You see there, Edgar?"

He pointed to a crack in the surface of Atherton that had the appearance of a narrow letter *V* on the map.

The drawing revealed the bottom of Atherton as a series of much larger V-shaped segments pointing toward the bottom. Some of the *V*'s were thin, some were wide. Between them were vast, open spaces of — of what? It was hard to say if it was water or glass or something else. One thing appeared certain: The entire area looked unclimbable in the extreme.

Dr. Kincaid stepped back from the table and lifted his walking stick, pointing it straight out. "We'll find that crevice about an hour's walk in that direction. And somewhere far below there, the hidden place we seek to discover."

The walking stick was pointing away from the lake and to the left of the new grove. Edgar didn't have to look where the walking stick was pointing. He already knew where the crevice was.

"You don't have to show me where to go," said Edgar.

"Don't tell me," said Vincent, his eyes lighting up.

"You've already climbed there, haven't you?" asked Samuel.

Edgar looked at the faces around the table sheepishly.

"You've been doing it without telling us!" declared Isabel, punching him in the shoulder.

"Be careful!" Samuel said sarcastically. "He's going to need that shoulder to climb with."

"I didn't want to worry you," said Edgar. "But this is good news! I already know the place. And I have to tell you, that V-shaped crevice is a really good location to climb. The gravity doesn't pull me in as much there, and if I go down a little bit farther —"

"Down a little bit farther!" cried Isabel. She wound up for another shot at Edgar. "You're mad!"

Everyone, not just Isabel, did think Edgar a little bit out of his mind, especially after he divulged the whole truth. He confessed that he'd been secretly climbing at night, as he had always done since he was a little boy.

"Do you mean to say that you've been climbing all this time? From the moment Atherton became flat?" asked Dr. Kincaid. He could hardly believe his ears.

"I've already done a lot of exploring down there."

"Then you must know about all the —" Vincent began, but Edgar cut him off.

"I know about some of the challenges. But they're nothing I can't handle. It's not so different from the climbing I've always done."

In truth, the challenges were enormous, but he didn't want his friends to know about them. Vincent took Edgar's hint and didn't ask anything more. If Edgar really had gone straight down from the crevice on the surface of Atherton, then he'd probably been closer to the docking station than he knew.

"I suppose this means we don't need to train him," said Vincent. "It appears he's in fine climbing shape."

"Indeed," said Dr. Kincaid, wondering how Samuel's father could have missed Edgar slipping out night after night. But then Edgar was a tricky and quiet sort of boy. Dr. Kincaid had to imagine it would be hard to keep track of him.

"I guess we're going to be doing this more quickly than I expected," said Dr. Kincaid. "The only question now is whether or not Edgar can actually find the docking station."

Vincent knelt down in front of Edgar, Isabel, and Samuel and looked at each of them.

"I have only had one job to do on Atherton, and you all know what it is."

"To protect us," said Samuel. He loved Vincent for his bravery, his skill with weapons and fighting, his singular mission to make sure everyone was safe.

Vincent shifted his gaze to Edgar alone.

"Allowing you to do this goes against everything I was sent here to do. But I can't help thinking we were meant to reconnect. What if we could do some good for the Dark Planet?"

"We could bring some of the children here," added Isabel.

"Maybe so," said Vincent. "But this is the thing. We've only used the docking station a few times, and we've never gone there the way Edgar will be trying to go. Our way to the docking station was always through the inside of Atherton, the way it was meant to be approached. What Dr. Kincaid is proposing is that you go to the docking station from a direction we know nothing about."

"Actually, we know a little," said Dr. Kincaid, and then he turned the map over and read the words scribbled there.

"Below the crack in the surface lies the longest shard and the crossing of the bridge of burning stone. Beware the keepers of the gate. You must be quick and quiet."

No one else spoke as the true measure of what Edgar might have to face came into view. Edgar would not be entirely alone on the underbelly of Atherton.

Something was down there, awaiting his arrival.

CHAPTER
4

DOWN THE LONGEST SHARD

"Are you sure this is a good idea?" asked Edgar. The meeting was over and Samuel and Isabel had gone to the grove, leaving Edgar alone with Vincent and Dr. Kincaid.

"We can't arouse too much interest," said Dr. Kincaid. "Atherton is stable, but only a year ago everything was in total chaos. People are finally settling down and feeling normal again. I should never have involved Samuel and Isabel to begin with."

"But why can't they come with us, at least to the edge?" asked Edgar.

"Samuel and Isabel have parents," said Vincent. "They can't disappear all day and night without drawing attention, and once you start they'll want to stay as close as they can. Chances are this little adventure will lead to nothing at all, and if that's the case there's no reason to get everyone worried about the

Dark Planet. I agree with Dr. Kincaid. The best thing to do is to go alone for now."

Edgar felt terrible about deceiving his friends. They would want to come along, to see him off and be there when he came back. If they found out he'd left without them they'd feel betrayed.

"If you're sure that's the way it has to be," said Edgar, not hiding his displeasure.

"Let's go to the edge and see where our conversation leads us," said Vincent. "I'm still not sure about any of this. We may well be turning back before we know it."

But Edgar was sure. He knew he wouldn't rest until he found and entered the docking station. He needed to do it to fill the hollow feeling he'd so often endured: he was motherless — not like an orphan, but truly motherless. And Dr. Harding was dead and buried at sea, so Edgar was also fatherless, too. Samuel's parents and Dr. Kincaid and Vincent had been kind to him, but it wasn't the same. He had a powerful urge to find the Dark Planet and discover more about his past. If there was some part of himself hidden there — a note, a picture, a drawing — anything that would tell him more about the place of his making, he would keep on until the treasure was found.

"I believe I'll stay here," said Dr. Kincaid. "It's an awfully long walk. The two of you can scout things out and return with news."

Vincent lifted the rocks from the edges of the paper that lay on the table, rolled it back up, and slid it into his belt. He looked wearily at Dr. Kincaid and started down the path with Edgar close behind. Along the way they spoke of how far Edgar had gone down before and what he had encountered.

"You can't tell Isabel," said Edgar.

"It makes no difference to me what you tell your friends," said Vincent. "I'm only interested in keeping you alive."

Edgar began telling what he knew, reluctantly at first, but quickly became immersed in the telling.

"There's a lot of paths on the underside of Atherton that lead to nowhere."

"What do you mean?"

"Everything is shaped like this," said Edgar, holding two fingers in the shape of a V. "The paths down the side start wide and end narrow. Between the paths there's a glassy sort of orange that can't be climbed. It's smooth, like glass, and it's warm. There's one path that goes farther than the rest. It's all kind of hard to explain."

"Keep trying," said Vincent, curious but stern. He was determined to find out how dangerous it was down there.

"The farther down the longest path I go the warmer and lighter it gets. It's actually easier climbing in the light, and the surface is warm but not too hot to touch. The top of the V or path or whatever you want to call it is really wide, like a hundred feet. It gets narrower as I go and there are wider sections of glassy orange. It's like being surrounded by a warm lake of, I don't know, I guess like a lake of fire under a thick pane of glass. I think it might be too hot to hold at the very end, but I don't know. I've never gone all the way."

"The bridge of fire is all the way at the end, so that's challenge number one," Vincent noted. "If it can't be done there's no point going down at all."

"I didn't say it couldn't be done," Edgar said defensively. "I was close. I could see the very end. It's only about twenty feet wide down there, but there's plenty of room for me."

"Are there any other obstacles you're not telling me about?" asked Vincent suspiciously. "Anything that makes you think about the words on the map?"

Edgar thought of what Dr. Kincaid had said. *Below the crack in the surface lies the longest shard and the crossing of the bridge of burning stone. Beware the keepers of the gate. You must be quick and quiet.*

"There are holes," Edgar revealed.

"What do you mean, holes?" asked Vincent.

"About halfway down the longest path I start to find holes in the stone. I think something is living in them. I hear things."

"What do you hear?"

Edgar couldn't describe the sound. He shrugged. "I can stay away from them. There's room for me to quietly slip past."

"I don't know," said Vincent. This new element made him nervous. How he wished he could climb as Edgar did and find the docking station himself. "You should have told us this before. Dr. Kincaid will want to know."

They were near the crevice at the edge of Atherton and Edgar felt the familiar sense of his feet being pulled gently in front of him. It was a feeling he had come to love, a silent signal that climbing was close at hand. The pull would grow fiercer the closer they got, and along with it, Edgar's desire to touch the side of Atherton with his hands. He couldn't stand the idea of turning back.

"You know how fast I can climb," said Edgar. "I've been down there a bunch of times already and nothing's come out of those holes."

Vincent knelt down in front of Edgar and looked at the boy with a mix of concern and hope. Edgar didn't know quite how to read the expression.

"None of this is going to matter if you can't reach the bottom of the longest path," said Vincent. "According to the map, that's where you'll find this thing called the bridge of fire and the way into the docking station. But you're going to find something else as well and we don't know what it is."

Vincent was torn between his duty to protect this boy and the need to reconnect with the Dark Planet. If there was a chance Edgar could find his way safely to the docking station it could mean saving thousands more.

He thought of all the things Edgar had already accomplished on his own. He'd climbed a mile up to the Highlands and two miles down to the Flatlands. There was no reason to believe Edgar couldn't climb quietly past a few holes in search of a way to reconnect.

"Don't go any closer to the holes than you absolutely must to get by them," said Vincent, reluctantly making up his mind. "Now listen to me, Edgar. After you find the station you have to turn back. The last thing we want is for you accidentally to end up on the Dark Planet without us. That would be a disaster and it could happen if you're not careful. The docking station is —

well, it's what we call automated. By that I mean it can do certain things on its own."

Vincent shook his head. It was impossible to explain how the station worked and what would be found there. It was all so alien to Edgar.

"Just promise me you'll turn back once you get there. What you're trying to do is enter the docking station from the way *out* of Atherton. Dr. Harding left us a map and a few words, so he must have imagined it *could* be entered this way, but no one has ever done it before."

Then Vincent said what he was truly thinking, the only thing that seemed to make sense as he stood before a boy who could climb like a spider. "Something tells me Dr. Harding imagined it would be you who would follow this path someday. There's certainly no one else who could do it."

Edgar could hardly wait to start down the side of Atherton. "I can do it, Vincent. I know I can."

Vincent touched Edgar on the shoulder and turned more serious. "Remember — turn back the moment you feel the slightest concern. The heat can tire you out and make your hands dangerously slippery from the sweat. Don't make the mistake of thinking you can do more than you're capable of."

The two began walking once more. Very soon they were on their bellies, crawling up close to the place where Edgar would start. In this particular spot, the flat surface of Atherton had cracked wide open. The crevice started at the edge of Atherton and jutted in for a hundred yards, where it created a gap of fifty or more feet across. Edgar felt a growing exhilaration as he turned and kicked his feet over and into the long chasm.

"Remember," said Vincent. "To the docking station and back and no more, and only if you can manage it. I can't come down after you. No one can. But I'll wait for you."

"You shouldn't expect my return until after nightfall," said Edgar. He secretly knew that he could get to the bottom in only a couple of hours if he wanted to. But he didn't want to be in the least bit rushed in case his plans changed. "Six or seven hours, I would guess."

Vincent nodded, astounded by what Edgar was capable of. Seven hours of climbing up and down the side of a wall of stone? He wondered what Dr. Harding had done to Edgar that made him so strong.

"Be careful," said Vincent.

And with that, Edgar was gone. Faster than Vincent believed possible, Edgar was so far down the crevice he could only barely be seen.

Edgar will be gone a long while, Vincent pondered. *I must talk to Dr. Kincaid alone.*

With that, Vincent set off at a quick pace in search of more answers about Edgar, the Dark Planet, and the docking station.

●

Very soon Edgar was out of the crevice that had been cut into Atherton and climbing on the outer surface. There were many paths he could have taken that led down the side, but he knew which one was the longest and started down at its wide beginning. For a long time there were no holes at all as he'd remembered, but then the way down started to narrow and the first of many holes came into view. It was three feet around and there was plenty of room to avoid the glowing orange edge of the path.

Edgar heard the strange sound as he passed by — a swishing, like something moving back and forth inside, and a hissing. *I can't understand why any of this is here,* thought Edgar, the face of Dr. Harding clear in his mind. *What were you thinking?*

Edgar had to travel slowly in order to remain perfectly quiet as he went farther down. As he moved, the holes became more numerous and difficult to avoid. He was dripping with sweat from head to toe and it was beginning to make his hands slippery as Vincent had feared. But Edgar had filled his pockets with gritty dirt that he could use to dry his hands when needed.

The bottom of Atherton was truly made for climbing, and this was his great salvation. There was an endless supply of easy handholds to choose from.

"Now comes the hard part," Edgar whispered. He had come to the end of his knowledge of the bottom of Atherton. Removing a small rabbit skin tied to his belt and filled with water, Edgar drank what had once been cool water from the lake. It had turned warm, but the water revived him nevertheless.

The farther down the shard one went the narrower it became; and all the while the holes grew larger. It was hard not to imagine that whatever lurked inside was getting bigger as well. It seemed like the most inopportune time to be climbing closer, and yet he had no choice. Either he would have to cross very near the largest of the holes or turn back. There was no other way down.

Seven holes, he thought, seeing what lay beneath him. *If I can just get past them it looks clear on the other side.* The path was now only twenty feet across, with a great sea of glowing orange on either side.

Edgar could feel his pounding heart race faster and faster as he passed between the first three of the seven holes without hearing or seeing anything. Then he moved between the cluster of remaining four holes and stopped stone-cold.

He looked back at the first three holes where a familiar clicking sound had begun, now more loudly than before. It grew even worse as the sound echoed from holes he had yet to pass by. His hands slippery and sweat dripping into his eyes, Edgar realized with terror that he was trapped in the middle of a field of holes from which unknown creatures were about to emerge.

Edgar glanced up and saw two beams of white light coming from inside one of the holes he'd passed. He was totally frozen with fear as the head of a creature emerged, encrusted with sharp chunks of glowing red and orange stones. The beams of light came from its hollow eye sockets.

The outrageous creature opened its huge mouth and lunged out of the hole, down toward the climbing boy, and slammed its jaws of stone inches above Edgar's head. Orange slime slid from its mouth as it recoiled in a flash of light, as if its tail were attached to a great spring that pulled it violently back into the hole. It crashed back and forth against the surface of Atherton, howling horribly.

The moment the lights were gone the two other holes Edgar had passed lit up with dancing white beams of their own. Two monsters shot out of their holes above Edgar and their horrible teeth went *SLAM! SLAM!* against the rock. If a person could climb and run at the same time, Edgar was doing just that as he charged recklessly down the side of Atherton.

"Dr. Harding! What's wrong with you!" cried Edgar as the monsters flipped wildly back into their holes.

Whatever was dripping from the mouths of these stone-encrusted monsters was melting the very surface of Atherton. It fizzled and crackled and let off a rancid black smoke.

From below, Edgar heard the clicking and hissing and snapping of jaws. Another monster, its rock-covered head glowing sickeningly, was out of its hole, and it appeared to be sniffing the air. It turned its awful sockets of light on Edgar and disappeared with a grinding sound.

That thing is coiling up down there, thought Edgar. *It's going to spring!*

Edgar practically dove to one side in the wildest, fastest climbing maneuver he'd ever imagined. He was almost rolling out of the way as the beast sprang, swinging its head and snapping uncontrollably in the open air. Orange slime flew everywhere as the monster reached the end of its hidden spring and snapped back.

Edgar watched in horror as he saw his leather water bag melt and steam, covered in deadly sludge. The orange goo fizzed all around him, but there was yet a path to the bottom. Edgar became so focused on escaping through the field of seven holes that he didn't realize how far he'd gone.

Soon, without a clue of how he'd done so, Edgar found himself not only through the field of holes but well clear of them. Looking back, he saw four more beams of light emerging, but

Edgar was far enough out of their reach. They only screamed in anger when they trained their hollow eyes on the distant intruder.

Edgar breathed a long sigh of relief, but his eyes were filled with concern. By coming this far he had trapped himself behind a wall of monsters waiting for his return.

What am I going to do now? he asked himself, looking up at the perilous way he'd passed through. *I can't go through that again. I'd never make it twice, especially trying to climb up instead of down. They'd have me for sure.*

Another twenty feet beneath him, Edgar spotted the largest hole of them all. From what Edgar could tell given the angle, it might be as big as ten feet around.

Edgar glanced to his right and left. Everything he saw was orange and glassy. It looked as though the inside of Atherton was filled with a lake of fire and covered with a thick, foggy glass.

"I have to get out of here," Edgar told himself. He quickly chose his route and imagined how fast he could climb past the remaining hole, and then he was off and moving like a startled spider. He glanced inside the great hole as he passed by, expecting to see two beams of light.

But there was no light, no sound.

What's this new trick you're trying to play on me? thought Edgar. He had come to see Atherton as a living, breathing creature full of every kind of surprise. Just because he didn't see any light didn't mean something wasn't about to try to eat him.

Edgar's hands were growing so hot from the surface he

could hold on with only one hand at a time, letting each hand cool off every few seconds.

At last Edgar came to the very end of the longest path down the side of Atherton. The great hole sat much closer to the bottom than Edgar had realized at first. There were only a few feet on the other side, and he hung there, hot and scared half to death. His hands started to slip as he tried to figure out what to do.

"There's no place left for me to go," said Edgar, pulling himself up and peeking into the hole. There was nothing, just a dull silence and a dark passageway. He lifted himself and sat down at the very edge of the hole.

He felt heavy. At first he thought this was because he was tired, but he soon realized that gravity was now pulling down on his feet more than it had on the surface of Atherton. He found that even the simple task of walking was difficult, as if he had giant rocks tied to his feet. Even his face felt as if it were being pulled downward.

"What is this place?" Edgar said, though it came out slurry and weak.

Along the walls of the hole Edgar could see that something had been here before. The walls were — what was it? — *scraped*. Something big had passed through here more than once. Something *really* big. It was wide enough to span the space and touch the walls as it passed through. Edgar took two steps forward and then, to his great surprise, he heard a new sound from deep inside.

Whatever it was did not sound happy to see him.

CHAPTER

5

ACROSS THE BURNING
BRIDGE OF STONE

Teagan awoke with a start in the Silo. The whole world of the Dark Planet seemed to have turned ominously quiet apart from a single sound in the night. The sound of a bender being put to work on a child.

"They took her while we were sleeping!" shouted Teagan. She glanced over, still hoping she might see her closest friend in the shadowy light drifting in from the hallway. But Aggie was gone. Only her covers remained in a bunch at the foot of her rusted old cot.

"Quiet, Teagan," said a small voice from another bed. "Or they'll come for you, too."

They were all awake now, so everyone had heard when the bender snapped against Aggie's skin out in the hallway. They had heard her cry, and its haunting echo. Red Eye and Socket kept the door to the barracks open for a reason.

"Leave her alone!" said Teagan, sitting up in bed without a clue of how to stop them. And then she thought of the one person who might be able to help them and called out her name.

"Hope!"

"Teagan, no!" said the same small voice. "Lie down and act like you're asleep, you fool!"

But it was too late. Red Eye's horrible shadow appeared in the doorway. His head was a misshapen silhouette of goggles and tousled hair. The bender swished back and forth in front of him as he entered barracks number three.

There was another *snap!* from the bender in the hall, and the sound of Aggie's wince. Teagan began to cry. She hated the Silo so much it was almost more than she could take. She was very near doing something stupid like jumping out of bed and running to find Aggie in the hall. She dreamed of having the bender herself and using it on Red Eye and Socket, beating them until they ran outside and were eaten by the monsters that lurked there.

"Hope's not going to help you. She knows better than to interfere in our business," said Red Eye. "The only person we answer to is Commander Judix, and she gave us free reign of this place a long time ago."

The mere sound of the name Judix caused a wave of quiet gasps from many of the beds. Judix hadn't visited the Silo in a long time, but the Commander's power and cruelty were legendary.

Red Eye stood over Teagan's bed, glaring down at her and running the hard edge of the metal whip against the rusting iron frame of her bed. He wiped his filthy nose on his even filthier sleeve. The light had made his eyes and nose run uncontrollably so that his face was damp and sickly in the soft glow of the room.

"It's okay, Teagan."

Teagan turned to the doorway and saw Aggie staggering in. Her voice was shaky, as if she were in shock, but Teagan also heard the ever-present resolve in her best friend's voice.

"They're done," said Aggie, trying to gather herself together. "Just shut your eyes. Go back to sleep."

Teagan closed her eyes, overcome by a feeling of helplessness.

"That's what we like, a good little worker who gets her sleep at night," said Red Eye. He swung around and looked over the cots. "We're going to work all of you even harder than usual tomorrow because of this madness with Aggie. Get to sleep! All of you! If I hear one more peep out of this barracks before morning, every one of you's gonna be sorry."

Socket laughed from out in the hallway, but it was not the big laugh he usually used. He was still hurting as much as his brother from the light they'd been exposed to. There was no hiding the fact that the two men were in pain.

When the door was shut and the room was dark again, Aggie whispered as quietly as she could.

"It wasn't that bad. Socket hardly knows how to use that thing."

Teagan knew Aggie was only trying to put on a brave face, but she didn't say anything. She just reached over and held her friend's hand. A few minutes later, when Aggie thought Teagan was asleep, she began to cry quietly.

"Move over," said Teagan. She crept into Aggie's bed and held her friend as close as she could. Aggie cried and cried, her whole body trembling. But after a while she calmed down and started breathing heavily. Teagan hugged her close and stayed there a little longer. It wouldn't do to be found in the wrong bunk in the morning, so she crept back into her own bed and tried to fall asleep.

Aggie was a strong girl, but she'd just received the most dreadful beating in the long history of the Silo.

●

The strange sound of an unseen monster weighed heavy on Edgar's mind as he crept forward ever so quietly. A warm, faint wind blew into Edgar's face. He assumed it was coming from the keeper of this place, a creature blowing gusts of hot air past sharp teeth, waiting for Edgar to arrive.

He thought of Dr. Kincaid's words, *the burning bridge of stone,* and he began to wonder — could this be the very place? He was, generally speaking, at the end of the longest shard. And the monsters he'd encountered outside were the last thing he'd come to. *Beware the keepers of the gate.*

"If it's true I've passed the keepers of the gate," Edgar said to himself, astonished at his own good luck, "then this must be the way to the docking station."

He rose to his feet with some effort and peered down the long tunnel in which he stood. It led straight into the heart of Atherton, and it was dimly illuminated in a way he'd never seen before — with a kind of blue light.

Where is that coming from? thought Edgar. He looked back at the opening of the tunnel and saw tiny blue dots dancing toward him. They were coming out of small holes in the ceiling and the floor. First there were ten, then a hundred, and then a thousand little blue bugs in the air.

Edgar wanted to reach out and touch them, and he very nearly did. Isabel and Samuel had seen firebugs. They had known the allure of touching them, of wanting to join with them in their charming little dance.

"I can see why Isabel wanted to touch them," said Edgar. "They are appealing little killers."

The thousand firebugs became two thousand, and soon there was a thick fog of glowing cobalt between Edgar and the outside world.

"Only one way to go now," said Edgar. He was afraid of what lay ahead, but he also knew that if even a few firebugs touched him he would never make it back to the surface of Atherton alive.

Fortunately, the firebugs remained just a few feet beyond the opening. They appeared to be trying to come nearer to Edgar; the warm wind must have been too much of a struggle for their delicate wings. They hung in the air, fighting to stay aloft in the heavy gravity.

It's really too bad they can kill me, thought Edgar.

Now that his fate had been determined, Edgar forged on. It was an eerie feeling, walking toward the inside with no way of escape, and he dreaded the idea of dying there alone.

Edgar's route turned into a climb again, though not a very steep one. When he neared the top the tunnel was glowing orange and yellow. Above him flowed a channel of liquid, a river of molten rock behind a ceiling of solid glass. The glass kept the river of fire from flowing into the tunnel where Edgar stood, but it seemed to Edgar that touching the ceiling could be hot enough to set him on fire.

Without any warning whatsoever the warm wind stopped. All was perfectly still inside the tunnel for a few seconds as Edgar realized the danger of what had just happened. He was suddenly paralyzed with fear.

"The firebugs," Edgar whispered. Soon he would be surrounded by thousands of the deadly creatures.

Edgar's mind raced. What could he do? He looked every which way and saw nothing that might be of use to him. He gazed back along the distance he had come. It was quite a long way to the opening, but already a fog of firebugs had halved the distance. They were merrily dancing toward him without effort.

Edgar tried to remember what Isabel and Samuel had said about the Inferno. He knew he couldn't let firebugs touch his skin, but his legs and arms were exposed. He didn't have anywhere near the amount of clothing he would need to cover himself completely.

"There has to be a way!"

Firebugs by the thousands were coming in a soft wave within twenty feet of him, glowing through the middle of the tunnel. The force of gravity was having a very real effect on their journey as they lolled along in the center of the cave. They were thick as a cloud at the level of Edgar's feet, thinner like a light fog at his eyes, and — what was this? At the top. At the top!

Edgar's mind raced with an idea that might save him. At the very top of the cave, in that last one or two feet, there were no firebugs at all. Gravity was pulling them down, and this provided Edgar with a chance.

With a swarm of firebugs ten feet off, Edgar leaped into action. He began scaling the side of the tunnel. It was scraped and grooved all around, and it would have been easy to climb if it hadn't been for the heavy weight of his own limbs. It took all of his effort to climb up to where the tunnel curved at the top, to clench his toes into a crevice and hold on with his fingers.

Hanging on to the ceiling of a cave was a nearly impossible task, even for Edgar, but it was made twice as hard by the constant pulling of gravity from beneath him. The cave wanted Edgar on the floor, not on the ceiling, and it pulled relentlessly. And then there was the heat. The river of fire ran slowly in a ribbon down the middle of the cave, five or six feet away, but it was still ghastly hot where Edgar held on.

The first of the firebugs flew beneath Edgar. They, too, seemed to struggle to stay so high in the air. They didn't appear to have the ability to see or hear anything.

As the swarm of swaying bugs moved under Edgar, his fingers and toes started to slide. It was quickly becoming painfully difficult to hang on, and he had to constantly reset his hands.

He craned his head around in the foot of space he had and watched. The sea of firebugs looked like cool, misty water he could fall into and be refreshed, which made it the worst kind of temptation. If it were possible to die a thousand deaths in a matter of seconds, Edgar would do just that if he let go.

The procession of glowing blue was beginning to thin and he could see the last of them working their way up the tunnel.

There were new sounds coming from up there as well. *Zap!* *Zap! Zap!* Firebugs were being devoured amid the snapping sound of something big and menacing.

There were only a few bugs left now — easy enough to dodge — so Edgar climbed down the side and rested his aching hands and forearms.

"I wonder what's up there," said Edgar. Seeing the very last of the firebugs disappear, Edgar followed slowly behind. He climbed up and into the rising part of the tunnel and watched as the cloud of firebugs continued in front of him.

When Edgar crested the top he saw that the river of fire over his head grew wider, closer, and unbearably hot. The whole ceiling of the tunnel was clear like glass and everything behind the glass was molten lava.

I shouldn't be here, thought Edgar, terrified by the power of the place he'd stumbled into. *This is no place for people.* Whatever this place was, though, he was certain a lot of energy was being created and stored.

Directly ahead was the end of the tunnel, where a giant, eyeless creature was gulping down thousands of buzzing firebugs. It was the same as the stone-encrusted monsters he'd seen outside — except far larger. Its head alone was covered not in stones but glowing red boulders. Supercharged beams of white light shot from its empty eye sockets. The monster's head swung back and forth in a cloud of blue. It didn't seem to be bothered by firebugs bouncing off the sides of its molten head. The head was eyeless, noseless — *senseless* but for the great rock-coated mouth that ate everything in its path.

Its body snaked back into the rocks. This thing and the tunnel were one — the thing and *Atherton* were one! There was no separating them.

This must be the keeper Dr. Kincaid spoke about, thought Edgar. *I don't know how to get past it. I shouldn't have come down here!*

The monster appeared to be drunk on firebugs as its head slumped forward and then sprang to life again. Edgar stood at the top of the main tunnel where it split like a T. The monster was down the left side, and on the right lay a passageway leading, Edgar guessed, to more trouble.

I can't go back out, and if that thing finishes with the firebugs it'll come after me next. I've got no choice but to run as fast as I can to the right.

The firebugs were thinning out fast when Edgar made his move. He made the fateful guess that this creature, like the others outside, was attached to Atherton like a spring. If he could move quickly enough he might be able to outrun it.

The monstrous head was energized from its dreamy meal of glowing blue bugs. Its head lashed hard and the lights from its empty eye sockets locked on Edgar. Someone had entered its realm, and the giant stone-covered beast was not pleased. Its head slashed forward, firebugs and flaming boulders flying every which way. Parts of the monster actually broke free, careening toward Edgar. Orange froth sizzled and charred the walls black.

The mouth of the beast opened full and wide, big enough to swallow ten Edgars in one crashing bite. Out of its mouth flew thousands of firebugs and streams of lava. The stone jaws slammed shut short of Edgar, but the wave of hot air sent fire-bugs flying everywhere.

As the monster careened backward on its own internal spring, its head smashed back and forth against the tunnel walls. The deafening noise of rocks crashing into each other sounded like the world was coming to an end. The movement created a draft that pulled at Edgar's shirt and dragged the fire-bugs back into the mouth of the monster.

The beast, battered and angry, retreated into the rocks and disappeared from view. Edgar felt unbearably heavy and tired. The weight of all that had happened on his journey finally top pled him to the ground.

Little did Edgar realize that he was staring down the tunnel to the very place Vincent and Dr. Kincaid had dreamed about. Edgar was closer than he knew to something he couldn't have imagined.

A way back to the Dark Planet.

CHAPTER

6

A LEAP OF FAITH

"What do you mean he's not back yet? He shouldn't even be *gone* yet!"

"How could they do this?" Isabel went on. "It's like they tricked us — tricked Edgar! — so they could get what they wanted."

"Try to stay calm," reasoned Samuel. "We don't even know for sure what's going on yet."

The two of them were standing in a grove of second-year trees tying strings around clusters of figs along with a number of other adults and children who might be able to hear them. Samuel was trying to keep her from giving too much away.

"How can you say that?" said Isabel, her words like a storm against a door that might break free at any moment. "They sent us away. They knew we wouldn't let him go to the edge alone, without support . . . without us *there* for him. It matters, Samuel. You know it matters to Edgar."

Samuel couldn't deny that Edgar was doing something that might very well get him killed. For all his strength and skill and courage, he was still only twelve and without parents to protect him.

"Do you think Edgar is easy to fool?" asked Samuel. "I mean, do you think he would let this happen if it wasn't what he really wanted?"

"He wouldn't do that — not without at least telling us first."

"I heard them talking," Samuel revealed. Isabel had agreed to let Samuel secretly go back to Dr. Kincaid's cave, and he'd arrived just as Vincent returned to the cave. He'd heard everything they'd said.

"What did you hear? Tell me!" Isabel shouted.

"Only if you keep your voice down," cautioned Samuel. "Everyone on the tree line is listening."

Isabel let out a grumbling sort of sigh. "Just tell me what you heard," she whispered.

Samuel didn't have the will to hide anything from her piercing eyes, framed with those thick black brows.

"Vincent and Edgar went together, but Vincent returned alone. I crept in between the giant rocks to listen. I didn't understand at first because he started speaking to Dr. Kincaid about things on the Dark Planet. But they weren't talking, they were arguing. Dr. Kincaid sees things differently from Vincent."

"How do you mean?"

"It seemed to me that Dr. Kincaid would . . . I don't know . . . risk more in order to reconnect with the Dark Planet. You know how Vincent is always protecting everyone? Well, Dr. Kincaid seemed to think it was time to start protecting people on the Dark Planet. Vincent wasn't so sure it was worth the risk."

Samuel was trying to hold back the truth, but his resolve was crumbling before Isabel's very eyes.

"There's something you're not telling me, Samuel. Spill it or I'll load a fig in my sling and go see Dr. Kincaid myself. I'll *make* him tell me."

"You wouldn't," said Samuel, knowing what a good shot Isabel was with her sling.

"I would!" insisted Isabel.

"Okay, just calm down. I just think it's a lot more complicated than we realize. I mean, what if we really could save a lot of people? How much risk is that worth? I don't think Dr. Kincaid *wants* to risk losing Edgar. I think he feels he has no other choice."

"He's willing to sacrifice Edgar to reconnect, isn't he?"

"I'm not sure it's fair to say it that way. Dr. Kincaid is trying; it's just not that simple."

"Of course it's simple! We're talking about Edgar!"

Isabel's voice had risen once more and this time one of the adults was walking toward them.

"What's the matter, Isabel? Is Samuel not doing his share of the work?" It was Lars, a good friend of Isabel's father. The last thing she wanted was her parents finding out about this.

"He's keeping up just fine," said Isabel, trying to muster a convincing smile. "We were just talking about my reading lessons — it's very hard, and I've been getting frustrated."

This was a good lie if ever there was one. Samuel read better than most in the grove, because he had long been a citizen of the House of Power before its collapse. The formerly illiterate population of Atherton, including Lars, Isabel, Edgar, and all of the former residents of Tabletop, had struggled mightily with the effort to learn to read, and many eventually gave up improving their skills in favor of a simple life of work.

"I know exactly how you feel," said Lars. He glanced at Samuel and secretly wished he could read as well as the young boy from the Highlands. "Reading's not for everyone."

"Oh, I like to read," said Isabel. She wasn't willing to feign laziness for a second. "It's just that Samuel is trying to teach me some *advanced* reading, and it's challenging." Lars frowned, already turning to go.

Samuel glanced down the row of trees and then out toward the blue lake. "I think we should get out of here. If we leave now maybe we can get to the crevice before he comes back. We could be waiting there for him. He'd like that."

"Maybe he would and maybe he wouldn't."

She decided she'd like to be there when Edgar returned so she could tell him how mad she was that he had gone off alone without telling his two closest friends.

"Let's finish this row. When we come to the end we'll sneak away and find him."

Thick veins of yellow and gold glowed soft and warm along the stone walls where Edgar stood. He had come to the end of the passageway. It was slightly wider here, but other than that, it had the appearance of a dead end.

Edgar was suddenly gripped with the alarming realization of his own hunger and thirst. Could he die in here? The thought scared him, more because he was alone than anything else.

He touched one of the walls and found it trembling ever so slightly. Looking back, the passageway was entirely empty. There was nothing but walls to touch, a floor to walk on, a ceiling to look at.

"I wonder what Isabel and Samuel are doing. I bet Isabel is mad." Talking to himself made Edgar feel better, less hungry and afraid. "She's going to kill me if I ever get out of here."

Lifting his heavy feet with great effort, he closed the final distance to the wall at the back of the chamber. When he reached it, he touched it, he pushed against it, and then he kicked it.

Nothing happened.

This is a disaster, thought Edgar. He was really trapped this time. There was a gigantic monster blocking the way out that spewed molten rocks and firebugs. And even if by some miracle he could make it past, it wouldn't matter, because there were seven more monsters waiting for him on the outside of Atherton.

He ran his hand over the surface of the passageway and, overwhelmed by a feeling of total despair, he punched the wall.

Edgar crumpled to the ground, holding his throbbing knuckles. And then, in the dim yellow and gold light of the room, he spied a hole near the floor about twice the size of his closed fist.

It had blended in at first, but there was no doubt of its existence now. It was black as night inside as he peered down the gullet of the hole.

Why are there always holes? I hate holes! thought Edgar, shaking his hand until the pain started to go away. He was imagining what might happen if he reached inside. Something might eat his hand. Something might grab his hand. Or maybe, just maybe, a treasure of some kind would be hidden inside, like the book he'd once found on the cliffs leading to the Highlands.

Edgar looked all around the room one last time for other holes. None. He crouched in front of the hole and imagined what might be inside. A minute passed. Then another. Finally, he put his fingers a little way inside the hole.

The wall inside was smooth as glass, which he hadn't expected. It felt alive with slickness, and Edgar was sure his fingers would be wet when he pulled his hand back out, but they were not.

He put his hand back in, a little deeper this time, and his heart raced at the thought of having his fingers bitten off. He took a series of deep breaths and tried to calm down, then he shut his eyes tight and reached deeper still.

His fingers touched a handle. Surprised, he quickly pulled his hand away, but then he wrapped his fingers around it and pulled. It wouldn't move, so he tried to turn it. The handle spun and clicked to the right. He tried pulling on it again, and this time the handle moved toward him.

Should I keep pulling? he wondered. It seemed the only natural thing to do. He had to pull hard on it, but eventually the handle came flush with the wall. When Edgar let it go it wanted to slide slowly back into the hole, so he pulled it back and turned it to the left. This locked it into place, where it stayed.

Edgar had no idea what he'd just done. He turned toward the back wall, once so hard and immovable, and saw that it was changing before his very eyes. The thick yellow veins of light had turned molten red. The veins widened more and more, until there were no veins at all but a throbbing wall of heat.

"What have I done?" said Edgar, his voice trembling and unsteady. The place seemed to have come to life and he feared for his life all over again.

Edgar scrambled for the handle and tried to turn it back, but it had locked into place. Whatever Edgar had set in motion would continue whether he liked it or not. He could wait and let the room dissolve into lava or run down the passage and face a monster waiting to tear him to pieces.

The center of the back wall began to melt. Edgar expected it to flow across the floor and overtake him, but instead the section of wall slid down into the ground. It appeared to be hollow below the back wall, so that the liquefied stone simply fell away and left a wide opening that could be passed through. Under the opening lay a wide, bubbling orange cauldron of lava.

Edgar approached the opening cautiously and felt the heat grow with each step. It became so hot he could barely stand it and thought his clothes would ignite into flames. The thin hairs on his forearms shrank and twisted as if beaten down by the destructive power of heat. A charred black rim surrounded the opening, and whatever lay on the other side was hidden by a layer of hissing steam.

Edgar stepped back, away from the heat, and tried to think.

If he jumped through the opening he might well be leaping into an open oven on the other side. Or, just as horrible, the weight of gravity might pull him down as he tried to cross over. He didn't even want to think about what it would feel like to sink into a boiling vat of melted Atherton.

Edgar looked in the direction from which he'd come and knew he couldn't get out. He gathered all his courage, took two deep breaths of hot air, and ran as fast as his legs would go.

I can't turn back! I can only jump with everything that's in me.

And so he did.

Station Seven was a metal and glass building that hovered over a lifeless, rock-encrusted cove on the Dark Planet. A web of entangled steel beams suspended the station in the air, where it was safe from the toxic sludge that drifted in and out each day.

At the vast window of Station Seven sat a woman looking at the shadows of a forsaken wood outside.

"It's quiet tonight," she concluded. "Too quiet."

The woman brushed a hand across her brow and returned her arm to rest on the rail of her chair. There was a coldness about her, as if the Dark Planet had made her heart turn to stone. She held a vacant but powerful stare into the night beyond the window.

"What will you do?" she asked. As usual there was no one in the wide open room to hear her. She had long ago fallen into the habit of speaking to herself. There were few others for her to hold a conversation with, and besides, she preferred to be left alone.

The woman was having one of her frequent recollections of a conversation with Dr. Luther Kincaid. Eight years ago — had it been that long? Eight years of silence, and in those eight years, the Dark Planet had grown much darker still. And Station Seven? It was but a shell of its former significance. Almost everyone had fled with the arrival of the Spikers.

"You will bring him back," the woman said forcefully, replaying the words she'd said in that distant conversation. "You will find a way."

There was a visible change in her face — a cringing of hate and regret — as the face of Atherton's maker came into her memory. The madman Dr. Harding. She could not think of him for a single second without being overcome with anger. For a long time she had gone every day down one of the three passages to visit his laboratory.

"He'll come back and finish what he started," she would say.

After a year of waiting she grew bitter. She had trusted Dr. Kincaid. Every resource at her disposal had been freely given, all of her formidable powers of persuasion put to the test to gather anything and everything he requested. But a year more had passed in devastating silence. Not a sound or a signal. Nothing!

Her anger turned a sharp and treacherous eye toward everyone who had been involved in the making of Atherton. Thousands of others had once walked the halls of Station Seven. She turned on them, hating them for their failure to find a solution.

And then, all at once it had seemed, something had died inside the woman at the window. Her moral will collapsed and she sank into grief. It happened on the day of the third year passing without a sign. A new bitterness filled her eyes, and everyone saw. She drove all but the most hardened away and set her course in a new and cruel direction. From that point on, Station Seven was, for all intents and purposes, abandoned and forgotten like so many other places on the Dark Planet.

It was said that she had lost her soul in the making of Atherton.

The woman at the window could have gone to another station and continued to lead and to work. She had certainly been asked. She had been president *and* supreme ruler in better times; she was brilliant, and she knew how to control people. But she had long ago made her choice. Her reputation was sullied by the failure of Atherton. In the failing world of the Dark Planet, this remarkable woman at the window had been forgotten along with Station Seven.

Her name was Commander Judix.

Every corner of the Dark Planet is failing, she thought to herself. Of those who remained, scattered on the bleak surface of the Dark Planet, no one went outside. And no one ever visited Station Seven. Dr. Harding had seen to that by filling the forsaken wood with Cleaners and Spikers.

Commander Judix was the only person who occasionally visited Dr. Harding's abandoned laboratory at the end of a darkened passageway. She would allow no one else to enter. In the five more years that had passed without the slightest sign of life from Atherton, Commander Judix had taken to visiting the lab less frequently, a nearly forgotten disaster from a more optimistic time. There were more pressing matters at hand.

And so it was that a small and distant signal could have been detected but was not. Inside the laboratory there was a little blue light blinking on a slick black surface. Soon the blue light would move, but would anyone from Station Seven even know it had appeared?

Commander Judix sighed and touched a pale yellow button on the arm of her chair.

"Shelton," said Commander Judix. "Come to the window."

Commander Judix heard the faraway echo of approaching footsteps. It would be a while before the footsteps reached her. Station Seven was a place made for thousands, but only a few dozen remained. When someone moved, the place became haunted by the long echo of metal-soled boots on an endless metal floor.

She had made a decision about the Silo and needed someone else to share the bad news. There was guilt over what needed to be done, though to be fair, this was not what kept her awake at night. Where the children were concerned there were always those who would try to oppose her. In the face of a dying world, Commander Judix shared no such feelings. It was a matter of hanging on as long as one could by whatever means necessary. A person's age had nothing to do with it.

Hanging on wasn't easy, either, since the world had become fragmented beyond all reckoning. There were the seven stations, separated by great distance and failing lines of communication. Commander Judix hadn't formally heard from any of the other stations in over two years. There were human outposts scattered everywhere, gigantic metal buildings filled with people trying to survive in the daily onslaught of so many threats. One such outpost was but twenty miles inland from the beach where Station Seven sat alone.

Sometimes there were stragglers — mostly children — who slipped into the forsaken wood and couldn't find their way out again. The older a person was, the more devastating it was to be outside at all. But there was a magic age, or so it seemed, in which a person could be out quite a lot and still survive.

4200 days old and you could be outside for days at a time and still live. It wouldn't even bother a twelve- or thirteen-year-old. Before that, the human body was too fragile and there were awful side effects to overexposure. And after 5000 days — almost fourteen years old — things started to swing the other way again. The eyes would begin to sink deeper and darker. Soon, these children couldn't go outside at all without goggles and masks, which weren't always easy to come by.

It was this magic age of 4200 days that had kept Station Seven afloat as the Dark Planet grew darker and more dangerous.

Commander Judix finally saw Shelton's watery reflection in the glass.

"Yes, Madam?"

Shelton was a grave, humorless man. He hadn't always been that way, but the circumstances in which he found himself seemed to have drained all happiness from him. He had resigned himself to waiting for the end and knew it would come — probably sooner than later.

Commander Judix spun around in her chair. She was the

only person at Station Seven who could not be heard moving around, because she had no legs. She rolled from place to place in complete silence and was fond of sneaking up on people because it was something she could do that no one else could.

"How many 4200s at the Silo?" she asked. Eleven and a half years old sounded so young. Commander Judix was much more comfortable calling them by the number of days they'd been alive. 4200 days sounded like a long time to have lived in a fallen world.

Shelton was terrified by the sound of her voice. She had ruled the most powerful hemisphere, then commanded the entire world as it fell apart before her very eyes. She had been powerful beyond imagining, controlling armies and weaponry he couldn't calculate. And in this isolated world of Station Seven she remained the supreme ruler. It was an inescapable fact that, like King Henry or Queen Elizabeth, she controlled everything within her realm from the wheelchair throne she sat on.

"At last count — that would have been four days past — there were only two 4200's, a girl and a boy," answered Shelton in a shaky voice.

"Are you positive that's all there is?" asked Commander Judix, alarmed. "No one new in three months' time?"

"I'm afraid not, Madam. The wood has been very quiet as of late. And we lost two more of Grammel's batch last week. Most of what he's leaving behind isn't making it to 4000. He finds them along the way, you know. They're too young to be standing on the banks waiting for someone to save them. He only wants them if they're old enough and strong enough to work outside."

The number of new children had been dwindling fast for months. Commander Judix knew this. Where once there had been one or two children every week stumbling into one of the traps in the forsaken wood, now there were hardly any. And Captain Grammel was bringing nothing but 2000's who were far too weak to survive life in the Silo. Only a year ago there had been nine eleven-year-olds at the Silo, but they were gone now. The pipeline wasn't filling up as it once had.

"Send the transport farther out, past the wood if you have to."

Shelton could already imagine the conversation he would have with the dwindling transport team.

"It will be hard to convince them," he said. "They say the Spikers and Cleaners are fighting over territory more and more. The forsaken wood is a hazardous place, to say the least."

A mad rage boiled under Commander Judix's skin as she thought of Dr. Harding and the mess he'd left behind.

"Grammel will be here in four more days. If we can't produce at least three children, he's not going to leave us a hundred days' worth of fuel."

Shelton was thinking of the children in the Silo. Only two elevens, but there was a big group of tens. Six boys and four girls. And there were nines and eights — at least a dozen of them in all. That made . . . what was it? Twenty-four children. And only two elevens!

"It's a shame Grammel won't take them younger than 4200," said Shelton.

Grammel used the same device as Shelton, Red Eye, and

STATION SEVEN

FORSAKEN WOOD

CLIFFS

TOXIC FOG

POWER STATION

CAPTIAN GRANNEL'S BOAT

THE SILO

PASSAGEWAY OF LIES

LAB

STATION SEVEN   THE YARDS

MILES

Socket to measure the age of the children. If the tip of the device was touched to skin it would produce a reading, right down to the minute, of how old a person was.

"Maybe I could convince him. Captain Grammel's probably finding it slim all along the coastline," said Commander Judix. "He may well take whatever we can give him."

"Hope won't like this," said Shelton. "She'll make a terrible fuss."

"Then do your job," said Commander Judix. She had turned on him with an accusing tone, as if Shelton were the sole reason for their troubles.

Had she heard him? It wasn't a few Spikers in the forsaken wood, it was a pod of them, and that meant a queen. They couldn't let anything that big near Station Seven, but without Grammel's fuel the power station would stop running. What then? The air would run out, and the water, too. But most appalling of all, the electric shield would come down. They'd be unprotected. The Cleaners and Spikers could get in.

"I'll make them go farther out," he said. And then, thinking like the coward that he was, he added, "You know, a ten-year-old could be almost 4000 days old. We have ten of those in the Silo. I could check them to be sure."

Commander Judix didn't look at Shelton. She couldn't look at him without wanting to run him down with her chair. Is this what she was left with? Cowards and weaklings and fools! Everyone else had fled long ago. But what choice did she have? Spikers and Cleaners were rampant in the forsaken wood. She would have to start conserving fuel, running the power station on reserve. Soon, so very soon, the shields would fail and leave Station Seven open to attack.

They took my legs before — and my family. What would they take this time?

"See how many days old the tens are," she said. "And tell Red Eye and Socket what's going on. Don't say anything to Hope until we have to. You still have time to make this right."

The words stung in Shelton's mind as Commander Judix spun her chair around on its wheels and rolled away in silence, leaving him standing alone in a giant, empty room.

Grammel. Shelton couldn't stand the captain of the supply ship. Every hundred days, like clockwork, he would come on the churning waters of the acid-soaked sea. Moored at the hundred-yard tip of the stone jetty, he would pull the horn and send billowing plumes of black smoke into the air. Shelton could actually imagine the man's face, completely covered in soot and smiling from ear to ear, rows of white teeth flashing as he plugged in the fuel hose. Grammel's ship was huge and ugly, spewing a filth into the air that was as much liquid as smoke. The ship left everyone and everything in its path covered in rancid soot.

"You'll take the tens," whispered Shelton. "You'll take them or we'll have your precious ship and everything in it."

But a ship without a captain wasn't likely to set sail again, and eventually the fuel would run out for good. Then what would he do?

A little while later Aggie woke with a start as she always did, disoriented in the ever-present darkness of the Silo. She never seemed to get used to it.

"Wake up, Teagan," she whispered. "I think it's morning."

Teagan rolled groggily onto her side and reached out her hand. This was their habit — to hold hands in the early morning. Then, to whisper as they waited. Soon the door would fly open. Red Eye and Socket would barge in.

"Today is going to be a better day," whispered Aggie.

"I think you're right," said Teagan.

In truth, they were scared of what the day would bring. But they needed the reassurance that the other wouldn't be destroyed by the Silo or the people who ran it. The two smiled at each other in the dark and put their goggles on, and then they both heard the bolt pulled back and felt the rush of air as the big metal door burst open. Some of the children woke with eyes closed tight, fumbling for goggles.

"Green team is assigned to the drying room! Red to the vines and orange to the planting. On with you now!" cried Red Eye. He was in the worst kind of mood imaginable. His head was throbbing, which made him angrier than usual at this hour. He looked at Aggie, picked up the end of her bed, and flipped it over on top of her.

Socket cackled as Aggie hit the metal floor and scrambled out from under the overturned cot.

"Get up! Out of these beds and moving!" said Red Eye, turning his gaze on the rest of the room. He was hunched over more than usual from a poor night's sleep. Glancing back at

Aggie he yelled: "And pick up that filthy cot or you'll be sleeping on the floor."

Aggie and Teagan turned the rusted shell of the cot back over and set the rumpled mattress on top. They both groaned quietly. The drying room was one of the worst jobs in the Silo.

Anything but the drying room. . . .

CHAPTER

8

THE DOCKING STATION

As his feet left the ground, Edgar felt so impossibly heavy it was hard to imagine not dropping like a stone into the boiling pool below. And the heat was virtually unbearable. He was sure the steam had burned every hair off his head and the eyebrows from his face. His shirt was almost certainly in flames, his shorts torn free by fire. It felt as if it was cooking his skin, his brains, everything.

By some miracle Edgar felt his toes touch the other side. He had an immediate and highly distressing sense of falling backward that took his breath away and gave him the extra burst of adrenaline he needed to lean forward and out of harm's way.

He lay on the ground and rolled away from the heat as his limbs came back to a lower temperature. He felt his arms. The skin was still there. He slowly reached his hands up and touched his head. He laughed out loud at the joy of finding his full head of black hair still there. And his clothes, too — they were all intact. He stepped farther away from the opening, and then turned to see something he would never forget.

The object was a full thirty feet across at least and rose twenty feet into the air. It was, in a word, gargantuan. It was shaped a lot like an egg, perfectly round for the length of its middle and tapering off at both ends. And it was solid black. The object hovered several feet above the floor of the space, suspended by two wide black pins that stuck into the sides of the room.

What in the world is this thing? thought Edgar.

The object had one other feature that kept Edgar at bay. All along the deep black surface were spikes the likes of which Edgar had never seen. They appeared to have grown out of the object like razor-sharp roots in every direction. A million needle points, the tip of each one glistening in the yellow light of the room — and ever so slowly, randomly in and out, they moved as if trying to feel the air in the room. They seemed . . . could it be? Yes — they were *alive.*

Edgar looked down the line of the wall and saw that the deep grooves in which the wide pins sat ran down the sides of the room. It looked like the stone walls had been gouged by something hard and spinning.

"This moves," whispered Edgar. "It moves down the line and past the opening. And then where?"

Edgar crouched down and peered under the object. The moving spikes were there as well, leaving only a few feet to crawl under. On the other side was what appeared to be a door, but did he dare go under the million black spikes?

I'm standing in the path of this thing, thought Edgar,

wondering what it would feel like to be rolled over if it started to move. And if the thing fell down while he was under it . . . well, he couldn't imagine. There would be nothing left of him.

Despite his fear, Edgar resolved to lie on his back and creep ever so slowly along the floor. The spikes moved in and out, closer to his face as he went, as though they were trying to sniff Edgar as he passed below. He felt his breath catching in his throat in little bursts.

"Don't think about it," he said. "Think of something else. The grove and the lake. Swinging in the trees . . ." As he recited his memories of the world above, his breathing slowed and he continued moving until at last he reached the other side and stood up with a great sigh of relief.

It was darker on this side, but soft orange and yellow light crept in through thin veins in the stone walls. He took a few steps toward the door at the back of the room.

"This must be the way in — from the inside of Atherton," said Edgar. "The way that's blocked."

And it was exactly as Dr. Kincaid had said it would be. When Edgar opened the door he saw a few feet of tunnel, followed by a wall of dirt and stone as if the ceiling had caved in from above.

Edgar turned around and noticed something important about the gigantic black object: The back side had an opening that led inside. It was pitch-dark beyond the opening.

Edgar edged forward cautiously, trying to be perfectly quiet. *What if this thing is alive and doesn't like visitors? What if I wake it up? It could shoot a thousand arrows at me.*

His choices were severely limited. He had no desire to crawl underneath again; only monsters and firebugs awaited him on the other side. And the way inside Atherton was blocked. It seemed then to Edgar very much like he had been made to come here. His options, like a lit fuse, led only one way and seemed to vanish behind him. . . .

Stepping inside seemed to ignite something within. Fuzzy light appeared — and to Edgar's dread, the light was blue.

"This thing is full of firebugs!" cried Edgar. But as he turned to run he had a feeling he was only partly right. Something different was going on here, something new.

He took a few more tentative steps, placing him at the center of the object, truly inside, and all at once he saw from where the light had come.

Firebugs indeed surrounded him on every side, but they were everywhere and nowhere all at once. The ceiling was filled with dancing blue dots and so was the floor. Edgar reached out his hand and touched — what was it? It felt like the glass Dr. Kincaid had shown him that surrounded the lantern in the cave.

As Edgar moved his hand along the smooth and warm surface, the firebugs grew thick and mimicked the shape of his fingers. He pulled his hand away and saw that the shape of his hand remained in the blue light, then slowly disappeared as the firebugs moved off.

He placed his hand on the glass again and watched the firebugs gather from the other side, then pulled his hand away. He leaned in close so his nose was almost touching the glass and watched with growing interest as the firebugs slowly began to drift off.

Without warning, there was a tremendous *BANG!* on the surface as the glistening head of a cave eel smashed into the glass. Firebugs flew like sparks and Edgar jumped back, falling on the floor with a shout. The body of the cave eel slithered past and back into darkness, and Edgar marveled as he realized it was *swimming*.

"There's water — or something *like* water — behind the glass."

For the first time, Edgar really looked around and saw the inside of the vessel. The glowing blue of firebugs softly lit his way as he walked back and forth. It was a big space — twenty feet in length or nearly, and big around on every side. He could see the shadows of swimming cave eels as they swept by here and there. Soon he had counted seven but was sure there were more.

Edgar had arrived at one end of the vessel and there he found rows of black chairs, fifteen chairs in all, plus a separate set of six chairs facing one another. Between the six chairs was a wide block of black stone or glass. Edgar sat down and saw firebugs immediately filling the inside of the chair beneath him.

"Everything is connected," said Edgar. "It's like a living thing."

The chair was now aflame from the inside with a million tiny dots of hovering blue. The outside of the chair was soft but clear, like glass that had lost its ability to stay solid. Edgar

THE RAVEN

THE "LIVING" SPIKES
PULSE AS THOUGH
BREATHING

CLOSE-UP VIEW

ENTRY DOOR

RAZOR — SHARP

PIN POINTS

RAVEN CROSS-SECTION

MADE OF
GLASS OR
STONE

looked at the seat next to him and saw that something had been left there.

"Who was here last?" Edgar asked himself. He knew the answer to the question. It was Dr. Harding. He would have come here one last time before closing the way in for good.

At first glance the thing appeared to be a common piece of wood. It was four or five inches long and about the same width, and it was maybe an inch deep. When Edgar picked it up he found that it was heavier than he'd expected, and older, too. It was marred at the corners as if it had been dropped a great many times. In his hands it felt like something not of wood or stone but on the verge of being one or the other. All along the edges were words that had been burned into the surface, a large number of which Edgar could not read. And there were numbers — *lots* of numbers.

"I should have paid more attention to Samuel's teaching," said Edgar. He was newly embarrassed at his inability to read very well. He had learned some basics, but it had only been a year and he hadn't taken to studying as much as he'd hoped.

Edgar leaned forward in the chair and held the block in the blue light. The words were burned in thin, black lines. Taking up most of one side was something that looked like a map. On the side he'd been looking at — the one with the map at the center — there were two words at the top. One word he could easily read, the other he could not. I–N–S–I–D–E A–T–H–E–R–T–O–N.

"Atherton!" said Edgar. "But what's this other word?"

He tried to sound it out but had a most difficult time of it. Frustrated, Edgar flipped the wood over and tried to read the words on the other side. At the top was a word Edgar could spell but not pronounce or understand.

S–I–L–O.

Beneath the four letters was a code of sorts, etched just as big as the word S–I–L–O.

L–I–F–T–B–5.

Under the large word and the code there were many hundreds more, but none of them were nearly as prominent. Numbers, sentences, whole paragraphs burned in with some kind of thin, precise instrument. The instrument of a madman, thought Edgar, because he knew this could only have been done by Dr. Harding when he was quickly turning into the monster he had become — Lord Phineus.

"I wish you were here with me, Samuel. You could read this to me, like you've read to me before." Edgar felt totally alone in the quiet of a million firebugs. He examined the edges of the block, turning it in his hands, feeling for a notch. Just as he was thinking there was nothing there to find, he held the item by its corners and — more by accident than on purpose — pushed and played at the opposite ends. The two sides slid apart down the middle to reveal a hollow inside.

There were two things hidden in that space. The first was the tool that appeared to have been used to write on the outside of the wood. The sharp tip of the instrument reminded Edgar of the spikes that covered the vessel he was sitting in. Inside the instrument glowed dozens of tiny blue dots

"Firebugs," remarked Edgar, wondering how they could have gotten there.

Edgar picked up the pen and touched the tip to a clear spot

of hard wood on the inside. He drew the pen down and it left a thin black mark and a tiny waft of smoke. Edgar twisted and turned the pen over the surface. It was as if it was melting the wood away in the thinnest of perfect lines and swishes. He was drawing on the wood with a firebug pen.

"I like this thing," said Edgar, holding it up and seeing how it filled the air with soft blue light.

He placed the pen back in its resting spot and picked up the other item hidden inside the tablet. The item was small and flat and smooth, like a perfectly shaped skipping rock. And it was solid black like so many other things Edgar had come to find in this place. He pressed it, tapped it, and walked around the vessel in vain searching for a place to insert it.

Whatever the small object in his hand was it didn't seem to have any purpose, so Edgar set the disk down on the flat black table of glass before him and returned to searching the wooden tablet for clues. The moment the disk hit the table, Edgar's life was altered forever.

It was the key to everything, and without realizing it, Edgar had just used it to make a long-awaited connection with the Dark Planet.

CHAPTER

9

THE RAVEN

A rush of warm wind filled the vessel when Edgar dropped the disk onto the black surface of the table. This sent Edgar into a panic, because the moving air was accompanied by a sound from the general area of the door he'd entered through. Edgar jumped up, started for the opening, and found it closed to the outside world.

I'm trapped in here.

Edgar returned to the table. Millions of tiny blue dots were dancing beneath the glassy surface. And what was more, they were coming together in ways Edgar had never seen before. They flew randomly at first, covering every square inch of the surface, but then they began to organize. It looked like someone was under the table drawing with a glowing blue pen. Whoever it was who made the drawings — if a person it happened to be — was a talented artist. The firebugs danced into position, huddling together in different places, and before Edgar's eyes a scene began to form.

What are you trying to show me?

Soon there was a cluster of firebugs at the very center about the size of the tip of Edgar's finger. "I know you," said Edgar. "You're Atherton."

At the bottom corner there grew a much larger circle — bigger than Edgar's head, and darker, too. "And you," he said, a little wary of naming the place, though he couldn't say why. "You're the Dark Planet."

Firebugs positioned themselves all through the open space between the two clusters. They looked like a night sky, sparkling as stars are made to do. A series of figures was forming along the right edge of the table. It was like magic. First, a thick fog of blue dots, then half of them dropping away, leaving the faces of those he knew quite well.

The face of Dr. Harding appeared first, drawn out in blue, at the top. Below him the face of Dr. Kincaid, then Vincent, and after that the faceless shape of a head. Beside each face was a cluster of bugs that made the shape of a thumbprint.

"What am I supposed to do?" said Edgar. He held his hand over the table and decided to touch the faces first, which produced no result. His finger then brushed over the faceless head and all the faces disappeared at once. In their place were three new faces, none of which Edgar recognized. But there was one that he liked the best, because it was a boy his own age, not a man. The boy looked familiar in a strange sort of way, and Edgar wondered if it was himself he was looking at.

He put his thumb on the cluster next to the face and the

firebugs burst out in every direction. The blue dots reformed into a word and a question mark. Edgar felt a chill despite the warmth in the room as he read what was there.

HELLO, EDGAR.

It was scary seeing his name appear like that, floating into view as if rising from the deepest part of a lake. The word evaporated and the face of Dr. Harding reappeared. And then, to Edgar's amazement, the glowing blue face of Dr. Harding began to speak.

"I had a feeling you might find the docking station. I can't say that I'm happy you take such risks. What father could be happy about a thing like that?"

"Can you hear me?" asked Edgar. "Where are you?"

Edgar was struck by an impossible thought: What if Dr. Harding were alive inside this strange vessel? Maybe he'd only hidden here, waiting for Edgar to return! He eagerly touched the warm glass where the face appeared. "Come out of there!"

"I made this recording for you, Edgar," said Dr. Harding. "I'm not here, in case that's what you're thinking. A trick of technology, I'm afraid. Chances are I made this recording many years ago and things have unraveled as I'd suspected they would."

Edgar couldn't understand and demanded an explanation. "How can you be here and *not* be —"

"Listen to me, Edgar," the image interrupted. "If you're here then a lot has already happened. Atherton has collapsed, which you have managed to survive. I am, no doubt, dead."

"No! You're not dead! You're right here," said Edgar. He knew the face wasn't really Dr. Harding, but he was so lonely and frustrated he couldn't quite let go of the idea. "You're alive!"

But the blue head wouldn't respond to Edgar.

"I can't tell you how important it is that you listen to me now," said Dr. Harding. "You *must* do as I say. Everything depends on it. First and foremost, you cannot trust anyone on Atherton. No one, including Dr. Kincaid and Vincent, has any idea what Atherton is really for. This was entirely necessary given the circumstances. No one would have believed, no one would have trusted, no one would have had the patience required . . ."

Without warning, the firebugs began drifting off, and Dr. Harding's face started to melt into a watery mix of black and blue.

"Come back!" said Edgar.

Dr. Harding's voice became garbled and slowed down, but then the firebugs reconstructed his face and he was speaking as before. Edgar had missed something.

". . . and so you see, I can't trust anyone else with this task. If my experiment has gotten this far along, well, it's you and you alone who must finish it. Things will have gotten very complicated down there. Dr. Kincaid and Vincent are not bad men, but they will only get in the way of what you have to do. They answer to people on the Dark Planet."

The face of Dr. Harding looked straight at Edgar and it nearly broke Edgar's heart. There was his father, right in front of him, smiling at Edgar with approval.

"This thing you're sitting in is called the Raven, or at least that's what I've always called it. I made it like I made you and Atherton. It's alive, just like you and Atherton are alive. It's very easy to operate if you follow its lead and trust its actions. It will take you to the Dark Planet. You need to go there alone and finish what I began."

"What!" shouted Edgar. The firebugs moved off again and Dr. Harding's face dissolved. Apparently, the bugs didn't like it when Edgar interrupted. He stayed very quiet and the face returned one last time.

"How can I say this? You and Atherton and the Raven, the three of you are connected, if you will, by the same raw material. How else could you do all the things you do? I know, I know — this sounds terrible — but it's the truth."

There was a pause in which Dr. Harding seemed to wonder what he should say next.

"You're going to need a little help," he continued with greater concern in his voice. "You were always a solitary little boy on the Dark Planet, but hopefully you've made at least one friend on Atherton. Give the tablet I've left behind to someone you trust, someone who can read. Something important needs to happen here on Atherton while you're away. But keep Dr. Kincaid and Vincent out of it. Now that you have the keys to the Raven, they'll think they can help on the Dark Planet. But trust me, Edgar, their good intentions would lead straight to Judix, and that's exactly what can't happen."

"Who's Judix?" asked Edgar. "What are you talking about?"

The face on the screen turned away from Edgar, as if it had heard someone or something coming near when it was recorded. The face turned back and began to drift into blackness.

"Go to the Silo first, where I lived as a boy, where everything began. Be careful who you trust."

The firebugs danced and moved and Dr. Harding disappeared.

"Come back! Don't leave me here alone!" said Edgar. But the face of Dr. Harding was gone. There appeared an outline of the Silo so that Edgar would know what it looked like. Then it vanished, replaced by the image of Atherton and the Dark Planet in their places, surrounded by a night sky of blue dots.

Edgar was now unable to imagine an outcome in which his feet weren't firmly planted on the Dark Planet. If Dr. Harding had lived in the Silo as a child, he had probably first imagined Atherton there. Edgar was sure the Silo was where he would find the answers to his most troubling questions. Where did he come from? What had gone wrong with the man who had made him? What was the purpose behind Edgar's existence?

He touched the oval disk that had started everything in motion. It was warm and slippery, like a small pool of shallow water, and yet it was also solid. Edgar slid the disk off the surface and let it drop into his other hand. The firebugs receded until only darkness remained on the table and Edgar heard the sound of the doorway opening.

He could escape this place and take his chances on the outside with all the dangers that awaited him.

Looking back at the table, Edgar had a sudden sense of clarity about the place he found himself in. He set the disk back on the black surface, heard the door shut, and watched the firebugs return and form the map of Atherton and the Dark Planet.

"I can command this thing to move," said Edgar, smiling in wonder at the thought of it. "I know I can."

He felt it in his bones, as though he and Atherton and the Raven really were connected by some unknown essential material.

Reaching out over the black surface Edgar touched the big cluster of blue that made up the Dark Planet. Words appeared.

Silo / Station Seven

Edgar couldn't read the second word and he didn't care about the third. All he saw was the word "Silo." Dr. Harding's last words rang in Edgar's ears.

Where I lived as a boy, where everything began.

On a whim, Edgar touched the much smaller cluster of blue representing Atherton. The flat surface exploded with blue dots that formed into three concentric circles, one on top of the other, each one a little bit bigger than the last.

"This is an old map of Atherton," Edgar noted. "Things have changed."

Leaning over the surface, Edgar saw that it was indeed the surface of Atherton. So detailed was the map he could see the House of Power in the Highlands, the grove and the other villages in Tabletop, and Dr. Kincaid's boulder-strewn home in the Flatlands.

Much of what Edgar was looking at was no more. Everything inside the smaller two circles was belowground and under water, but the outer circle — the Flatlands — remained. It made Edgar wonder about the Dark Planet. Had it also changed? Maybe it was already dead. Maybe the Silo wasn't even there any longer.

"I have to find Samuel and Isabel before I go," said Edgar. Was he really saying that? Leaving for the Dark Planet? It was such a gigantic idea. If only he could give the wooden tablet to his friends. Samuel could read and decipher it.

Edgar reached out and almost touched the very place where Dr. Kincaid and Vincent lived. At the last second he realized that if this were to set something in motion as he suspected it might, he would not want to find himself at Dr. Kincaid's doorstep.

Edgar moved his finger closer to where the grove would be and touched the place on the map where he wanted to go.

The vessel moved ever so slightly and Edgar scrambled into one of the six seats around the table. He picked up the two tablets and slid them back together again with a snap. There was a grinding noise from outside, but Edgar heard only a faint whisper of sound. All through the walls, ceiling, and floor of the vessel, creatures were moving and firebugs were glowing brighter.

Edgar had awoken the Raven and it had begun to move.

"You're not a machine," said Edgar, petting the armrest instinctively. "I know that word. Dr. Kincaid told me about machines. They're cold and dead, that's what he said about machines. He said the Dark Planet was full of them. But you're not like that, are you? Neither one of us is like that."

Edgar felt confident the Raven was moving faster now, though he had no way of knowing for sure. He watched the eels swimming all around him in the murky black. Their mouths opened and firebugs tried to escape their predators. They left blue trails of quickly dying light.

Without warning, Edgar felt a pull on his legs and back from the seat he sat in. He felt glued to the chair by an unseen force.

The Raven had begun to roll and gain speed, but it remained fairly calm inside. Already the Raven had moved past the giant stone-covered monster and watched it cower in fear of a million spikes. The Raven was virtually indestructible, and she was more useful than Edgar knew.

She came to the point in the tunnel where it dropped off violently, and this time Edgar felt the surge of speed. He couldn't move his limbs as the Raven went faster still. The seven rock-encrusted cave eels that had waited for Edgar's return heard the spiked beast coming and cowered deep in their holes, snapping their jaws in nervous fear.

The Raven shot through the hole and into the open air around Atherton. Silent and stealthily it flew, rising as if invisible in the dark night until it landed ever so quietly on the surface of the Flatlands.

●

It was night on Atherton as Edgar moved quietly over a rocky surface peppered with clumps of green grass. The Raven had landed to the right of the grove, which meant Edgar would have to pass through a wide pasture.

Edgar had begun his adventure climbing down the side of Atherton in the late morning of the same day and found it hard to believe so much time had passed. He was hungry, thirsty, and tired. Though he pressed on soundlessly as he neared his destination, the sheep in the pasture saw his approach, scurrying off in clusters and *baa*ing as they went.

"You're bothering my sheep."

Edgar jumped back and lost his footing, dropping the tablet with a bang as it landed badly on the rocks below. It was the shepherdess Maude, out watching the herd much later than he'd expected.

"Sorry, Maude . . . I was just passing through on my way to the grove."

Edgar and Maude knew each other well. They both understood the secretive nature of the other.

"I see," said Maude. She was a portly woman with a round face, known for her strong personality.

Maude leaned against a shepherd's staff and clicked her tongue in the direction of the herd.

"Edgar's not going to hurt you. He's only sneaking back from someplace he doesn't want anyone knowing about."

Maude raised an eyebrow at Edgar and locked her eyes with his in the dim light of night. She was worried about him, but she also wouldn't pry or try to stop him. After all that Edgar had accomplished in the past she had learned to let him go about his business.

"I have to leave for a little while," said Edgar, knowing Maude would understand.

Maude stabbed the end of the staff into the dirt and looked off toward the lake.

"Where are you planning to go? There's not much around the other side."

She had been all the way around the lake in search of pastures and found nothing better than the ground she stood on.

Edgar didn't answer. He had discovered a crack along one

side of the tablet. The two sides were still stuck together at the middle, but in the faint light Edgar could see that one had been damaged.

"What have you got there?"

"Something I found. I'd like Samuel to have it, because there's a lot of writing."

Then and there Edgar struck on an idea.

"Would you give it to him for me?"

Like the majority of people on Atherton, Maude couldn't read. She didn't want any part of books or words, so there was no risk in having her discover what the words said. She took the tablet and examined it curiously.

"Where are you going, Edgar?"

Edgar hesitated before answering, but in the end he knew he couldn't leave his friends without telling them where he'd gone.

"I'm leaving Atherton, but I'll be back. Make sure you tell them I'm coming right back. I won't be gone long."

"What do you mean, leaving Atherton?" asked Maude, stricken with fear for the boy. "You're not making any sense, Edgar."

"Tell Samuel there are things hidden inside," said Edgar, pointing to the tablet. "If he can get the two sides to slide apart. And tell Isabel I'm sorry — I'm really, really sorry. I didn't have a choice. I had to go."

"Go where, Edgar?"

Edgar looked back toward the Raven, hidden in the night. He simply couldn't imagine leaving his friends without telling them.

"The Dark Planet. To find out why we're here."

This news came as a shock to Maude. The Dark Planet? The words rang in her head and she knew them. There was a buried memory that would not surface, but it left a lingering feeling. And, oddly, a smell. Like something burning, but what? She sniffed the air deeply but it was gone. *My memory is playing tricks on me,* she thought. She shook her head and looked again at Edgar.

"I'll give this to Samuel," said Maude. She knew from experience that Edgar was venturing out on his own and that he'd have it no other way. She removed a pack from around her shoulders. Inside were figs, bread, and a leather pouch of water. Maude had often come out in the night, only to find herself sleeping with the sheep and waking hungry and thirsty.

"It's my breakfast," she said, holding out the bag. "Take it with you. Who knows where your next meal will come from?"

"This is just what I needed!" said Edgar. "Thank you, Maude!"

"And I'll tell them where you've gone."

Maude put her arms around Edgar and they embraced for a long moment. For Edgar it felt like Atherton itself was holding him and wouldn't let him go. It aimed to keep him here, to keep him from knowledge it didn't want Edgar to have.

"Are you sure you want to do this?" asked Maude. "What if you're about to see things you were never supposed to know about?"

Edgar pulled away and backed up a few paces, sure Maude was going to try to stop him.

"I can't stay here, Maude. I just can't."

He steadied Maude's pack on his shoulders and walked away, expecting Maude to follow. But she didn't.

In the deepest part of night on Atherton, Samuel and Isabel waited at the edge of the crevice for their friend to return. They wondered where he had gone and vowed to wait all night if they had to. They fretted over his safety and guessed at what he was doing.

The Raven moved in silence, invisible against the dark sky.

Samuel and Isabel couldn't have known that before their very eyes, as they looked out over the edge, their closest friend was leaving Atherton without them.

PART
TWO

THE SILO

If ever I return,
It will be on Gossamer's wings.

Dr. Maximus Harding
Into Hidden Realms

CHAPTER

10

THE FORSAKEN WOOD

Sunrise on the Dark Planet was the saddest time of all. At night a person could look out from the sterile safety of Station Seven and imagine everything was perfectly fine. There was so much less devastation to see when things were truly dark, and this made the dawning of each new day all the more depressing.

"What was that?" said Commander Judix from her bed. She thought she'd heard something from the direction of the forsaken wood.

Cleaners and Spikers looking for food?

Lacking evidence, her dismal outlook always pointed to the worst possible scenario. If only she had allowed herself to imagine what had *really* made the sound. She would have discovered the arrival of a vessel from the forgotten world of Atherton.

She opened her eyes and saw the time. Six a.m. Another hour, maybe two, and she would have to face Hope, the acting mother in the Silo next door. It was an encounter she looked forward to with a mounting sense of dread.

Escaping her bed and flopping down in the safety of her chair was a complicated business, but one she was proud to handle on her own. She had always preferred to manage these difficult tasks herself without the aid of some idiot feeling sorry for her. And she didn't want any fake parts attached to her, either. Her legs were gone and that was that.

Commander Judix rolled her chair to a small window and looked out. To gaze at the forsaken wood in the pale morning light was to see the shattered remains of what once was. The trees were last to go. They looked for all the world like a stand in the deepest part of winter, or a burned-out forest reaching helplessly towards the sky. It was the smog that made a person realize the trees could never return. It snaked through grey limbs, strangling their trunks. And somewhere in there were monsters of a kind Commander Judix couldn't think of without trembling.

She rolled away from the window and opened a cooling unit. There was a small plastic bottle of milky water inside and she removed it, mixed in two spoonfuls of white powder from a container, and gulped it down. It left a chalky white film that made her compulsively chew and lick at her waxy lips until the feeling went away. There were small bars of food in the cooling unit as well, and she took one, eating it without the slightest emotion.

Commander Judix rolled in front of a mirror and pinned up her brown hair. She hadn't washed it in nine days, not because there was no water, but because the thought of having it dry and brittle after a good scrubbing was almost too much to

112

bear. After five days her hair was soft as silk. She could run her fingers through it for hours and not tire of the feeling. Soft hair was something she could control, a small but meaningful pleasure she hated giving up.

Looking again at the time, Commander Judix decided there was probably enough of the early morning left to ride down the corridor to Dr. Harding's laboratory. She hadn't been there in so long, but things were getting desperate. Against her better judgment she couldn't help but maintain enough hope to at least check the old lab every few weeks. What if the blip returned and Atherton came back online?

"I wonder what bad news today will bring?" she said. She didn't have to wait as long as she'd expected for trouble to arrive. Already she could hear the familiar sound of footsteps coming down the corridor that led to the Silo. From the distinctive long stride and a light step, she could tell that Hope was coming. *Remember who's in charge here. Don't let her push you around.*

Commander Judix rolled to the door and opened it.

"I won't let you take them. They're too young."

Hope had long since given up saluting or offering any other signs of respect. As far as she was concerned this was not the president or the supreme ruler. Station Seven was no longer a command post doing important scientific work. It was an outpost of the apocalypse like all the others. Some of the old rules of behavior simply didn't apply.

"You're calling a little early this morning, don't you think?"

"You can't have them," Hope declared. She was a tall, graceful woman with black skin. Her hair was very short and peppered

with white. She had the fierce eyes of a mother protecting her children.

"We have no choice," said Commander Judix, engaging her chair. Hope jumped out of the way as it passed by and started toward Dr. Harding's laboratory.

"Don't do this, Jane," said Hope. She watched as Commander Judix's chair stopped, spun around, and motored back. Hope had called the commander by her first name, something she hadn't done in a very long time.

Commander Judix looked up at the tall woman in front of her with icy resolve. "We agreed that if you stayed you wouldn't make trouble. Coming over here — *badgering* me this way at six in the morning — and calling me that *name* . . . it's a lot of trouble all at once."

Hope knew she was on shaky ground. She commanded almost no power at Station Seven, less it seemed as time had gone on. She had come to the Station as a doctor, but it was the children who made her stay long after almost everyone had fled. It was Hope's job, in the face of so much darkness, to keep the youngest abandoned and orphaned children of the Silo from dying before her eyes.

"You told me you'd never go below 4200," said Hope. She was fighting mad. "You let two tyrants run the Silo and ship these kids off to God knows where" — Hope trembled momentarily — "Shelton said you might even take a *ten*-year-old. You can't do that, Jane! I won't let you take them."

"Stop calling me that name!" Commander Judix screamed with such force her emotionless, pallid face actually shaded with color.

They heard steps clattering from two or three different directions, the empty tin echo bouncing everywhere. It was hard to say how many people were on their way.

"If I ask for a ten-year-old, you'll give me a ten-year-old," said Commander Judix, trying with all her might to remain calm. "Or would you rather I shut this whole operation down? Where will all your precious children go then?"

Hope knew the awful truth. There was only one person who could shut down Station Seven, and that was Commander Judix. She alone kept the station running. It had been her sickening idea from the beginning, but it was also a sort of insurance policy. Every ten days she went to a keypad and punched in a series of nine numbers. If the numbers weren't entered, the power grid would go into irreversible shutdown. Within a few days the air filters would fail, the defenses would be down, everything would be over.

"I know where I'll go when I don't enter the numbers," continued Commander Judix. "I'm a former leader of the free world. Just because this place has failed doesn't mean I can't escape. I've already held on for years longer than anyone else would have. There are plenty of places in this broken-down world where I can sit this out in peace and quiet until the very end."

She was lying, of course. Station Seven was better than most other places on the Dark Planet. The remaining enclaves, scattered across the globe, were overcrowded, disease ridden, and always short on food and water.

"What's happened to you?" asked Hope.

"When was the last time you looked outside?" asked Commander Judix. "Our choices become more limited every day. Our choices become *harder*. And I have to make those choices while you *babysit*. Stop questioning me!"

"You've compromised too much," said Hope. She had a burning anger of her own. Even as Commander Judix turned her chair and rolled away toward oncoming footsteps, Hope would be heard. "Did you enjoy your breakfast this morning, Jane? They risked their lives to make it for you — did you forget about that?"

"They receive from me a safe place to sleep, free from Cleaners and Spikers and the menacing smog of the outside!" Commander Judix had turned. She'd decided she didn't want to talk to anyone approaching her nor visit the laboratory. She wanted to be left alone.

Commander Judix had rolled back into her room. She was about to close the door in Hope's face.

"Jane, please — don't do this. Give them at least until they can stand it outside."

Commander Judix grabbed the edge of the door. "Go back to the Silo where you belong."

She flung the door shut, thinking all the while of her lost mother and father and sister, all of them lost in the forsaken wood because of that madman Dr. Harding and all his monstrous mistakes. And that name! No one around here ever called her Jane, only her family had called her that. It burned her insides to see their faces and hear them calling her name. *Jane! Jane!*

It was God's sick humor she was alive at all.

After Edgar ate all the food and drank all the water Maude had given him he had a hard time keeping his eyes open. He was tired and the Raven was so warm inside. He made the longest part of the journey to the Dark Planet in his sleep, unaware of the impossible speed at which he was traveling.

Just before dawn he arrived in the atmosphere of the Dark Planet and it stirred him in his sleep, if only for a brief moment. The outside layer of the Raven spun violently, but the inside remained still and steady. It wasn't until the Raven landed on the Dark Planet, ripping through a grove of trees on its spinning final descent, that Edgar was finally jolted awake.

"Who's there?" said Edgar as he awoke in the chair. Whatever force had held him down was gone now and he was free to move. Soon he was on his feet, stumbling around in the near dark.

"You look tired," he said to the Raven, noticing the empty blackness of the glass walls. There were firebugs scattered here and there, but no cave eels. It looked to Edgar like the Raven would need some time to restore energy before she could travel again.

Is it really possible I've left Atherton? thought Edgar, rubbing his eyes as they grew accustomed to the paltry blue light. As the full force of what he'd done dawned on him, he felt very lonely and afraid.

"What have I done?" he said, and looking at the lifeless walls of the Raven, added, "and what if I can't get back home?"

Edgar looked at the flat, black disk lying on the now lifeless table. The disk would fit in his pocket, but he was afraid to pick it up. He knew what would happen if he did.

Are you ready for the Dark Planet? he asked himself, trying to put on a brave face. *It can't be as bad as the Flatlands once were, right? At least this place won't be crawling with Cleaners.*

Edgar had landed the Raven in the same place it had always landed, hidden in the depths of the forsaken wood.

"Here we go, then," said Edgar, placing the black disk in his pocket. He heard the door slide open and saw the foggy air emerge. It was murky outside, but stepping through the door he quickly realized it wasn't completely dark, only dim like night on Atherton. The air smelled like nothing he'd ever smelled before. It was a sharp scent he could actually taste on his lips. He had a hard time breathing it in and began coughing.

The fit of noise set off a series of other noises Edgar hadn't expected. Some of the sounds were horrifyingly familiar.

"Cleaners," whispered Edgar, totally surprised to hear the ghastly roar of a monster he knew all too well. "And by the sound of it, big ones."

He stood in shock, unable to move his feet as he listened. The earth shook and a sound like breaking bones and slamming jaws came rapidly closer. If this really was an approaching Cleaner, it would have huge teeth attached to a set of jaws wide enough to cut Edgar in half. It would have a hundred rattling bony legs and a long, hideous body with an underbelly that sucked up everything in its path.

The smog was thick through the barren tree trunks as Edgar peered out. It wasn't until he caught the first glimpse of the creature that he finally turned and dove back inside the Raven.

With a quick flick of his wrist Edgar pulled the disk from

his pocket, tossing it toward the table like a skipping rock. When the disk touched the table it stuck, as though it had been pulled down by an unseen force. The door *whoosh*ed shut with little more than a few seconds to spare. If he had taken a moment longer he would have shared the space with the chomping head of something very big and hungry.

"What was *that*?" said Edgar, breathless with terror. He wished he could see what kind of monster he faced. He felt the Raven rock back and forth and heard the sound of an animal crying out in pain.

"Whatever's out there just touched you, didn't it?" asked Edgar, thinking of the million razor-sharp spikes that covered the Raven's shell. "You haven't been here for a long time. Maybe they forgot what they were dealing with."

Edgar felt a mix of emotions as he heard the beaten creature move off. On the one hand, he was safe inside. He could already see more firebugs emerging in the black walls, floor, and ceiling. Soon enough, he could turn the Raven around and go back home.

But another part of him was dying to go outside and explore, regardless of the dangers. He'd faced down cliffs and Cleaners and floods before. The Dark Planet was a challenge he wanted to overcome.

"I wonder . . . ," said Edgar. He tapped the table and firebugs returned. A map of the world outside of the vessel emerged. On one side was a body of water that appeared to go on forever, its beach surrounded by a forest and jagged rocks. On the beach a building was indicated by a square, and from the building a line led outward to a tube-shaped structure at its end.

"And there I am," said Edgar, pointing to a small, oblong image in the trees. He looked carefully at the map and decided the tube-shaped structure had to be the place called the Silo. It looked so close, perhaps only a short walk away.

Scanning the image, Edgar noticed that about halfway through the forest, between the Raven and the Silo, there appeared to be a series of giant holes.

"If there are holes, there are cliffs leading down, and I could hide in there if I needed to," said Edgar. "Unless something lives inside them."

Edgar sat down and took a deep breath. Like so many times before, he knew his mind was already made up.

Edgar picked up the black disk again and the door opened. The firebugs darted away, and the tails of cave eels pulled back into the deepest part of the walls as if the Raven knew the forsaken wood was poison and wanted nothing to do with it.

Edgar peered out the door. Seeing and hearing nothing nearby, he stepped out onto the barren surface of the Dark Planet.

Dawn had passed into morning and the haze of smog was a level lighter, though still murky, like looking through muddy water cut through with sunlight. Pollution lay thick and heavy through an endless stand of desolate trees.

Edgar looked for some mechanism that might shut the door from the outside, but there was nothing to be found. This should have alerted Edgar to another way out from the inside, a way that could allow the door to remain shut, but he didn't make the connection.

You'll have to make do on your own until I come back.

Edgar pocketed the disk and started off, keeping an eye on the widest of the trees in case he had to climb one in order to hide from an oncoming threat. He looked back at the Raven, but it had already disappeared in the thick smog of the forsaken wood.

CHAPTER
11

THE KEY TO MULCIBER

"I'm never going to forgive him. Never, ever, ever."

Samuel sat next to Isabel and listened to her grumbling as they watched Maude walk away. Maude had done what she had promised, giving the tablet to Samuel and telling the two of them where Edgar had gone. But Maude didn't have the will to involve herself any more than she had to. She and her husband Briney's life had returned to its normal state of simplicity and she liked it that way. If trouble was coming she'd deal with it on arrival and not a moment sooner.

"You'll have to forgive him," said Samuel. "It's what he does, and he knows you'd only want to stop him. You can't make him stay safe and cozy all the time. He'll come back. He always does."

Isabel stewed a little more. Samuel looked in every direction to be sure they were alone by the water's edge. Satisfied, he lifted the tablet from where it had been placed between the rocks.

"What do you think it is?" asked Isabel.

"It's two-sided," said Samuel, trying to pry the two halves apart with his fingernails. "And they come apart, or at least I think they do. Maybe there's something hidden inside."

"Here, let me see it," said Isabel. Samuel reluctantly handed it to her. Isabel gave it a brief glance, then held it over her head so she could smash it against the rocks.

"What are you doing!" cried Samuel, reaching up to take it from her. "We have to be careful with it. There's a lot that needs to be read on there."

"Here, you can have it," she said, pushing the tablet into Samuel's hands and beginning to walk away all in one fluid motion. She felt he was punishing her for not knowing how to read better.

"Wait — Isabel, please. I didn't mean anything by it. Let's look at it together and see what we can figure out."

Isabel ignored him. Neither Edgar nor Samuel seemed to understand how a friend was supposed to act.

"Come on, Isabel. I said I was sorry. I need your help on this. I can't do it alone."

Isabel stopped but didn't turn around right away. She took out her sling, set a dried fig inside, and began swinging it over her head. *Fwoosh, fwoosh, fwoosh* — faster and faster it went until *snap!* she let it fly out over the water. Samuel watched until it went so far he almost lost sight of it, a tiny black speck against a deep blue sea of water. The effort made Isabel feel better.

"Let me see it again," she said, turning. She would leave if he wouldn't trust her with the tablet.

Samuel hesitated before holding it out toward her. When Isabel took it she ran her fingers over the letters that covered one side. She could feel them, etched as they were, and it was a new sensation she liked. Like Edgar before her, she quickly figured out the second word at the top. A–T–H–E–R–T–O–N. "Atherton! That's what it says," she said proudly.

"You're right," said Samuel. "Let me have a look."

She held it out.

"And that other word, I think you know that one as well."

Isabel wrinkled her brow so it fell low over her eyelashes. Her long black hair fell over the sides of her face as she concentrated on the letters. First, she said something that sounded like *in-sid*, but right after, without any help, she changed her mind.

"Inside — inside Atherton!" cried Isabel. But then she realized what she'd read. Samuel saw that she was shaking, a look of terror on her face he'd only seen once before.

"It's all right, Isabel. Don't think about it."

Isabel handed the tablet back to Samuel and turned away. The inside of Atherton held the Inferno, which had almost killed Isabel not that long ago.

"It's just a tablet, Isabel. We don't have to do anything with it."

Deep down there was nothing Samuel wanted more than to read the tablet top to bottom, to absorb every single word and number. It fascinated him beyond all reason.

"I think we should set it on fire," said Isabel. "Whatever it says can only bring trouble."

"We can't do that. And I don't think we should just give it to Dr. Kincaid. There must be a reason Edgar wanted *us* to have it."

"I still say we should get rid of it," said Isabel.

"We can't do that! What if there's something important here? This is the work of Dr. Harding — that's obvious. We can't just destroy it, Isabel."

"Then you read it. I don't want to read any more."

Samuel was secretly glad Isabel didn't want to read the tablet. He offered to let her sit by the water's edge while he gave the tablet a good long look.

After what seemed like hours to Isabel but was actually only a little over thirty minutes, Samuel set the tablet aside in the rocks. He moved over next to Isabel and the two gazed out over open water.

"I don't want you to overreact," said Samuel, "but there are some things you need to know."

Isabel squeezed the hard, black fig in her hand, trying to stay calm.

"Promise me we're not going back through the Inferno," she said. If Samuel could guarantee that this message didn't lead to a river of fire with firebugs and cave eels, she was willing to at least listen.

He smiled the smile of someone who knows something special and is dying to share it. "I promise," he said. He saw Isabel nod ever so slightly, and taking the cue, he began pointing to different parts of the tablet.

"There are a lot of numbers, mostly in sets of five, so they must have unlocked some part of Dr. Harding's brain. You remember when we were inside his laboratory before, how there were so many five-digit numbers, and how he used them to lock things away in his mind? Well, I think the ones on this tablet must be important. He obviously carried this around with him in the absence of journals. These numbers are burned in. They're permanent."

Isabel became more interested in the tablet and pointed to a group of words trapped inside a circle. "What's that say?"

Samuel recited the words he'd already read and thought about. "Birth of the Nubian, the making of the Inferno, the fall of Atherton, the flood, an altered state of Cleaners, the chill of winter."

"That sounds — I don't know, it sounds like a list of some kind," said Isabel.

"Maybe it's a list of things that are going to happen. If that's what this refers to, then the list appears to be in order, or at least it could be. Maybe the Nubian came first, at the beginning — you remember those?"

How could Isabel forget the giant winged creatures inside Atherton, the way they had tucked their wings and dove, their glistening black beaks as sharp as arrows aimed at her and her friends?

"Then came the making of the Inferno," said Isabel.

"The fall of Atherton and the altered state of Cleaners — those have both happened," he said.

"That only leaves the last one," said Isabel, looking at the words and trying to remember what Samuel had said. "The . . . chill of winter, right?"

"That's the strangest of them all," said Samuel. He looked at Isabel. "Do you know what winter is?"

She did not, because there had never been anything like winter on Atherton.

"Some of the books I used to read in the Highlands talked about winter. It's a time when everything turns very cold and —"

"And what?" asked Isabel. She pierced right through Samuel with those brilliant dark eyes of hers. It was impossible for him to keep secrets from her. He couldn't figure out how Edgar had done it.

"In the time of winter everything dies," said Samuel.

"When you say everything, you mean *everything*?"

Samuel didn't know how to respond. He hadn't ever had any real experience with winter, so he didn't really understand it.

"I don't know for sure. But there's something else about winter, and it might be more important given what these words say. Winter is really cold."

"And you know what else is really interesting?" said Isabel. "The chill of winter is the last thing on the list. What do you suppose that means?"

"It means we're coming to the end of one thing and the beginning of another. This is really important."

"I wish we could show it to Dr. Kincaid."

Samuel and Isabel trusted Edgar more than anyone else. Until their friend returned, the tablet was theirs to protect. They weren't sure exactly why, but they couldn't share it with Dr. Kincaid or anyone else just yet.

"There are all sorts of things on this tablet. I haven't even begun to understand it all. The other side is full of things that are completely beyond me. The Silo, Station Seven, Spikers, the lost garden — it's all so confusing. And then there's this."

Samuel pointed to the left corner of the tablet, where he saw a collection of lines and markings and words almost too tiny to read.

"What is it?" asked Isabel.

"It's the key to Mulciber," said Samuel, reading some of the words. Seeing Isabel still didn't quite understand, he spoke more directly, pointing to a long word of eight letters.

"That word right there — THEYARDS — that's the word, Isabel. It will open the yellow door."

The yellow door. They'd long wanted to open it but had never known how. The eight-letter combination had been kept from them by Dr. Kincaid and Vincent.

"Are you thinking what I'm thinking?" asked Isabel.

Samuel just smiled. They had the key to Mulciber! They could actually get back inside Atherton.

"We could just take a quick look around," said Isabel. "We don't have to go very far, right?"

"Absolutely!"

Samuel loved the idea of adventure almost as much as Edgar did, and going back inside Atherton was the most adventurous thing he could think of.

"You see there? That's the Inferno," said Samuel, pointing down a path on the map so delicately burned into wood. "But this map leads in the opposite direction."

Isabel could see that he was right.

"But where does it lead to? And why would we go back in there?"

She secretly loved the idea of having an adventure of her own to tell Edgar about when he got back and was beginning to hope it would work. There was something very appealing about taking up this challenge while their closest friend was on a far-away quest of his own.

"It leads here," said Samuel. His finger followed the jagged path of a burned line. It went every which way, rising and falling, passing words and markings. Near the end, the markings increased and took on the form of something Samuel had read about in books.

"I think those are snowflakes," he said. Isabel crinkled her nose and leaned in closer. She'd heard of snow but had no memory of having ever seen it or felt it.

At the very end was a set of four words Isabel had seen only a moment ago.

"'The chill of winter,'" she whispered.

"There's a secret hidden inside Atherton that no one else knows about. Not even Edgar. Maybe not even Dr. Kincaid."

"We'll just have a look, that's all," said Isabel. "We can always turn back and get help if we need it, can't we?"

The two smiled at each other and nodded.

"Of course we can," said Samuel. But he had no intention of turning back. His mind was aflame with curiosity. He wanted the chill of winter to be his discovery whether Isabel went along or not.

CHAPTER

12

SPIKERS

Edgar didn't have to walk very far before realizing he'd made a terrible mistake. The smog of the Dark Planet swirled on a sea breeze, and the sound of giant, pounding feet came from behind him. As Edgar turned in a circle, every direction looked exactly the same. Grey tree trunks, sick with disease, rose all around him. Here the world was colorless in the extreme, a deep monotone fog pervading everything. And he was having trouble breathing.

Edgar had made the catastrophic error of walking away from the safety of the Raven without leaving himself a trail to follow back. He couldn't have imagined how quickly the vessel would dissolve away in the haze.

I'm lost, he thought, coughing into his arm as quietly as he could. Something was tracking him as he moved.

The sound of approaching creatures was coming from more than one direction now, but in the soupy smog Edgar couldn't say for sure where the first attack would come from.

Time to climb, he thought. The idea of climbing calmed him down at first, but when he dug his fingers into the tree trunk in front of him, he had an unpleasant surprise: Things he'd never seen before began crawling out of the rotting wood. They were the color of dirt and decay, a shade above monochrome. It took all of Edgar's will to hold back a scream as he released the trunk and shook his hands.

The sound of pounding was coming from three directions now — or was it four? — and Edgar spun around. When he faced the tree trunk again he knew he had run completely out of options. Whatever was after him had arrived.

Don't think, just move! Move! thought Edgar. He took hold of the tree trunk and climbed fast and furious into the smog above.

The bugs were long and many legged with slippery shells that twisted and turned like a snake. As they emerged from the rotting tree trunk with startling speed, one of them crawled over Edgar's hand. He froze, holding his breath and expecting to be pierced or pinched with unseen claws. But it only left a slimy path on the back of his hand as it passed over.

While Edgar looked at the bug crawling away he felt another moving up his arm and heading for his armpit. Edgar held on with his other arm and shook it free, watching it twist and spin toward the ground in the open air.

This must be what the Cleaners are eating out here, thought Edgar.

He'd only climbed six or seven feet up the side of a dead tree but already the ground was invisible below. Looking up, Edgar saw that things were a little bit brighter, and so he quickly scaled another ten feet, flicking creepy crawlies as he went. Now he could see the tops of the stand of trees in every direction, a sea of weather-beaten spikes emerging from a boiling cauldron.

He was startled by the sensation of a slimy creature that had made its way under his shirt and around to his back. "Get off me!" he cried.

He realized right away that he'd spoken too loudly, because the sound of giant steps from below came quickly to a stop. All was quiet in the forsaken wood and Edgar knew something had heard him. He thought he heard sniffing from twenty feet below, but he couldn't be sure.

Without warning, there was a loud chopping sound from below and the tree in which Edgar was perched was cut free at the bottom with one swipe. As it toppled, Edgar had no choice but to jump. He slammed flat into another trunk, smashing his face hard and nearly bouncing free into the air. Another loud *thwack!* and a second tree toppled over to his left.

He climbed higher still where the air became brighter, and then Edgar began leaping from trunk to trunk, making his way across the forsaken wood as trees fell behind him. Looking back, he saw the shadows of something from below that looked like a giant hammer rising and crashing into the earth.

Edgar jumped three more trees away and then stopped, clearing all the crawling bugs from his arms. A second bug had traveled all the way to Edgar's head and made a nest of his floppy hair. He was trying to disentangle its squirming four-inch body with shaking fingers when he heard a sound he knew all too well.

Clang! Clang! Clang! Clang! Clang! The sound of breaking bones.

"Cleaners," whispered Edgar.

The clanging of thousands of bony legs rushed beneath him. He could see the shadows of Cleaners shooting past in a herd toward the falling trees.

I've never seen ones that big, Edgar thought in awe. He could only make out their shadows, but it appeared these Cleaners were two or three times bigger than any that had lived on Atherton.

They must be thirty feet long or more! he thought. Two bites and Cleaners this big could remove every trace of Edgar from the Dark Planet.

Edgar had to leap with all his strength in order to get across the gap between dead trees — maybe ten or eleven feet — each time grabbing a lower hold on the next trunk, forcing him to climb back up again. At each landing the bugs would churn out as if trying to escape an approaching menace. But Edgar scrambled on, just ahead of the falling trees behind him.

All at once, there was a commotion like nothing Edgar had ever heard before. It reminded him of the sound of crashing cliffs on Atherton. The earth shook and trees snapped. A fight between monsters was on.

Edgar heard the screaming and ripping and biting. He could see the shadows moving like awful puppets in a violent show of power on the ground behind him.

High in the trees, swaying through the smog, came something that must have been fifty feet tall. The creature must have been the queen of the pack. She was laser focused on the ensuing battle and didn't notice the tiny presence of Edgar as she passed by, but Edgar got a good look as she rumbled past. He couldn't see any legs, only the long, loose neck lolling back and forth. At the end of the neck was a beak that looked for all the world like a ten-foot spike. A wide helmet of rocky bumps that ran down the whole length of its wobbling neck surrounded the back of the queen's head. Two red slits for eyes pierced the smog as if they were lit from the inside.

Edgar watched as the sharp hammerhead rocked back lazily on the round weight of the head and then — *FOOOSH!* — shot down with staggering speed. A sound of screaming pain ripped through the forest.

The queen's head lolled heavily back into the air. In the maw of the beast was a gigantic skewered and squirming Cleaner, its legs flailing and clicking in shadow as Edgar looked on in disbelief.

Keep going! Edgar spurred himself on. *Get away from here!*

Edgar's emotions got the better of him and he sobbed and coughed, jumping from tree to tree in search of an escape from the forsaken wood. The sound of violence grew softer until he was far enough away that he felt confident he was alone. The creatures who ruled this place seemed to be at war with one another, all of them at once involved in the fight so that the rest of the wood was surprisingly calm.

Edgar's arms ached and he felt grimy with slime from all the bugs that had crawled along his skin. He could feel blood dripping from more than one place on his head and face from crashing into tree trunks over and over again.

By the time he scurried to the ground, something new was already on the approach — he could hear it — but it wasn't like anything he'd heard before.

What new monster have you unleashed on me now? he wondered bitterly, wiping his eyes dry and thinking of Dr. Harding. Adventure on a dying planet was not as appealing as he'd imagined from the safety of Atherton.

"I can't go back up there," said Edgar. He had been lucky not to fall, but jumping really wasn't his greatest strength and he knew he had already been pushing his luck. One wrong move and he could fall and become seriously injured. And then what would he do?

And so Edgar ran as fast as his legs would carry him. The sound behind him was somehow even more threatening than the idea of coming face-to-face with a Cleaner, because he'd never heard it before. His imagination conjured up a giant creature with many teeth and swordlike claws.

Edgar kept going, dodging between trunks until the trees disappeared unexpectedly. He stopped short but not fast enough, tumbling over and into one of the holes he'd seen on the glowing blue map.

He free-fell, but not as far as he thought he would. After about thirty feet he found that something broke his fall. It was a net of some kind, covering the hole like a soft, sunken lid.

Edgar struggled to make his way to the edge so he could climb out as quickly as possible, certain that it was home to the giant creature he's seen hammer its spiked head into a Cleaner.

When he reached the top and peeked over, he came face-to-face with what had been following him.

●

"You've wandered into a very dangerous place."

Shelton had followed the instructions of Commander Judix and took the search team out at dawn in search of children. What a brilliant stroke of luck to find a child in one of the traps!

"Who are you?" asked Edgar, lowering himself down on the wall and thinking of how he might escape. Whoever stood above him was wearing some sort of mask that made him sound like he was talking from the back of a cave. He had goggles on as well, so that his face was completely obscured. By the looks of him, Edgar couldn't be at all sure the figure was human.

"I'm Shelton," said the man. "There's a place I can take you that's safe. It's *inside,* away from the smog and the monsters. And there's food and water."

"I'd rather stay here," said Edgar. He didn't like the sound of Shelton's voice. It reminded him of the way people had talked in the Highlands, as if Edgar was stupid and they could trick him. The man looked back over his shoulder and two others came alongside, whispering in their weird voices.

"Get out of there," said Shelton, looking down at Edgar. "The Spikers are headed this way. We can't stay."

"Spikers?" said Edgar, aware that Shelton was probably talking about the hammerheaded things he'd seen in shadows.

"Trust me, you don't want to be out here alone when they show up."

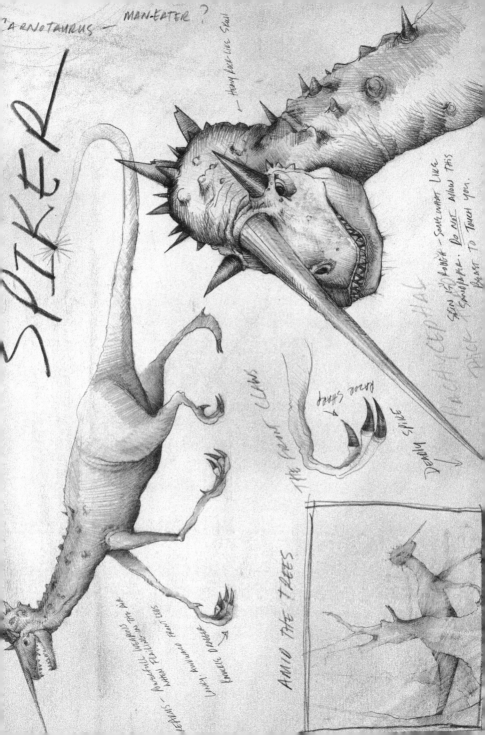

"Where would you take me?" said Edgar, reaching for clues to what sort of circumstance he'd stumbled into.

"It's called the Silo," said Shelton. "You may have heard of it. There are people who will take care of you."

Shelton could see he had finally struck on something that was likely to get things moving. He couldn't have known that he'd used the one word that would get Edgar into the armored transport.

Edgar scurried up the side of the hole with amazing speed and dexterity.

"How do we get there?"

"You're a good climber!" said Shelton, betraying his happiness at having found a healthy child in the forsaken wood. "That will come in handy at the Silo. Do you happen to know how old you are?"

Edgar didn't answer. The question sounded loaded with meaning he didn't comprehend.

"No matter," said Shelton. "We can figure it out later."

Shelton moved to the side and Edgar saw the transport team for the first time. Through the haze sat a machine. There was something about it that scared Edgar almost as much as the sound coming toward them. Edgar didn't like the idea of getting inside of it. It was all metal and rust, big and loud like a monster in its own right.

"We really must be going," said Shelton, trying to move Edgar along by placing a hand on his back and giving a little shove toward the armored transport. The boy wouldn't budge. Shelton leaned down and stared at Edgar. "You've arrived in the worst place on earth. I can get you out of here and take you someplace safe, but we have to leave *right now.*"

Before Edgar could protest any further two men grabbed him, one on each side, and hauled him up off his feet.

"We're getting out of here!" said one of them. "And we're not coming ever again. You can tell Commander Judix we're through!"

The two men dragged Edgar forward onto a ramp as he yelled to be let go.

"Quiet, you!" said the man on Edgar's other side. "You'll get us all killed."

Once inside the transport the ramp lifted with a *whish* of air and shut Edgar inside. The two men moved forward to the front and Shelton stayed with Edgar in the back. All three of the men removed their goggles and masks.

"You'll like the Silo," said Shelton, trying but failing to hide his fear of what was coming. He moved past Edgar toward the front and screamed. "Move this thing! They're almost here!"

The transport lurched forward loudly on a grinding circular shaft below. It was more like a tank than a truck, and it barreled over dead trees as it gained speed. Edgar felt like he was inside the belly of a monster and it had begun to move, to take him someplace and digest him.

"You tricked me!" cried Edgar. "This thing is alive!"

"What do you mean, alive? It's a machine, you stupid boy," said Shelton. Now that he had Edgar in his grasp it was best to hate him. It would be easier to give him up to Grammel later.

"And stop fussing so much. You're almost more trouble than you're worth."

Edgar looked around the space for an escape. He was about to leap for the closed door to see if he could get it open when Shelton stepped in front of him.

"Sit down and stop thinking up dumb ideas," said Shelton, pointing some sort of weapon in Edgar's face. "We're not out of danger just yet."

The ride was very bumpy inside — nothing like riding the Raven — and Edgar banged his head more than once. There were four Cleaners, all of them twenty feet long or better, chasing the transport out of the forsaken wood. They reached the edge and the Cleaners hesitated, as if beyond the edge of the wood lay some hidden danger. The moment the transport was free of the trees, Shelton screamed into a device he held to his face.

"Turn it on! Now! Turn it on!"

Edgar heard the sound of at least two Cleaners screaming from outside. They had come up against something neither they nor a Spiker could overcome. Not even the queen Spiker could make her way past whatever energy protected Station Seven, the Silo, and the beach these structures stood on.

Shelton glanced out the inch-thick glass of the armored transport front window. He sighed deeply, knowing they'd narrowly avoided letting a monster out of the woods and onto the beach. He wondered how long it would take Cleaners and Spikers to get inside Station Seven if the energy for the shield ran out.

He didn't think it would take long.

CHAPTER

13

INTO THE SILO

"Bring him to the usual place and we'll come right out and get him," said Red Eye. As he placed the receiver against the wall, Socket walked over to investigate.

"New one coming in?" Socket asked, genuinely surprised. It had been quite a while since anyone had been brought to the Silo. He had gotten in the habit of lying awake at night, rubbing his pulsing eyes, and wondering just how many people were left on the Dark Planet.

"What is it, a boy or a girl?" Socket wiped a finger across both goggle lenses, which did nothing to clear his sight. His eyes itched fiercely behind the glass.

"A boy — and they think he might be 4000 or better. Said they couldn't get a good reading for some reason. I'm in no mood for trouble, I can tell you that."

Red Eye's head was still pounding as he glanced across the drying room floor and scowled at Aggie.

"Get your head down! This doesn't concern you," he yelled.

Aggie and Teagan began tamping once more, but Teagan couldn't help but whisper while they worked.

"Did you hear that?" asked Teagan. "They've found a boy."

"How could I miss it?" Aggie flinched as she moved to a different drying bed, kicking pockets of white dust off the floor. "At least those two will be busy this morning. Maybe they won't bother us."

"I wonder how old this boy is and what kind of shape he's in."

"Prepare for the worst," said Aggie. She was aware of how easily Teagan got her hopes up. "Chances are he's been out there a long time. You know how they are when they come in like that."

They both knew what happened when children stayed outside too much — hollow eyes, pale skin, difficulty staying still. Kids like that were usually moved out of the Silo the day they turned 4200. The older boys could be especially difficult to handle and often didn't last more than a few months.

"It looks like Socket didn't hold anything back this time," said Teagan. The girls wore olive green shorts and sleeveless shirts like all the other children in the drying unit that day. There were long red lines across the backs of Aggie's legs and over her arms. They'd given her lashings on every limb.

"I'm fine. It's just so hot down here," said Aggie, running her dusty hand across the stubble of blond hair on her head. "This room makes everything hurt more."

"SHUT — YOUR — MOUTHS!" screamed Red Eye. He was in a horrible mood even by his own standards and couldn't bear to hear the annoying voices of children who should be working. The very idea of a new recruit — a disruptive 4000 boy, no less — gave him a raging headache.

Red Eye and Socket made their way to the riser that ran through the middle of the drying room, located on the bottom level of the Silo, where the white powder was finished. When Socket walked past Aggie, he leaned down and yelled at her so everyone could hear.

"If this here bin's not empty, you're not going to the barracks."

He laughed and wiped his goggles uselessly again, looking at his brother for approval.

"Come on then," said Red Eye. "Let's get out of this heat and let them work."

The two men clanged onto the platform and held on. A moment later the platform rose on a hydraulic tube and they were gone.

"I hate them," said Teagan. "I wish I could get one of those benders and give 'em some of their own medicine."

"We all hate them, but there's not much we can do about it."

The voice had come from a boy among them named Vasher, who was working at a drying bed alongside a younger boy named Landon. Both had tightly cropped hair and the same olive green shirts and shorts as Aggie and Teagan. They were skinny like all the other boys with dark-ringed eyes and ashen skin crying out for a sunny day. The four of them — Vasher, Landon, Aggie, and Teagan — were the green team, one of four teams that worked in the Silo. They always worked together during the day, then parted at night to separate girls' and boys' barracks.

"They'll put him with us in place of Ramsey," said Landon. The four glanced at each other in silent agreement that this was possible. It had been ninety-one days since they'd taken Ramsey, the former fifth member of the green team. Vasher would be the next to go, then it would be Aggie's turn. It was something none of the remaining four liked to talk about. They didn't know where children went when they left the Silo. Only that they never came back.

"Let's just keep working. It won't do any good to slow down," said Teagan, thinking of Aggie and how she wanted her to rest as soon as possible. Both boys nodded their agreement. They talked nervously about the new boy and what he would be like. Would he be older and meaner?

All four members of the green team had come from a sprawling compound fifty miles down the beach. Tens of thousands of people lived there, many of them orphaned children, and the circumstances were so horrific people often wandered off in search of something better.

"I was thinking of my dad this morning," said Teagan. She cried about her parents sometimes. "He was a lot like you, Aggie. Headstrong and confident."

"Do we have to dig all that up again?" said Vasher. He was the biggest and oldest of the group. "Let's just get the work done so we can get out of here."

Vasher didn't like all the carrying on about parents. It was the same story over and over again, and the older he got the more annoyed he was by it all. Parents left the compound searching for someplace better and never came back. And when the day came that kids couldn't wait anymore, they went looking for their parents — and ended up in the Silo. It had happened to everyone on the green team.

Teagan wanted to lash out at Vasher, but Aggie looked tired and sore and she had to admit talking about their parents made everyone sad and less productive.

Red Eye and Socket rose on the platform and passed through the main chambers of the Silo. The platform ran the entire length of the middle of the Silo, from the drying room at the bottom to the engine room at the top. Red Eye and Socket ascended through the drying room and emerged on the other side into a high-ceilinged chamber with vines dangling everywhere.

"Faster, you yellows! Faster!" yelled Red Eye at the five children who were working there, pulling the bender from his back and *whap! whap! whapping!* it against the rail of the platform. "They're catching up down there!"

The sight of the bender sent the working children into a frenzy. They were all younger than Aggie and Teagan. Picking buds from the long vines was dangerous, but it was also one of the easiest jobs in the Silo. When the children got older they were usually moved to the next level up, which Red Eye and Socket presently passed into. This was the growing room, where the white powder found its beginning.

Thirty long rows of red bulbs the size of a man's head lined the floor of the room. Brown leaves fanned out in perfect form, which children tended and preened. One boy was carefully picking seeds from the tips of the leaves. A very tiny girl was trimming an overgrown plant. Two more were tilling the soil. The vines grew from the bottom of the bulbs, through the floor, and into the vine room below.

"You there!" said Red Eye, stopping the platform ten feet over a boy's head. "Stop what you're doing and go help with the trimming."

"Yes, sir!" cried the rail-thin boy of 3700 days. He came alongside the small girl at the trimming station and began carefully tearing bits of yellow off the edges of the otherwise orange, floppy leaves. The leaves and the seeds were used to make bars like the one Commander Judix had eaten a few hours before.

The platform continued on, rising through the planting room and into the barracks level, where the boys and girls slept. There were three barracks in all: one for the boys, one for the girls, and one where Hope cared for the very young children between 1500 and 2500. Only one level remained — the engine room — which was also where Red Eye and Socket slept. No one but Red Eye and Socket was allowed in the gloom and noise of the pounding engines.

"We'll take the new boy down to the drying room and put him right to work with the greens," Red Eye said as the platform arrived on the barracks level.

"Oh, no, you won't."

Red Eye and Socket whirled around and saw Hope, who had been standing next to the platform waiting for the new arrival. They had long grown weary of this meddling lover of cast-off children.

146

THE SILO

PROCESSING PLANT —
* USED FOR HEATING
AND ENERGY.

* HERBACEOUS PERENNIAL

BARRACKS

VINE ROOM

BRACTEOBE

STRINGERS

ENDRO-POCKET

BRACTAL

LUPOLAN GLANDS

— CONTAIN ESSENTIAL OILS &
RESIN COMPOUNDS

ING ROOM

BRACTEOBE
SEED

SOFT-CELL
INTERIOR

THIN HARD
SHELL

* BITTERNESS

FOOD SOURCE

"I had a feeling we might find you here," said Red Eye. "We've already placed the boy with the green team. Aggie's been slow today and they've fallen behind in the drying room. That girl is getting lazier by the minute."

He smiled, feeling his cheeks push against the bottom of his goggles.

"I hear Aggie had a beating last night. That true?"

Even with goggles to hide his eyes Socket's expression always gave him away. "She had it coming. The little monster tried to blind us!"

"We agreed you'd tell me before disciplining a girl. Did you forget about that?"

Red Eye laughed and spit sprayed from his mouth. His voice became grim and mean.

"We don't take orders from you," he said. "You're here by invitation only."

"She's already more trouble than she's worth," added Socket.

"If it's trouble you want, it's trouble you'll get," said Hope. She had a steely resolve that put both of the men back on their heels. They knew the truth: If push came to shove they'd have a hard time running the Silo without Hope. She had medical training no one else had. When kids became sick, which happened a lot, Hope took care of it. As for the little ones — the snot-nosed, whining little ones! — Red Eye and Socket couldn't stand them and refused to take care of them. None of the 1500's would ever become 4200's without Hope's mothering.

"Just stay out of our way," said Red Eye, regaining his confidence. "The recruits are mine to deal with."

"We'll see about that," said Hope. She put her hand in her pocket and Socket flinched, cowering behind his brother. Hope had another reason to be feared, but she almost never used it. The mere fact of its existence was enough to keep Red Eye and Socket from going too far.

The first of a two-layered bay door slid open on the outside wall of the room. This sent all three of them moving quickly down the hall that separated the two barracks. Hope, who was in the best health of all of the adults, had no trouble arriving at the bay door first.

"Do you *really* need to be here?" asked Hope. "Why not give me a few minutes to make a proper introduction?"

The two men looked at the door like two hungry lions awaiting the death of an injured animal. They weren't going anywhere. The second-layer door slid open and exposed the barracks to the outside world of the Dark Planet.

"He's late," said Socket, leaning out and staring down toward the ground. There was a metal grate for a landing. It was rusted almost clean through and didn't look like it had much chance of holding Socket's weight.

"I see him!" announced Socket. "He's coming up the ladder."

●

Moments before, Shelton had opened the door and shoved Edgar out of the armored transport.

"Up the ladder," he had said, "someone will be waiting for you." And then, without warning, Shelton had closed the door and driven away in a plume of flying dirt and rocks.

Edgar had been mesmerized by the sight of the Silo. The beach on which it sat was not covered in smog like the forsaken wood had been. Something about the wood had trapped the poison of the Dark Planet more thickly, but here, closer to the sea, there was a lonely breeze blowing steady with the burning smell of oil. He could see the Silo rising tall into the sky, narrow at the middle, wider at the top and bottom. It was covered in a cake of rust and decay that flaked off in Edgar's hands and turned powdery and dry.

"Hurry it up! We can't keep this door open all day," Socket yelled from above. Edgar had begun climbing the rusty ladder, taking special care not to grab the rungs that looked like they might pull free in his hand. He instead chose to hold on to the rails along the sides to pull himself up.

"He's a strong climber," said Socket, turning back toward Hope and Red Eye. "*Really* strong."

"He only wants inside," said Red Eye. "He'll slog off as soon as there's work to be done. You can count on that." But Red Eye had no idea what he was dealing with until Edgar crawled inside the Silo to safety.

Edgar stood up, not the least bit breathless from the effort. As the door *swoosh*ed shut behind him he became aware that he was trapped inside the Silo, the very place of his maker's childhood.

The three people who stood in front of him were each, in their own way, surprising to Edgar. There were Red Eye and Socket, with their wild hair and goggles and benders at the ready, waiting to whip a new and unpredictable boy into shape. They were pale and thin, mean and unhappy.

Hope, on the other hand, put him immediately under her spell. He'd seen dark-skinned people on Atherton before, so that didn't surprise him. She was tall and lanky and looked down at him as if her only duty in the world was to take care of him. With patchy gray hair and big, dark freckles beneath sorrowful eyes, she was soulfully beautiful in a way that couldn't escape notice by a frightened boy of twelve from Atherton.

Socket bobbed up and down to get a better look at Edgar through his cloudy goggles.

"Something's been beating the life out of 'im."

"He's fine," said Hope. Even with the bruises and scrapes from hitting the trees, Hope could see that there was someone very special in front of her. "This boy's never been outside."

"Has, too!" cried Red Eye. He'd been thrown outside to fend for himself as a child and it made him furious to look at this seemingly perfect creature before him. "Where have you been hiding, boy? *Where?*"

Edgar hadn't thought up what to say. In his awestruck encounter with the Dark Planet it hadn't occurred to him that he might not look like everyone else.

"You better start talking," said Socket.

Red Eye and Socket had both been thrown out of a compound at a young age for beating up younger boys, and the thrill of picking on someone small had never left Socket. "We can get the information from you whether you want to give it or not."

Socket dragged his bender across the metal wall of the Silo and it scraped sickly.

"I just . . . well, I don't really remember where I came from," said Edgar. "I've been lost for a while."

It was the best lie Edgar could come up with and it didn't even come close to tricking Hope, but it did seem to work well enough for Red Eye and Socket.

"Maybe some work will jog your memory," he said. "And there's plenty of that to be had. Move!"

He stepped aside and guided Edgar to walk in front of him.

"The day is already half over," said Hope. "In a few hours I'll see you in the barracks. I'll have some food and water waiting for you, and we'll have a look at those cuts and bruises."

Socket dug down in his greasy pocket and pulled out a bar. "He can make it a few hours without drinking up all the water and eating our food," he said, taking a bite.

"Get him Ramsey's old olive greens," Red Eye told his brother.

Socket scurried off and Edgar glanced around the metal landing, overcome by the idea of Max Harding living in this Silo. Everything about the Dark Planet was so much worse than he'd imagined it would be.

Hope knelt next to Edgar again and looked deeply into his eyes.

"You *are* something different, aren't you?" she said. She was especially surprised by his skin and his eyes, which were both full of life and vibrancy. "Wait until the girls get a look at you."

Edgar smiled awkwardly and Socket came banging down the metal floor, throwing a green shirt at Edgar.

"About time," said Red Eye, who hated to be kept waiting. "Put that on and move!"

Edgar was shoved forward onto the round platform, followed by the two men who had taken him captive. Edgar surveyed everything very carefully while he changed his shirt. As they descended from level to level, he noticed one thing above all that interested him greatly. All through the Silo there were metal beams and girders. The ceilings, the walls, even some parts of the floors on the different levels were crisscrossed with an endless array of hand- and footholds. This place was made for climbing.

When they arrived in the drying room Red Eye nearly threw Edgar off the platform. "He's one of you now," said Red Eye to the green team. "But don't get used to it. He'll be leaving along with Vasher in . . . what is it, Socket? Four days?"

"Four days! Four more days and you're both shipping out. And we'll get double our reward! Ha!"

Aggie and all the other members of her team were looking at Edgar slack-jawed, as if they'd never seen a boy before in all their lives. Edgar didn't look like a person born on a dying, poisonous planet. They were completely captivated.

By nightfall they would find Edgar even more interesting than he looked.

14

THE WAY OF THE YARDS

"I can't believe we're doing this," whispered Isabel. It was very early in the morning and the crisp, clear light of a new day was just underway. Dr. Kincaid and Vincent were back at the edge of Atherton searching for any sign of Edgar, which left the cave empty when Samuel and Isabel entered.

"We're only going to take a quick look around," said Samuel. "We don't have to go any farther than that if you don't want to."

But Isabel knew better. Samuel had packed enough food and water to last for days. He was planning on a big adventure whether Isabel went along or not.

"Come on," said Samuel. "Don't you want to see if the lock will open? It's all we've talked about."

Isabel wasn't so sure. "Are you positive it leads away from the Inferno?"

"Positive," Samuel assured her.

Isabel nodded, more enthusiastic than ever, and the two went deeper into Dr. Kincaid's cave. The small bag at her side containing her sling and dried figs made Isabel feel more confident.

When they reached the back of the cave they found Dr. Harding's bed. Edgar had woken up right there after falling into the Flatlands, back in the days when Atherton still had cliffs. It was the place they had laid Isabel when they'd escaped the inside of Atherton before. She remembered waking there, the way her head had felt like it was half filled with sloshing water. But mostly she remembered how she'd stood at the edge of the newly formed lake for the first time and felt her heart breaking.

"The last time I did this everything changed," said Isabel. "There was a village — *my* village — and the grove. When I came out, the places I loved were all gone."

"You don't want to come back and find things changed a second time, is that it?" asked Samuel.

That wasn't exactly right, but it was close. Isabel looked over her shoulder at the growing light of morning seeping into the cave.

"I *am* curious to see what we'll find inside. But I worry I'll come out and find the new grove has been overrun by monsters or the whole place flooded and destroyed. I think about things like that all the time."

"Back then there were also dangerous cliffs and Cleaners crawling everywhere," Samuel pointed out, walking past the bed and reaching down toward the round yellow door that was hidden on the floor of the cave. "You had almost no food or water and Mr. Ratikan to deal with every day. But those things are changed for the better now. My entire world is gone. The Highlands are under water and I'll never see them again. There was a lot I liked about that place, but I like the new Atherton a lot better and I don't think it's going to change again. I think this is the world we're going to live in from now on."

Isabel thought of Edgar and let herself imagine that he was doing fine and that he would soon return in one piece. Her mind began to fill with the pending adventure and she knelt down next to the door.

"Let's get on with it," she said. "They could be back anytime and we don't want to be caught opening this thing. Can you imagine what they'd say if they saw us?"

Samuel's throat tightened at the thought of missing this chance and he went straight and fast at the dials on the yellow door. Eight of them were embedded in the center so that he could only see half of each spinning dial. There were millions of combinations, but he had the one that would open it memorized from the wooden tablet.

T–H–E–Y–A–R–D–S

He entered the letters, each of them clicking into place on its dial, and heard the hissing sound of the round door releasing. Samuel took the handle in his hand and pulled.

He and Isabel drew in a sharp breath. The yellow door was open and the inside of Atherton lay in wait. A source of light was pulsing softly far below.

"It's a long ladder," said Samuel, his voice shaking with excitement. "*Really* long."

"You didn't mention that before," said Isabel. She was

starting to wonder whether Samuel was cut out to lead their adventure.

"Vincent carried you on his back when we came out. You were —"

"I was almost dead, I know," said Isabel.

Samuel took out the tablet. In the dim light of the cave he had to hold it just right to read it.

"You see this here?" he said, reading four words next to the etched map. "There will be light."

"So we won't need any," said Isabel. "Like we talked about."

The two had agreed that carrying a lamp or fuel to burn would be difficult, and it appeared now they wouldn't need it. Samuel just wanted to make sure Isabel still agreed.

"Then it's settled," he said, putting the tablet back into the pack. "We'll go down and see for ourselves. If things turn dark we'll come back."

Isabel got down close to the hole and took the first rung of the ladder in her hands. She had a pack of her own and it was awkward creeping over the edge, but she managed it and began climbing down. Samuel followed, grabbing the inside handle of the yellow door and pulling it down over them.

"What are you doing?" said Isabel, looking up and seeing Samuel's feet along with the bottom of the door about to be shut over them.

Samuel tried to hold the door upright, but it was heavy and from where he stood, he could only hold on with one hand.

"We don't want them to find it open," said Samuel, struggling to hold the round door. "And we have the combination now — we can open it back up whenever we want."

"You don't know that!" cried Isabel. "Don't let it go! Push it back!"

But it was too late. What little strength Samuel had gave out. The door crashed down toward him as he ducked out of the way and held on with both hands.

There was a crushing echo down the long hole as the two listened carefully for sounds from below. What if they'd disturbed the Nubian, or something worse?

"I don't suppose we could make our arrival any more obvious," said Isabel.

"It's heavier than it looks!"

"Can you see the dials?"

"I can. I'll unlock it so we know we can get out."

Isabel listened carefully, because she thought she'd heard something familiar. It was very faint at first, but as she listened to the clicking of the dials she heard something else growing louder. Samuel heard it, too.

"I know that sound," said Samuel, stopping on the Y of T–H–E–Y–A–R–D–S and looking down toward Isabel. They both heard a distant shriek booming through the inside of Atherton.

"The Nubian," said Isabel. "They know we're here."

Samuel turned quickly to the dials and went on through A and the R and then D. He knew the flying beasts with black talons and razor-sharp beaks couldn't reach him all the way up where he stood on the ladder, but just knowing they were inside terrified him.

"Last letter," said Samuel, clicking in the S and pushing on the door. There was no hissing sound of opening and no clicking of some locking mechanism letting go. Samuel pushed with all his might.

"Get on with it, Samuel," said Isabel. "My arms are getting tired."

The sound of the Nubian grew nearer as Samuel uttered the exact words Isabel did not want to hear.

"The yellow door won't open."

●

It didn't take Samuel and Isabel long to figure out that staying where they were would do them no good. They would only grow more tired with the weight of the packs. And the longer they waited the greater the chances of falling as their arms grew tired. There had been arguments about whose idea it had been in the first place and why they hadn't told Dr. Kincaid and Vincent, but in the end Samuel and Isabel resigned themselves to the truth: They were stuck inside Atherton and needed to find another way out, if such a way even existed.

They climbed down the hundred and twenty-seven rungs on the ladder and found themselves standing on firm ground. A wide tunnel ran off in two directions.

"Let's look at the tablet," said Isabel, listening for the Nubian. As Samuel removed the tablet, Isabel pointed to the wider of the two ends of the tunnel, where she was certain the horrible sound of flying beasts was coming from.

"We're not going that way, I don't care what that map says."

The light at the bottom of the ladder was very much like the light Edgar had encountered as he'd made his way toward the Raven. It was a soft light, orange and yellow, and somehow everywhere and nowhere all at once. They saw it radiating through cracks and chasms in the ceiling, the walls, and the floor, but they couldn't see its source.

"It's that way," said Samuel. He glanced down the corridor, away from the threatening sounds. This would have pleased them both if not for the fact that the way Samuel had pointed to was also the darker of the two. The sound of the Nubian began to trail off, like they'd turned a wide circle and were flying away.

"They're probably farther away than they seem," said Isabel. "Sound really carries in here."

She glanced down the darker corridor and wondered what to do. "Let's walk a little way and see where it leads." Isabel could be quite brave in circumstances like these, where their choices were few and the stakes were high.

Samuel followed behind her and they passed through a series of wide chambers lit from deep gaps in the ceiling and walls. After a hundred or more steps, Samuel began to wonder if they should turn back.

"Isabel," he began, "I don't know where this leads, other than the words at the end — *the chill of winter* — and that doesn't sound like a way out." Samuel felt awful. He'd been so excited for the adventure, and already it had turned deadly and frightening.

"I know," Isabel said, unsure of how to proceed.

"Maybe it's time we broke this thing open, as you suggested. What if there's something inside that could help get us out of here?"

Isabel took the tablet from Samuel and held it near weak light emitting from a crack in one wall. She thought she could see the ladder they had come down as she looked at the map. What she saw stunned her.

"If that's the ladder, then this is a lot farther than I thought." Isabel pointed to the obvious destination, where those words sat cold and alone inside an etched circle — *the chill of winter.*

"That's days away from here," said Isabel, looking at Samuel with pleading eyes.

"Then it's a good thing we brought some Black and Green and water," said Samuel, trying to be enthusiastic. "We're going to need it."

"And you're right about something else. This map doesn't look like a way out. All I can see for sure is that it leads far away from where we came in."

"The yellow door," said Samuel. He thought about it a moment, feeling a glimmer of hope as he imagined Vincent opening the door and coming in after them. But the moment passed as he remembered what he'd written on a note he'd left for Dr. Kincaid.

"Why did I say we were going to the other side of the lake to search for Edgar? Stupid! Stupid! Stupid!"

"Quiet, Samuel!" Isabel whispered. "Who knows what you'll wake down here?"

"But they'll be searching for us along the edge — *up there* — and no one is going to imagine what we've done."

Isabel spied a long edge of sharp rock with light creeping out from somewhere below. She walked over, half angry and half curious, and bashed the edge of the tablet against the rocks. The tablet slid open.

"I hope we didn't break something," Samuel said as he came over to her.

Isabel slid the two sides apart and drew in a breath. The moment she set eyes on the firebugs trapped within their case of clear glass she threw the tablets down and backed away.

"Get away from them!" yelled Isabel. Samuel was carefully picking up the tablets, and something more.

"They'll kill you, Samuel! Don't touch them!"

But as far as Isabel could tell it was already too late. It appeared as if Samuel had picked up the firebugs and had trained a cluster of them to dance in his hand.

"They're trapped," said Samuel. "See?" He held the etching instrument out toward Isabel and she jumped back.

Samuel couldn't help laughing just a little at the strange object he held in his hand. "It's warm, but it appears to be harmless. And there's something else here you're going to want to see."

Samuel picked up one half of the tablet and held the glass end of the pen filled with firebugs.

"Look here," he said, and she came a little closer. "This thing is used for writing." He touched the sharp black end of the pen toward the inside of the tablet, and made a letter *I*, then an *S*, and so on, until he'd spelled Isabel's name in thin lines of burned wood.

"The tip looks like something I've seen before," said Isabel, curious. "It looks like the beak of a diving Nubian, don't you think?"

Samuel nodded in agreement. It did look startlingly similar

to the flying creature they'd encountered on their last journey through the inside of Atherton with its razor-sharp black beak.

"This is what I wanted you to see," said Samuel, holding the glowing tail end of the pen lower on the tablet. There Isabel saw a series of words, which Samuel read out loud.

"'Gon to find SILO. Do not wory. I am ok. I wil be bak soon.'"

"Edgar!" said Isabel. "He wrote that — I can tell he wrote it!"

"I really need to work with him on the spelling, but the message is clear. He's fine, Isabel. He always comes back if he says he's going to."

"And he'll be back soon," said Isabel, repeating the words on the tablet. "Do you realize what that means? We're saved!"

"We are?" said Samuel.

"When he comes back he'll see we're not there and he'll know — he'll know we came down here."

"You're right! And he'll tell Dr. Kincaid. All we have to do is wait here. We have food and water. We could last for a week if it came to that."

Without thinking, they hugged each other. The embrace was awkward but comforting, and when they released each other an unexpected warmth remained.

"Did you hear that?" said Isabel. Her expression had gone suddenly cold. She could barely hear it at first, but there was definitely a sound from the direction of the ladder leading up to the yellow door.

"We should never have left the base of the ladder," said Isabel.

A whipping and snapping sound was coming toward them. Whatever it was that crept up the corridor, it had smelled something new inside Atherton and become curious.

"Run!" said Samuel. He already had the pen, the map portion of the tablet, and his pack — and Isabel had hers — and so they were off at a tear, away from the advancing creature.

The other half of the tablet was left behind in the rocks, which was a shame, because there was information there that might have helped the two understand that what they were doing was more important than they knew.

15

POWDER BLOCKING

"And you say he's at least 4000?" asked Commander Judix. It was the first potentially good news she'd had in quite some time.

"It's hard to say. We couldn't get a clean reading," said Shelton. He had returned from the forsaken wood and gone straight to the same giant window he'd stood at the night before. "I think the reader was acting up, but he's at least 4000."

"That's odd," said Commander Judix, puzzled by a reader that wouldn't work. It worried her that yet another piece of technology was failing with no way of replacing it. "Tell Red Eye to try his. We need a clean reading or Grammel will complain. I can't give him a reason to short us this time."

She looked pensively into the forsaken wood. She could already imagine the meeting with Grammel.

"Was this new boy hostile or troubled like the others? Grammel won't like it if he's too old."

"Ma'am, I assure you, this boy is at least 4000 and healthy as a horse on Atherton."

He regretted speaking of Atherton the moment he'd done it. There had been a time when all good things were called Atherton things — the air on Atherton, the water, the trees, the animals, the people — everything was so much better on Atherton. But the mere mention of the place had long been taboo.

"Why must you always be such a fool?" said Commander Judix. "Get me a reading as quickly as you can. Grammel is going to be early."

"What do you mean, early?"

"I received word this morning. He's going to be ninety-seven days instead of a hundred. Apparently, a rancid wind has been at his back and he's short of help. He'll be very pleased we have two."

Shelton so hated Grammel that the idea of him showing up in — could it be, only one more day! — well, it fully ruined his morning on the spot. It drove him near mad that such a buffoon could have so much power over Station Seven.

"Get on with it!" said Commander Judix, seeing that Shelton was daydreaming. He'd been doing more of that lately and it bothered her. "The reading's not going to take itself."

"Yes, ma'am, right away." Shelton began to leave, but turned back at the last second. "Oh, one more thing."

Shelton paused, rubbing his chin as he tried to think of how to put it. "He looks . . . well, he looks different."

Commander Judix thought this sounded like trouble. "How do you mean?"

"It's hard to describe. I guess he's not as sickly as one might expect."

Commander Judix sent Shelton away with a wave of her hand. *Not as sickly as one might expect?* This was sounding better all the time. It wasn't that far across the plain to the forsaken wood. This boy must have come from a long stay at one of the outposts and kept a mask and goggles on. Maybe he'd come from a rich family that could afford an underground hideout. Who knew? Who cared! The fact was she had a very valuable thing in her possession, a rare asset ideal for bargaining.

Commander Judix thought of what a wonderful stroke of luck this was. She would get another hundred days of fuel, maybe more since Grammel would be early and she had such a good crop of new help. She'd already been working out a plan to get more children during that time. Whether they liked it or not, Shelton and the transport team would go out past the forsaken wood into places they'd always stayed away from. Plenty of children crawling around out there that would love a chance to live in the Silo.

Yes, things were definitely looking up.

⬤

"What's your name?" asked Aggie.

Red Eye and Socket had gone up on the platform to check on the vines. The tube that held the platform was still like the trunk of a lonely tree. If it began sliding down into the ground they would know the two goggle-headed monsters that ran the Silo would be on their way back down.

"Don't you have a name?" Aggie persisted. Edgar glanced around the hot room, trying to get his bearings. The Silo was starting to worry him. Would he ever be able to escape and get back to Atherton?

The light in the drying room was rather dim, and it struck Edgar that this was true of every room he'd entered so far. There were no windows at all. He'd noticed some of the children wearing dark goggles as he passed through each of the levels, but no one on the green team was wearing them except the oldest boy, Vasher. Everyone else had their goggles either propped on their foreheads or hanging around their necks.

"I'm Edgar. It's my first time in the Silo."

Edgar had never seen children like these. They were even skinnier than he was and their eyes were tired. But the most striking thing was their close-cropped hair, especially on Aggie and Teagan. He asked Aggie about this and she seemed embarrassed by the question.

"I'm afraid you'll get yours cut soon enough," she said, looking at the mop of black hair on Edgar's head and wishing for all the world she still had hers. "Red Eye makes us keep it this way. He says it's easier to keep clean, less likely to get in the way. I think it's just another way to control us."

Aggie was equal parts spellbound and bothered by Edgar's presence. What right did he have to look so fresh and new? She should look healthy like that. But it was also this unexpected vitality that drew her interest.

"What are those things over his eyes?" asked Edgar, motioning toward Vasher, who was busy working and staying quiet.

"We all have them, but most of us don't need them unless there's more light. There's not really any rhyme or reason to it. Being outside affects some people's eyes more than others," said Teagan. Edgar could tell she liked explaining things. "Anyway, they're called goggles, and they protect our eyes from light. Vasher's only wearing his because sometimes he gets headaches lately. He seems to feel better with them on, but I think it's all in his head. I mean, look at this place! There's hardly any light at all. Very depressing! Red Eye and Socket are the worst. They're really sensitive to the light, so they leave all the old lights off unless they absolutely need them on. You should have seen what Aggie did to the two of them last night!"

Edgar looked at Aggie curiously, but she quickly changed the subject.

"Where have you been living? You look better than anyone I've ever seen come in here."

Edgar didn't know how to answer Aggie so he shrugged and pretended not to know where he'd been. "I don't remember a lot. I've been wandering awhile."

"Have not!" cried Vasher. No one even knew Vasher was listening from where he worked. He stared at Edgar, a rage building. "No one wanders outside for long and comes out looking like you."

"It's all right, Vash," said Aggie with a calm and steady voice. "He's not going to hurt you or try to take anything from you."

Behind the goggles, Vasher had the deepest-set eyes of the group, and they quickly scanned everyone in the room.

"He's lying!" accused Vasher. "He's from the station. He's come to spy on us." Vasher had been getting harder to control during the past few months. Sometimes he was perfectly calm, but other times, especially when his things or his position were at risk, he lashed out.

"I'm not lying," insisted Edgar. "I just don't remember."

Vasher looked at Teagan as if he might start to cry, overwhelmed by some other emotion that had quickly taken over. This is what always happened. If a person had been exposed to the outside for too long when they were very young, a day came when emotions ran amok and attention was hard to keep. It was why the really young children Grammel brought on the boat were of such questionable value. He'd find them on the beach, totally exposed to the outside world, and bring them to the Silo expecting them to grow up and be useful a few years later.

"It's okay, Vash — really it is. He's not going to take things away. He's nice, aren't you, Edgar?"

Edgar nodded and smiled at Vasher.

"And I'm a hard worker," he said. "Just tell me what to do and I'll do it. You'll see."

This seemed to calm Vasher down and he leveled off, going back to work with Landon but still casting a wary eye at Edgar every few seconds.

"Take this," said Aggie, handing Edgar a metal tube with a blunt end. "And use it like this."

Aggie had her own metal tube and she began tamping the powder inside the bin. The bin itself was about four feet across and three feet tall at the sides. It was a little over half filled with papery-looking buds that appeared to Edgar as if they were swimming in a vat of white powder.

"Why are we doing this?" he asked.

"It's how we make the white powder," said Landon, surprised that Edgar didn't recognize one of the most basic elements of life in the Silo. "You know about powder blocking, don't you?"

Edgar thought Landon looked like the youngest and weakest of the bunch. His eyes were bloodshot in a way that made Edgar's own eyes water when he looked at them. But Landon was full of energy and hopped around from place to place as he worked.

"I'm afraid I don't know about any powder. I've never seen it before."

Every member of the green team thought this was peculiar. They were constantly being told they were saving the world with the work they were doing. The powder blocks were sent all over — or so they thought — so people could mix the powder with whatever liquid they could find and drink it.

"They don't start out all chalky like this," said Aggie. She liked the idea of getting to know this strange new boy a little more. "The vines — you saw them coming down here, I'm sure — they make flowers that never bloom."

"The team in the vine room climbs up and gets them," said Landon, racing around a bin so he was facing Vasher. "The flowers, I mean — and they get dropped on the floor."

Aggie pointed to the ceiling. "Then the flowers that never bloom pass through a lot of holes that lead through heated grates. The grates shake them dry. When they finally fall through the ceiling —"

As if on cue, a dried-out white bud about the size of Edgar's thumb dropped out of one of the thousands of holes in the ceiling and landed in one of the many bins. There was an unmistakable sense that Dr. Harding had somehow been involved in what was going on here. It had his fingerprints all over it.

"When the flower curls up into a ball that way, it's ready to be tamped," said Aggie. Edgar thought the flower looked like it had caved in on itself, hiding from the scary world outside. "We smash the flowers, and the papery leaves get tinier and tinier until they turn to dust."

Teagan added, "This is also the hottest room in the Silo and the place we hate working the most."

"The vines are the best, though we hardly ever get to work there anymore. But we still climb the vines sometimes," said Landon in a sort of sneaky voice. "Right, Vash?"

"Quiet, Landon!" said Vasher. He glared at Edgar. "You know we don't talk about that, especially around someone we can't trust." Edgar saw right away that Landon thought of Vasher as a big brother.

"We don't get to work in the vines anymore," said Aggie. She, too, seemed to be hiding something behind her green eyes. Edgar was drawn to this mysterious girl with short hair and slightly sunken eyes. He could imagine her on Atherton in his beloved grove, walking beneath the trees.

Edgar felt sweat dripping down his forehead.

"Don't let that fall in the bin," said Teagan nervously. "We'll get in trouble."

"But how would anyone know?" asked Edgar, wiping an arm across his face.

"They test every block for purity before it goes out. They can tell if anything gets in there."

"What's a powder block?"

"When it's all dust, it goes over there and gets smashed."

Teagan pulled her goggles down over her eyes. There was a pair of long, stiff gloves hanging from the side of the bin and she put them on. Then she held her arms out and made a funny face as she walked like a monster toward Aggie. Her arms looked huge against the skin and bones of her slight body. Landon thought it was hilarious and laughed out loud.

"Back to work, you monster!" Aggie joked.

Teagan picked up a large metal cup and scooped white powder from one of the four corners of the bin where they worked. The metal cup had a floppy lid on hinges and she closed the lid with a clang, then walked to one of the metal walls in the room. She reached out a gloved hand and clumsily slid open a small door. Even from where Edgar was standing he could tell it was burning hot behind the door. Teagan took a deep breath and reached inside, dumped the cup quickly, and pulled her hand back out.

"It's full enough," she said, closing the door and taking hold of a lever that appeared to be in the down position. She looked at Edgar and smiled once more. "Better cover your ears."

Edgar set the tamper down and put his hands over his ears, but it didn't help very much. When Teagan pulled the lever up and locked it into place there was a sound of something moving behind the wall that was so shrill it made Edgar's head hurt.

Ancient iron grated against bearings in need of oil, moving walls of steel closer and closer as they smashed the powder into a block of concentrate.

"How long does it take?" screamed Edgar. No one could hear him. Less than a minute later the sound stopped for a split second then started right back up again when Teagan threw down the lever and locked it.

"All done," said Aggie at long last, touching Edgar on the shoulder ever so briefly to reassure him. "But we'll have to do it another five or six times before we finish these bins."

"Six more times?" said Edgar.

Teagan had opened a second sliding door. The gloves ran all the way up to her shoulders and she set her covered forearms along the sides of a block about the size of her own head. It looked like it was heavy — maybe ten pounds — and she struggled to lift it out and place it in a metal box at her feet. It would take a total of thirty to fill the container.

"Each one can feed a person for a month," said Teagan. "Well, that and the bars made of seeds and leaves. With the blocks, you have to break pieces off and mix them with water or it's awfully hard to choke down."

"Is that all you eat?" asked Edgar. "Bars and powdery water?"

Teagan nodded, gazing at Edgar with curiosity. "It's all anyone eats."

Edgar thought aloud without really knowing the words were coming out.

"Dr. Harding did this."

"What did you say?" asked Aggie.

"He said Harding — he knows about this place. I told you he knows! He's a liar!"

The blizzard was flying through Vasher's head again.

"They sent him over here to get me!"

Vasher held his metal tamper out into the open and pointed it at Edgar. It was not a formidable weapon with its wide, flat end, and if it were swung in Edgar's general direction he could easily dodge it. But if it were thrown . . .

"Calm down, Vash," said Aggie. She hated giving Edgar the impression she and her friends were living in absolute chaos. "We don't know anything about Edgar. Everyone's heard of Max Harding, you know that."

"I don't trust him," said Vasher, walking toward Edgar as he raised the tamper over his head.

Edgar darted away from the bin and took hold of a metal rail along one of the walls. With lightning speed he was on the ceiling, fingers and toes clawing along countless holes the size of his fist.

"He's fast!" said Landon. "And he can really climb. He'd be amazing in the vines!"

Vasher wouldn't be distracted. "I won't go! I won't let them take me!"

Vasher hurled the tamper. It was a good shot, heading straight for Edgar's head, but Edgar dodged it easily as he moved seven or eight feet along the web of holes in the ceiling in the space of a few seconds. Edgar let go with his feet and hung limp, then dropped the distance to the floor and stood in front of Vasher.

"I'm not here to spy on you," said Edgar. "I'm not from Station Seven. I'm not even from the Dark Planet."

"What do you mean?" asked Aggie, but in her heart of hearts she knew. She had heard — they had all heard — of a place where things were different. It was like a fairy tale, the only fairy tale, in fact, in which all the girls and boys were rescued and taken to a new world free of darkness and pollution and monsters.

Edgar didn't speak. Maybe he'd said too much too soon. But he couldn't stay on the Dark Planet for long, that much he knew. Every second counted in this wretched place if he had any hope of getting back inside the Raven and going home.

"Where are you from?" Aggie asked. She had liked Edgar on seeing him, but she was entirely mesmerized by him now. And that was saying a lot for Aggie, the often stoic leader of the green team.

"You don't really think? You can't be serious!" said Vasher. "That's not even real, Aggie! It's just a story Hope tells to make us feel better."

"But what if it is true?" said Teagan, unable to hide her optimism. "Hope and Dr. Harding — they were friends when he was just a boy. Maybe . . ."

"Shut up! Both of you just shut up!" yelled Vasher. "It's nonsense, all of it! He's come to make sure I'll go without giving them any trouble. That's all he's here for."

Everyone froze as they watched the tube lurch to life and begin moving lower. The platform was coming down. Another few seconds and Red Eye and Socket would be back, yelling at them.

Aggie looked at Edgar like no one had ever looked at him before. There was now a pleading hope in her despairing eyes, as if she thought Edgar had the power to remove all the terrible things in her world with a wave of his hand or a certain set of words.

"Have you ever heard of a place called Atherton?" asked Aggie, her voice shaky and quiet. For some reason she couldn't help herself and touched Edgar again on the shoulder.

"Aggie, no. He'll only break your heart," said Vasher.

Edgar looked at Vasher and saw that he wasn't holding his tamper. He'd thrown it only moments ago and the platform was getting very close. Edgar darted across the room with electric speed, grabbed the tamper, and tossed it through the air. Vasher caught it as Red Eye's boots came into view. Edgar didn't have time to get back to the bin and his own tamper, which he had set down in order to escape Vasher's advance. But his back was to the platform and so he was able to gaze into Aggie's eyes and tell her the truth.

"It's real. *Atherton* is real."

She was awestruck and held his gaze longer than she should have given the circumstances.

"Edgar!" cried Teagan. "Look out!"

But it was too late. Red Eye had already advanced on Edgar from behind. The bender was out and swinging. Edgar closed his eyes and waited. He'd been hit lots of times before by Mr. Ratikan's walking stick in the grove. But this was different. This stung like needles and seemed to cut right though the skin on his back.

Edgar never stopped looking at Aggie. He saw the marks on

her arms and could imagine this terrible man hitting her as he'd just been hit. He suddenly realized he could never leave the Dark Planet without taking Aggie and her friends with him. He had to get them out of the Silo.

Tears began to fill Aggie's eyes. In the unexpected silence Red Eye lurched around where he could see Edgar's face. He was frothing with anger.

"Why aren't you working?" asked Red Eye. He was in a rage as he turned to the rest. "He's standing in the middle of the room doing nothing!"

Red Eye turned on Aggie, his favorite choice on whom to dole out punishment, and he swung the bender to and fro in front of him.

"Is that the best whipping you can give?" said Edgar. All the children in the room gasped, but Edgar had to do something. He had to turn Red Eye's vengeful eye away from Aggie.

"This boy's mad!" said Socket, laughing and snorting from behind Edgar.

"Then we'll have to beat the madness out of him, won't we?" said Red Eye. He grabbed Edgar by the arm and hauled him toward the platform.

"Where are you taking him?" asked Landon. He could be fearless when the mood struck him. "Don't take him away — he only just got here. The passageway of lies can wait a little while, can't it?"

"Shut your mouth, Landon!" screamed Red Eye. "Or you'll be choking down powder with no water in it tonight."

Socket just cackled and wiped his goggles, crossing quickly to the metal bin of finished powder blocks.

"What's this? Only one more block while we was gone? You'll be here all night!"

He laughed some more and looked back at his brother who had stowed his bender. He took the reader from its holster and held it near Edgar's arm.

"Don't you listen to this boy, Lanny," said Red Eye, sure that Edgar was filling their heads with lies. "None of you listen to him! He doesn't have a clue what he's talking about."

Edgar had already felt the reader once and it stung terribly, like a shot of electricity that burned down to his bones. He flinched at the sight of the reader and tried to pull away, but Red Eye had a crushing grip and wouldn't let go.

"There's no passageway of lies here," said Red Eye, his voice like the hiss of boiling oil. He jammed the tip of the reader into Edgar's skin. "Now hold still so I can give Judix the good news."

Edgar felt like he'd been stuck through with a burning needle. When Red Eye pulled the reader away and looked at the screen he didn't say anything. No one could see his eyes behind the goggles, but his scowl turned sharper on his face as he glanced at the reader and then Edgar. The reader had never failed before. He had just used it an hour ago on a girl in the vine room. What was this nonsense?

"How old is he?" asked Socket, walking toward Red Eye. Red Eye couldn't stand his brother meddling all the time. He turned the reader off and locked it back in its cradle at his side.

"He's 4311," said Red Eye. Then, looking cruelly at Landon, he added, "Plenty old for the passageway of lies after a good long beating!"

"The commander will want to hear," said Socket, racing for the platform. "I'll tell her!"

Red Eye pulled the bender from his back with harrowing speed and swept it across his brother's path.

"Leave the commander to me," he said, and then by way of a reward he pushed Edgar toward his brother. "Take him to the engine room and make sure he knows who runs things around here. And watch for Hope. She won't like you beating him on his first day."

Socket pushed Edgar onto the platform and held him against the rail as the platform began to rise. Just as Edgar was about to rise all the way out of the room he saw Red Eye standing against a far wall, turning some sort of dial.

Red Eye had opened the door to the passageway of lies and gone to find Commander Judix.

CHAPTER 16

THE CENTURION

"Keep running!" cried Samuel. "Whatever it is has caught our scent and it's following us!"

Isabel had already loaded a sling and was ready to face the oncoming enemy when she felt something warm at her back.

"It's getting hot in here!" yelled Samuel.

"Run faster!"

Glancing back, Isabel saw a growing tower of red fire shot through with spiraling black smoke.

"This is worse than the Inferno!" said Isabel. "We're about to be set on fire!"

The extra light from the flames gave Samuel a chance to see his surroundings a little better. Whatever was behind them would soon catch up. Their only hope was if the tunnel narrowed far enough so whatever it was could no longer advance, or if they could find —

"There!" said Samuel, pointing to a small opening in one wall. Isabel saw it, too, and they both scrambled inside.

The sound of crashing feet and a snapping tail was practically on top of them and a new bolt of flames came shooting through the tunnel. Isabel burrowed deeper into the hole and Samuel followed, crunching his shoulder into her side and knocking her flat on the ground.

It was dark inside and they quickly discovered that the space they'd entered turned downward and opened up. When they stood, the opening was at eye level and they each looked out as flames drove past their line of sight.

And then, as quickly as they had arrived, the flames and the sounds of pounding feet and a snapping tail were gone. All was dark. Samuel sat down and pulled Isabel to the ground next to him.

"Should I take out the pen?" whispered Samuel. He'd put it in his pocket to hide the light, but now he wondered if it wouldn't be a good idea to look around.

"No!" whispered Isabel. "Just be quiet and let this thing pass so we can get out of here."

Outside the hole the tunnel glowed softly from seeping points of light hidden from their view. An enormous clawed foot stepped in front of the hole. The creature was tracking them, searching out the passageway.

Isabel felt Samuel touch her shoulder and shrugged away his cold hand. She listened as the monster outside crept down the descending tunnel and sniffed the air.

Samuel touched her again — his hands were *so* cold — and

this time she brushed him away, but soon felt his hand on her other shoulder and then on her head.

"Stop touching me, Isabel!" Samuel whispered. "You're scaring me."

"I'm not touching you," Isabel replied, shivering as she realized something truly terrible: Something was in the hidden space with them.

She could barely breathe. Isabel watched as Samuel took the pen from his pocket and blue light escaped. Like a nightmare growing in intensity, they began to understand what had happened. They were the intruders in someone else's quiet home.

Along the walls they could now see dark spheres entangled with long tentacles, glowing slick in the light of the firebugs. The many twisting arms pulsating along the floor were moving toward Samuel and Isabel, surrounding them, *touching* them. What had they found?

The long arms ensnared their legs and arms and wrapped around their necks, squeezing and pulling in every direction. There was no doubt — the creatures wanted to destroy them.

Samuel could feel the tablet being pulled away by one of the tentacles and lunged toward it, striking a twisting arm with the burning tip of the firebug pen. It burned a deep wound in the tentacle and the creature's grip loosened. He kept stabbing at the arms even as they crushed him.

"Samuel!" cried Isabel. She had forgotten about the larger monster outside as her neck and middle were squeezed tighter and tighter. Just about the time Isabel thought she was going to lose consciousness, she heard a terrible noise.

Whatever was outside had heard her scream Samuel's name. It was coming back. And before either of them realized what was happening, a monstrous black claw wrapped around them both at once and jerked them out of the hole.

Isabel and Samuel now saw the first creature that had been chasing them. It was covered in blue scales and had curved, piercing eyes. Black spikes ran all the way down the neck and over the powerful back, and the beast's crowning glory was a swordlike spike protruding from the bridge of its nose. Samuel and Isabel looked at each other, both of them sure it would be the last time.

Samuel saw the roiling slick tentacles around Isabel and the bodies of the creatures hanging heavy at her side. They appeared to have no eyes or nose, only the round pulsing body and the arms squeezing tighter and tighter around the two intruders.

Isabel screamed as the beast lunged forward, sure its great spike would punch right through her chest and out her back, splitting her in two. But Isabel felt nothing. She opened her eyes and saw the spike had gone right through the bodies of both creatures, slashing them into pieces until only a strong smell remained.

The huge beast sniffed them both — first Isabel and then Samuel — then its tongue darted out and touched Isabel's hand.

"He smells like burned figs," said Isabel, in a state of stupefied shock at the thought of being cooked and eaten. She was sure this thing was tasting her skin in order to decide whether or not to flame broil her.

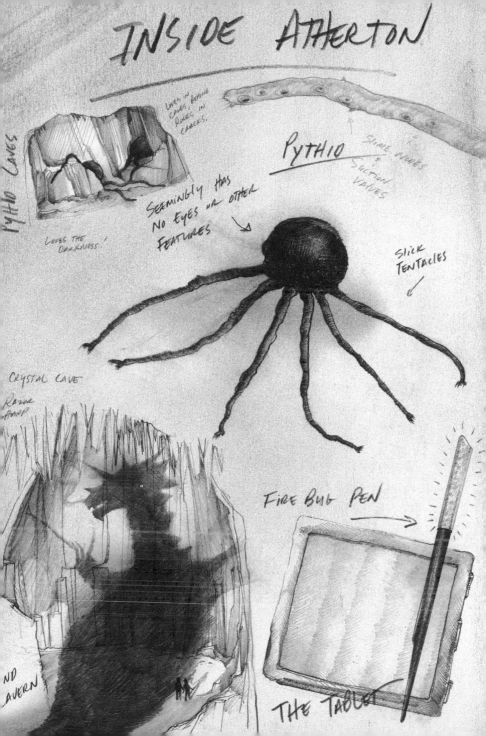

INSIDE ATHERTON

PYTHID CAVES

Lives in caves, behind rocks, in cracks.

Loves the darkness!

PYTHIO

Slime whiles & Suction valves

Seemingly has no eyes or other features

Slick Tentacles

CRYSTAL CAVE

Razor Sharp

FIRE BUG PEN

ND CAVERN

THE TABLET

"It's the Centurion," said Samuel, quite suddenly aware of what he was looking at. "It didn't occur to me until I saw the black horn on its head. It's not going to eat us, Isabel!"

"Of course it's going to eat us!"

"No — no, it's really not, are you, Centurion?"

The dragon pulled its head back ever so slightly. Its beautiful black teeth were slick and shiny, perfectly shaped and powerful beyond imagining.

"Could you put us down?" Samuel requested gently.

Amazingly, the Centurion set its bundle on the ground and released its claw. To Isabel's great pleasure the Centurion sat down and looked at them, tiny puffs of black smoke curling out of its nose.

"It looks . . . I don't know . . . happy or something," remarked Isabel. She rubbed her arms, her neck, her stomach. "What is this thing, Samuel?"

"Look here," he said, holding out the tablet and looking at the inside. He'd barely had a chance to start examining it before fire had started filling the tunnel behind them. "You see, it's a Centurion. Or maybe it's *the* Centurion. I don't know if there are any others."

The tablet had an etched figure of a spiked head encircled by words written in flames: *Gossamer. The Centurion made by my hand to protect. A dragon of the most excellent kind.*

"Strange name for a creature like this," said Samuel.

Isabel didn't understand the words "gossamer" or "dragon," but she liked the sound of Gossamer right away.

"What does it mean?" she asked.

"Well, I think it means delicate or soft, but this thing is anything but."

"Dr. Harding never does anything without a purpose. Maybe he's softer than he looks."

"He?" said Samuel.

"Yes, he," said Isabel. She crept forward with an outstretched hand and Gossamer leaned in close to her. He would not let Isabel touch the black horn, but he did let her touch the scales of his long nose.

"There's something magical about this beast," said Isabel, completely swept away by Gossamer's power and warmth. "He's much softer than he looks."

"Well, there you have it," said Samuel. He wasn't as sure as Isabel about touching a dragon. One swipe of the tail or flick of the head and Samuel would be cut in half. He searched the tablet for more about Gossamer and found a block of small words in one corner.

"Listen to this, Isabel," said Samuel. "'Imagined in my youth at the place called the Silo, where all grown persons but Hope were cruel. Forged by my hand in the secret realm of Atherton, this beast is made to love children but distrust all others. It is powerful and purposeful beyond all measure. A child must guide it homeward.'"

Isabel was overwhelmed by the grandeur of this beautiful creature in their midst "He's on our side," she said, her voice lyrical with wonder. "Who can be against us with a thing like this on our side?"

Gossamer's stomach made a noise neither Isabel nor Samuel

understood and Isabel stepped back, momentarily unsure of what was coming next. The dragon reached forward, gently nudging Isabel to the side, and put its claw inside the hole from which he'd rescued them. He did it in a familiar sort of way, like he'd done it many times before. When his claw came out he held one of the horrible things that had tried to kill Isabel and Samuel.

"What's he doing?" said Isabel.

"I don't have any idea, but I think I know what *that* is," said Samuel. He had found an image he'd originally thought was a sun on the tablet. It was round in the middle and it had wavy lines on every side. Drawn inside the circle was a word.

"Pythid," said Samuel. "It's called a Pythid, I think."

The Pythid squirmed in Gossamer's claw, wrapping its long tentacles around scaly fingers. Gossamer held the squirming glob away from Isabel and Samuel, dropped it, and proceeded to blow a stream of fire. The Pythid burst into flames and tried to scurry away, but Gossamer grabbed it by one arm and let it dangle in the air. He blew fire once more, toasting the skin on the Pythid until it was crispy black.

"Wow," said Isabel. "We're really lucky he likes us."

Gossamer set the Pythid down and took one of the crusted tentacles between two of its claws, ripping it from the round body.

"Yuck," said Isabel.

The dragon held the dripping arm in front of Samuel and Isabel, again with an expression that could only be assumed was a smile of some sort.

"I think he wants us to eat it," said Samuel. Gossamer turned back to the burned pile of Pythid and picked up the remains with his other front claw. He leaned his head back, dropped the whole thing into his mouth, and swallowed it without chewing.

"Maybe it tastes like rabbit," said Isabel. "At least it's cooked."

She reached out and took the crispy tentacle from Gossamer, and the dragon seemed to encourage her to take a bite. It was about the size of her own arm and appeared to be boneless. The end where it had been severed was steaming and bubbly.

Isabel shrugged. Gossamer had saved her. If he wanted Isabel to eat, then Isabel would eat. It was crunchy on the outside, soft and squishy on the inside, and surprisingly tasty. After some persuading, Samuel grabbed the other end and soon the two of them were holding a cooked Pythid tentacle between them, munching away happily in the presence of the most powerful creature on Atherton.

"I think we're going to be all right," said Isabel. "Let's take another look at that map."

"Look here," said Samuel. He'd been scanning the inside of the tablet and pointed to a set of words and symbols and numbers. He read the words aloud.

"'Lead Gossamer to the chill of winter, where all my work comes to an end.'"

Gossamer cooked and ate nine more Pythids while Samuel and Isabel thought about what the tablet said. Now and then the dragon marched down one of the tunnels looking for danger, and each time he came back with a squirming Pythid between his claws. Apparently, there was plenty of dragon food along the way.

"Are you ready to walk the yards?" Isabel asked at length. Samuel nodded. They had named the great and winding tunnel "the way of the yards" because of the combination that had gotten them through the yellow door.

With a very impressive new companion leading the way, it would take trouble of an even bigger kind for the two children to worry any longer. Unfortunately, that was just the kind of trouble awaiting them at the end of the long and dreary path on which they traveled.

CHAPTER

17

L–I–F–T–B–5

Red Eye waited in silence for two hours, wondering why he'd bothered to come in the first place. Two hours! The barracks would soon be shutting down for the night. He was hungry, thirsty, and tired of staring out the window into the gathering darkness of the forsaken wood. And they kept the lights so bright in Station Seven he had to keep his goggles on. Now the goggles itched his eyes and his head and he desperately wanted to take them off. Why had he requested a meeting with Commander Judix? If only he'd called instead.

"What can I do for you?" asked Commander Judix. She had rolled silently into the room and Red Eye leaped back in fright, touching the window. His hand was greasy and it left a smear.

"Don't touch the glass," snapped Commander Judix. "You know how I hate that."

She watched in disgust as Red Eye tried hopelessly to remove the smudge on the glass and only made it worse with his dirty sleeve.

"Leave it, you imbecile!" said Commander Judix, rolling toward Red Eye without a thought of slowing down so he could move out of the way. "I hope you run the Silo with a little more care."

Smudged glass wasn't the only thing Commander Judix hated. She loathed having to deal with Red Eye or his snarly younger brother in person. In fact, she couldn't remember the last time she'd actually seen either one of them up close.

Red Eye embodied everything she hated about the Dark Planet. The sick eyes set deep in their sockets, those revolting goggles, and skin so unnaturally pale. At least Red Eye didn't have that cackling laugh. How she hated it when Socket would screech in his unbearable way.

"The new recruit, Commander, he'll be ready with the other one," said Red Eye, so nervous he could hardly spit the words out. But he had so wanted to play the hero just this once, and to do it in person. He had even allowed himself to imagine there might be a reward.

"How old is he?" Commander Judix stared aimlessly at the forsaken wood through the giant window pane.

"4311," said Red Eye. It was the second time he'd said the number and he couldn't for the life of him imagine why he'd come up with the random digits to begin with. Why hadn't he chosen something closer to 4200?

"That's a little older than Grammel likes them. Is he edgy like you? Does he cackle?"

"No, ma'am, there's none of that with this one. He's not in the least bit nervous. He's an odd one, healthier than we've seen in a long time. But he's been trouble-free and hardly says a word."

"You could learn a thing or two from someone like that," Commander Judix said.

Red Eye thought of how Edgar was getting the beating of his life in the machine room, and this made him feel a little better in the presence of the commander's cruelty.

Commander Judix had already heard how healthy this new recruit was once before, and something told her it was a meaningful piece of information. But her heart and her mind were so bitter and determined, she couldn't quite get at it.

"Does he have a name?" asked Commander Judix, thinking it might jog something in her memory.

"I don't know," said Red Eye. He thought he might make up a name but had some concern that he'd soon forget it and be caught in a lie. He was having enough trouble remembering 4311 without adding more details to remember.

"Find out and tell Shelton," said Commander Judix. "I'll ask him in the morning and I want an answer. Do you understand?"

"I do," said Red Eye, nervously tapping the metal sole of his boot on the floor.

"You're sure about the number? It won't do for Grammel to get a different reading when he arrives."

"One boy of 4200 and one of 4311, both ready to work. That's what I'll deliver."

The boldfaced lie made his neck twitch dreadfully and Commander Judix couldn't stand looking at him anymore. She rolled away, calling over her shoulder, "Bring them to the usual place tomorrow just before dark."

Red Eye wished he'd never made the trip to see Commander Judix in person. He was in a cold sweat from head to toe as he began walking back to the Silo. He could lie about the reading when Grammel came. He could say it had worked before and he didn't know why it wouldn't work now. Captain Grammel would see this recruit and want him. Who wouldn't want a boy like this one? Everything would be fine.

"Now, about that name," he said to himself, wishing for something that would take his attention away from the pounding in his head. "I do so hope I'll have to beat it out of him."

●

"The powder blocks go across the passageway of lies just like the 4200s," said Landon. "Then we never see any of them again."

"What's the passageway of lies?" asked Edgar.

He wanted to know what a 4200 was as well but didn't want to ask too many questions all at once. The barracks door was still open, but the boys were lying on their bunks in the dark. Faint light crept into the room from the corridor that separated the three barracks. There were six boys — seven including Edgar — and all but Vasher were younger than Edgar by a year or more.

It was hard work in the Silo and sleep was a marvelous escape into a world of dreams that almost all the boys, including Vasher, were quick to take advantage of. But in every group of children there was always one who couldn't fall asleep until after everyone else was softly snoring. In this group, that boy was Landon.

"The passageway of lies is the corridor between the Silo and Station Seven," continued Landon, happy to have a night companion to talk to. "Red Eye and Socket say it leads to a place better than the Silo, a place we go when we get old enough, if we've worked really hard. But then other times, when they don't think we're working fast enough, they tell us what a party they'll have after we're gone and how our new home will be full of horrible monsters and bad dreams. We can't tell when they're lying, or if it's all lies, or if they have no idea where we go and just make things up when they feel like it. So we call it a passageway of lies. We're pretty sure it leads somewhere bad, right, Vash?"

Two bunks down the line Vasher didn't answer.

"He sleeps really good," said Landon. "I think it helps him forget he's next to go."

Edgar rolled a little to his left, trying to get comfortable. The bender had been painful, but not as bad as he'd imagined it would be. He had expected it to be awful, but it felt to Edgar like Socket had looked at Edgar's back and for some reason couldn't bring himself to scar it too badly. Still, he felt the welts and bruises as he moved.

"You ever hear of a man named Grammel?" asked Landon.

Edgar shook his head no.

"That's how I got here. Everyone else got lost in the wood and was brought here. Out looking for their parents is what they say. I suppose it's true. I never had parents around, far as I can remember. And I don't even remember how I got on the beach. I think maybe I was sent out for something or snuck out of the compound to see the water. This man, Grammel, found me. I was only five or six. Anyway, Grammel picked me up in his boat and dropped me here at the Silo. He said he'd come back and get me someday and we'd have great big adventures, but I don't think he's coming back."

Landon bit his fingernails for a few seconds but started talking again before Edgar could say anything.

"They count the days around here, did you know that? So I'm not seven and a half years old, I'm 2730 days old. A 4200 is eleven and a half. That's when they send you packing. You get used to the big numbers after a while. Not that you'll have a chance to."

"Thanks a lot!" said Edgar, laughing softly despite the bad news. Landon giggled, but he stopped short and glanced across the bunk at Edgar.

"I'm sorry you can't stay longer. You're nice to have around."

"Don't count me out just yet," said Edgar. "I might have a trick or two up my sleeve."

Landon was about to question Edgar when the familiar clanging sound of metal-soled boots drew nearer from the passageway. A moment later, the door creaked open and a dark shadow was cast along the floor of the barracks.

Red Eye walked in, rubbing the deep sockets of his eyes with his thumbs. He was glad to be back in the dim light of the Silo. Red Eye took four strides — *bang, bang, bang, bang!* —

and stood in front of Edgar's bed. He pulled the bender from his back and slapped it down across Edgar's shins with a loud *whish!* and a *snap!*

"Tell me your name," said Red Eye.

Edgar cried out loudly enough to wake all the boys, but none of them stirred. They all knew better than to get involved.

Edgar glanced at Landon in the pale light in a way that he hoped the younger boy would understand. *Why does Red Eye want to know my name? We better not tell him.*

"Peter is my name," said Edgar. He remembered the name from a story Samuel had used to help teach Edgar how to read.

"That's not what you told us before."

"What's that you say?" said Red Eye.

He walked three angry steps and lifted one of the bunks, dropping it with a loud boom that left no question that everyone was now awake. He stood in front of Vasher's bunk.

"He said his name was Edgar when we were in the drying room. I don't know anyone called Peter."

Red Eye moved the bender along the front edge of the rusted steel bunk where it made a noise like slowly ripping paper.

"How interesting," he said, glancing down the line of beds and seeing that Edgar had sat up.

He sidled down the row of bunks, a little thrill in his step at the prospect of attacking this healthy new worker who had caused him so much humiliation with Commander Judix. Red Eye had guzzled a tin of powdery water moments before and a chalky film lay heavy in the corners of his mouth like froth from a mad dog.

For whatever reason, he now placed all the blame for the current state of his terrible life in the Silo on Edgar. The splitting headache was no longer Aggie's fault, it was Edgar's alone. Touching the glass at Station Seven, the verbal abuse from the commander, his endlessly annoying brother — he wanted to destroy Edgar and now the little dirt ball had given him a reason to do it.

"We don't turn a blind eye to liars in the Silo," said Red Eye, arriving at the foot of Edgar's bed, his pulse quickening. "One bad lie leads to another, and then another, and soon the whole place is full of nothing but *LIARS*!"

Red Eye lifted the bender over his head and stared down at Edgar.

"What seems to be the problem in here?"

A tall figure stood in the doorway with her hand on the latch. Seeing he might lose his chance, Red Eye swung the bender sideways over the bed with an aim to crack Edgar right across the face, something even Red Eye had never done. But Edgar was much faster than Red Eye had thought. He leaped back, felt the wind from the bender and heard the tearing swish, but Red Eye had missed.

"Get away from that bed!" said Hope. She had a voice of sheer magic. It had the kind of power that made an enemy wish against his own will to be on her side. For the first time Red Eye seemed to lose his nerve. It wasn't that Hope had any authority over him; it was the weapon she'd gotten from Max Harding years ago that Red Eye feared.

Red Eye's breath shook with indecision, for he knew that Hope could bring him under control if he wasn't careful.

"You shouldn't even be in here at this hour," she continued, striding confidently into the room until she stood only a few feet behind Red Eye. There was something in her hand, but Edgar couldn't make out what it was.

"I was only tucking all the little monsters in for the night," said Red Eye, dropping the bender on his back where it made a *flit!* and disappeared. "This new one's been giving us some trouble today."

He turned to face Hope for the first time and a thick beam of red light pointed into Red Eye's face. The dreaded thing in her hand had been activated.

Like a tractor beam the light held Red Eye and wouldn't let him go. Hope moved her arm down and Red Eye collapsed to his knees.

"Let me go!"

It didn't sound like Red Eye was in pain, but rather afraid, like a ghost had entered his mind and was trying to scare him to death.

"I know you think you can torture these kids all you want," said Hope. "But just remember what I've always said. You're going to get what's coming to you in the end."

"Leave me alone!" Red Eye pleaded.

"And I'll remind you once more so you don't forget. If you ever try to get rid of me, every child in the Silo will have one of these little gadgets. Young Dr. Harding was pretty good about organizing things like this. He had a gift for it."

Red Eye was pretty sure Hope wasn't bluffing. Max Harding was legendary for protecting helpless kids in ways no one else could have imagined.

"The barracks is all they have," said Hope. The light continued to pour into Red Eye's sockets as he withered closer to the floor. "It's the only place they can escape and rest. I won't have you destroy it for them, not after how hard you push them."

"I won't come in again, I promise," said Red Eye.

The line of heavy, liquid red light fell away and Red Eye staggered to his feet. He shook his head and looked every which way.

"Curse Maximus Harding!" he screamed. "I hate him for ever existing!"

He was humiliated and angry as he went for the door, but he glanced back before vanishing out into the passageway.

"Sleep tight, *Edgar*," said Red Eye. "It's the only night you're going to get in my Silo."

With a great rumble Red Eye departed, and then every boy in the room immediately sat up in the soft light. All but Vasher. He rolled in a ball and refused to show his face.

"Everyone back to sleep," said Hope. She was their protector, their healer, and a soft voice to calm them down. "Enjoy your rest, my little angels."

They settled back in and Hope sat across from Edgar on Landon's bed. Hope didn't speak a word to him until he whispered a question. He'd been thinking about the red light he'd seen and what Hope had said about it.

"Dr. Harding gave you that?" asked Edgar.

"He did. The good doctor and I were close when he was your age," said Hope. "You talk as if you knew him."

"Oh, no, I didn't mean that — I've heard of him."

"So you know he used to live here? He didn't like it when people were mean."

"Why did he leave?" asked Edgar.

"He was very bright. They thought he could help."

"Help with what?"

Hope sighed deeply. "It's a long, complicated story with a not very happy ending. Let's save it for another time."

She patted her pocket softly.

"He made Red2O, this little device in my pocket, and he showed me how to use it. He knew how rough things could get around here." She glanced over her shoulder. "It's the only one, but Red Eye's just dumb enough to believe I've got a hundred of them and a plan. Keep it secret!"

Edgar smiled. "He sounds like a good man — Dr. Harding, I mean, not Red Eye."

Hope laughed softly and nodded. "I'm sorry you won't be staying with us very long," she said, looking at Edgar as he rubbed his shins. "But I guess you're happy to go after a day like today. How much worse can it be somewhere else, right?"

"Right," said Edgar. He wanted to tell her about Atherton, the Raven, Dr. Kincaid, and everything else, but for some reason he held back. What if she turned out to be tricking him? He'd been unable to trust any of the other adults he'd met on the Dark Planet, and he was more afraid than ever that he'd never get back home.

"Do you know where Dr. Harding slept when he lived here?"

Hope glanced over her shoulder and pointed to Vasher's bed.

"Right there. B five. B for boys' barracks and five for the fifth bed in the line of twelve. He slept there every night of his stay. A lot of empty bunks here now. I guess that's probably a good thing."

Edgar's head was reeling. L–I–F–T–B–5. It was the combination of number and letters from the tablet he'd found. Something was hidden beneath Dr. Harding's old bed! If only he could get Vasher out of it long enough to find out what it was.

Edgar had one more line of questioning for Hope before letting her slip away.

"What's the passageway of lies? Where does it lead?" If Edgar was going there, he wanted to know as much as he could before they took him.

Hope had been asked this question more times than she could count. She'd been sending kids off to sea for years and never told one of them where they were going, because to be fair, she really didn't have a lot to go on. She knew it was outside, and that was all she needed to know. Outside was a black lung, a hacking cough, a death certificate. She'd only ever said to be prepared for some things that might be a little hard, but that it would be an adventure.

Hope's life had long been about giving children a few years of hope, to take the edge off a bad place, to love them and care for them but never to scare them. And so she told the lie once more, hoping it would be the last time and knowing deep in her broken heart that she'd be saying it again before long.

"I can't tell you where the passageway of lies leads. No one knows for sure, I guess, least of all me. But it will be an adventure — that much I know — and you won't have to deal with Red Eye or Socket anymore."

"When am I leaving?" asked Edgar.

"The rumor is tomorrow night," said Hope, putting her warm hand over his. She felt for his pinky and found it missing, and this surprised her.

"Looks like you've been beaten up a little, after all," she said, gazing at the near perfect creature who had landed in the sad world of the Silo. She could already imagine this strong, healthy boy out in the open air turning pale and broken. "You best get some rest. And don't you keep him up all night talking, Landon."

She let go of Edgar's hand and glanced down at Landon, who appeared to be sleeping.

"Don't let him fool you," said Hope. "He's a little chatterbox."

Hope leaned over each boy whether they were sleeping or not and checked their covers. When she came back and touched Edgar on the cheek his heart skipped a beat. *Why can't you be my mother?* he thought as she disappeared out the door.

Not three seconds went by and Landon was already talking again.

"Got a surprise for you," he said.

There was a spark of light in the room and an old candle was lit. Landon wouldn't look directly at it, but Edgar had always liked the light from a candle and couldn't stop staring at it.

"That's great, Landon. But shouldn't you be getting some sleep like Hope said?"

"I got an even better surprise. You ready?"

Edgar was looking at the candlelight, thinking about how he might use it to help look under Vasher's bed.

"I'm ready," said Edgar. He was really starting to like this young busybody. He had great energy for such a gloomy place. Landon jumped out of bed and reached up next to the metal wall. A series of thick pipes ran every which way, and he tapped on one of them four times. A few seconds later there was a distant echo as someone tapped back, and Landon jumped out of bed.

"Come on, we have to go."

"Wait. Landon, there's something I need you to do for me."

"Anything! But we need to hurry. They'll wonder where we are."

Edgar was terribly curious about where they were going and who they would meet, but time was so desperately precious. He might not get another chance.

"This is going to sound strange, but I need to look under Vasher's bed."

Landon blinked rapidly in the candlelight. It was a small, soft light, but it still made his eyes sting at the edges.

"Vasher's not so bad. And he takes care of me. He's just scared, that's all."

"I know, Landon. I like him, it's just, well, this is going to sound really strange, but I think something is hidden there that will help us. I'm not going to hurt him or take anything from him. Really I'm not."

Landon didn't see the harm in lifting the bed and looking underneath, so he shrugged and got up. Edgar followed, and when they arrived at the foot of the bunk, he lifted it ever so slowly, just two inches above the floor. Vasher stirred but did not wake. Landon peeked underneath but found nothing.

"Try the posts," whispered Edgar.

Landon felt the bottoms of the metal pilings that held the bed. He shook his head, not finding anything, but Edgar wasn't satisfied. He held the bed with one hand, which was difficult because it was heavy, and he made a spinning motion with his other hand.

Landon took the hint and began trying to turn the bottom of one of the metal legs. Nothing. He moved around Edgar and tried the second leg, and this time the bottom part began to turn. He looked up, smiling excitedly at Edgar, set the candle down on its fat bottom, and began spinning faster with both hands. Soon the leg was off and he pulled it free. He dug out a rolled-up piece of paper and held it up in victory, then put the leg back where it had been.

When Edgar set the end of the bed down it made a small sound and Vasher sat up in bed.

"I'm not eating that! I don't care if it's all there is. I won't eat it!"

It was the gibberish of a dream.

"It's okay, Vash, lie down," said Landon softly. "No one's going to make you eat anything you don't want to."

"That's more like it!" said Vasher, lying back down and closing his eyes.

When Edgar and Landon were back at their beds Landon handed Edgar the folded-up piece of paper.

"He talks in his sleep like that. Sometimes he walks around, too. That's a little scarier."

"Thank you, Landon," said Edgar earnestly, sure this new clue would reveal something important.

"Do you have to look at it right now? They'll be waiting for us."

"Who'll be waiting?"

"You'll see," said Landon.

Edgar looked at the folded paper. He could hardly wait to open it, but he was also curious about who Landon wanted him to meet and where.

"Where are we going?" asked Edgar. And then Edgar heard Landon whisper just the kind of words he loved to hear.

"Stay close and I'll show you the way. We're getting out of here."

Landon pulled Edgar down the center row of beds and stopped short when he reached Vasher's bunk.

"Vash," said Landon, shaking Vasher's foot. "Wake up. We're going."

Vasher mumbled and rolled over. "Go on without me," came his exhausted voice out of the darkness. "I'm too tired."

The sound of grumbling came from a bunk nearby and Landon pulled Edgar farther along.

"He sleeps like the dead lately," whispered Landon. "That happens to boys when they go over 4000. I've seen it before."

They came to the slick metal wall and Landon blew out the candle, setting it carefully in the corner to be picked up on their return trip. The world was suddenly very dark.

"Something tells me you're a good climber, so you shouldn't

have any trouble with this. Just feel for my feet and stay close behind. It isn't very far."

Edgar nodded, then realized Landon couldn't see him and said: "Got it."

He could feel Landon moving above him and followed, gripping a series of round pipes before reaching the girders that snaked along the ceiling. The metal girders were very good for climbing, with wide gaps to pass through and crawl on top of like a spider.

"Be careful with this next part," said Landon. "We'll be going down."

Soon there came a T in the passage. The space was so small Edgar had to guide his feet back first, bending his knees then curving his body to get all the way flat at the bottom.

"This way," Landon called from a surprising distance down the corridor. Soft light crept into the duct as Edgar scrambled to catch up. And there was something else — roots or vines that crawled all along the sides of the passage like they were trying to take over the place. Edgar saw shadows dancing in front of him as Landon moved like a cat in the cramped space.

"Almost there!" Landon's voice echoed through the narrow passageway. "One more turn and you've got it."

The snakelike roots had turned lush and green, and the tunnel leading down was loaded with leaves shot through with pale light from below. Edgar had been crawling headfirst in the downward stretches and wished he hadn't this last time, because he could see as he passed through the thickest of the leaves that this passage would end in open air and hanging vines.

Landon's head popped into view as a silhouette against the dim light below.

"Just let go," said Landon. "You can catch a vine on the way out."

Edgar wasn't sure about this idea, and instead reached the opening and poked his head out into the vine room. The vines hung close together and they were full with green and yellow leaves. It was like a jungle held captive from the outside world.

Landon had slid down and hung well below the entrance now. "Getting back to our beds will be some work, but it's worth it," he said. He was hanging from one of the long vines, swaying softly back and forth.

Edgar heard something coming toward them, but he couldn't see what it was. Without warning someone slammed into Landon, sending him flying off to another vine and grabbing hold with a shout.

"Hey! We just got here! You could have waited long enough to —"

Landon couldn't finish what he was saying because someone else flew in from the other direction on a different vine and slammed into Landon again. This time he held on but only barely, flopping wildly through the air.

"Help me, Edgar! They're attacking!"

"What's happening?" yelled Edgar. He couldn't tell what was going on for sure, only that his friend was being clobbered. Edgar dropped out of the hole in the ceiling and grabbed a vine. He felt natural curls and loops in the vine that he could easily slide his feet into.

"Here they come again!" yelled Landon. "Grab another vine and head for the wall!"

Edgar moved as quickly as he could in the direction of Landon's voice.

"This way, Edgar!" he cried, and then right after, "*Ooommmph!*" He'd been tagged again and spun aimlessly below.

"Keep going for the wall! They can't get you there."

Edgar sensed something was heading toward him and he sped up, leaping from vine to vine and feeling the sting at every point on his back and legs where he'd been beaten by Red Eye and Socket.

Someone swished past, barely missing Edgar as they went. Whoever it was called out with a hooting sound. *Whoo! Whoo!* The hooting was returned from Edgar's left, and he barely had time to brace himself before someone flew overhead, grabbed the vine he was on from above, and plucked it like a guitar string. The vine wobbled violently and Edgar held on for dear life.

Just when he felt under control a second attack occurred, and this one did him in. The assailant flew past, chopping at Edgar's arms as they went. Edgar let go and free-fell backward, dangling from the loop that held one foot.

"Don't feel too bad," said Landon from below. Edgar couldn't see him, but if he had been able to, he would have seen that Landon was also hanging upside down. "They're really good and you're new at this."

Edgar was completely confused. What had just happened?

"Do you want some help getting out of that loop?"

The voice came from somewhere above Edgar. Craning his neck to see, he realized who it was.

"Aggie?"

"And Teagan," said her friend, hanging nearby.

Aggie looked better than when he'd seen her before. Her face actually had some color in it and her eyes seemed brighter and less hollow.

"Vash hasn't been showing up lately. It's nice to have a team of boys to beat again," said Aggie.

"Woooohoooo!"

Edgar heard the sound below him and wondered what Landon was doing down there.

"The best way down," said Teagan, "is to let go and fly." And just like that Teagan let go of her vine and dropped like a rock toward the bottom.

"But you'll get hurt!" said Edgar, grabbing a vine and swinging himself back up again.

Aggie pulled back and forth on two vines until she was swinging in a wide arc.

"Don't want to land on top of her," she said. And then Aggie dove free of the vine and howled all the way to the bottom.

"Come on, Edgar!" yelled Landon. "It's not that far! You can do it!"

Edgar couldn't see the bottom, but the voice didn't sound so very far away. Shadows danced everywhere, like he was in a thick jungle with a full moon above.

"We're clear of you, it's safe to drop."

Edgar took a deep breath and let go, falling fast through leaves and knocking countless flowers that would never bloom free from their vines. It snowed buds all around him, and below they formed a thick carpet.

Edgar tucked into a ball as he hit and it was pure magic. Soft golden buds exploded everywhere and broke his fall. He never did hit the very bottom, but the layers grew denser the deeper they went.

Edgar popped up on his feet and saw Aggie, Teagan, and Landon lying on the top of the sea of gold. Edgar's entire body except for his head was submerged in the deep golden sea.

"Happens every time," said Aggie. "Next time lie out flat and you'll stay on top."

She rolled along the top layer, light as a feather, until she reached the wall. Then she climbed up onto a vine, swung across until she hovered above Edgar, and told him to grab her feet. He did as he was told and pulled himself up. When the four of them all hung together again, pushing idly against the wall and laughing softly, the real talking began.

"They have to leave the lights on in this room or the vines will die," Aggie explained. "And Red Eye and Socket never come down here at night. Once they're locked away in the machine room they hardly ever stir. I'm not sure who discovered the ducts first, but kids have known about them for a long time. Most of them are too afraid to leave the barracks, but we come here and play when we're not too tired."

Edgar knew then he could trust them, that children on the Dark Planet were the same as children on Atherton.

"When we were in the drying room, you said something to

me," said Aggie. Her eyes sparkled in the golden light of the room, and even with the close-cropped hair and slightly sunken eyes she was very pretty. "You said Atherton was real. How do you know that?"

"What do you know about Atherton?" asked Edgar.

"Everyone's heard of Atherton, especially around here," said Landon. "It's our favorite story."

"How does it go?" asked Edgar, amazed that the truth might have passed into the things of legend and fairy tales.

"It begins with a boy named Max who lived here a long time ago," said Landon.

Teagan jumped in. She absolutely loved telling the story and couldn't help herself.

"Max was very small and super smart. No one could say where he'd come from, only that he wandered into the forsaken wood one day like so many others. Back in those days there was a place called the yards where they let the children out to play. That was before the Cleaners and the Spikers came, before the air got harder to breathe and everyone who stayed out too long got the sockets and the jitters."

There was some collective nervous laughter and Aggie looked down, rubbing her temple and closing her eyes. She didn't want Edgar to notice that she had been out a little too long, that it showed in her eyes. But Edgar couldn't have minded less.

"It was a sort of playground," said Landon. "There was an old merry-go-round and a slide with some steps missing, and there were neat statues of things that the kids would climb on. Plus a lot of dirt and sand from the sea."

Teagan jumped in. "Anyway, Max was small and the older boys picked on him. So he made all sorts of gadgets out of parts he found in the Silo. He would collect old motors and bolts and pieces of metal from the engine room. Back then you could do that, and you could get old chargers, too. And he would sneak away from the yards over by Station Seven and look through all the junk. There were tubes of this and that and wires and bottles of potion and lots of strange things! He would take them and make amazing inventions. The older boys stopped tormenting Max when a metal spider crawled on their legs at night and clamped down on their toes!"

"I love this part," said Landon. He was still young enough to hear the same story for the twentieth time and like it just as much.

"Max was more than just smart, he was different. He saw things no one else saw, had ideas no one else had. Under his bed was like a tiny laboratory filled with every kind of trapped bug and seed he could find from the outside. There were concoctions and witches' brews and tubes of glowing green. He made small bugs bigger and stranger and let them loose on the bigger boys. They were so afraid of Max!"

"He sounds like a little mad scientist," said Edgar, unable to keep his mouth shut as he heard of his maker's early exploits. But they didn't like that description and scowled at him, especially Landon.

"Then one day a very famous scientist — the most famous ever, in fact — saw Max in the yards and talked with him. He thought this small boy from the Silo might be a help to the people who were trying to fix the broken world. And so Max went to Station Seven, but he never forgot about the Silo. *Never!*"

"How do you know he never forgot?" asked Edgar.

"Because he kept coming back. All the time after that he would come back. He invented these vines and the seeds that never flower and the powder blocking and — well, he invented *everything*. At least that's what he did in the story I'm telling you. It was a long time ago, way before we showed up here, and no one seems to know what really happened."

"What then?" said Edgar.

"They say he invented the best thing there ever was," said Aggie. She was watching Edgar to see how he would react. "He made Atherton. And he put all sorts of creatures there, including Gossamer, the black dragon."

"The what?" said Edgar, finally finding something in the story that even he couldn't believe.

"The black dragon!" said Landon. "The one that has more power than any other dragon! Its only job is to protect children, and it lives on Atherton. But one day it will come back here and kill all the bad beasts in the forsaken wood."

"Oh," said Edgar, not sure how or when he would break the news to Landon that no such creature existed.

"And then Max went to Atherton and never came back," said Aggie, picking up where Landon had left off. She sounded a bit sad as she went on. "It's the only fairy tale we've got about the Silo, and it ends rather badly. Max Harding became Dr. Harding and made a new world for all the children. But then he disappeared and forgot about us. Some say he's coming back, but I mostly think that's just so they have something to believe in. I think it's just a story that gives some of us hope."

"Is the story true?" asked Edgar, turning to Teagan and Landon for help.

"I hope it's true," said Teagan. "I want to know what if feels like to breathe clean air and take a long walk outside under the stars at night. I haven't seen a star in a long time."

"Atherton's real," said Landon. "I know it's real, and I think Dr. Harding's coming back soon. I'm just about sure of it, actually."

"Really?" said Edgar, inspired by Landon's enduring spirit despite the fact that Edgar knew that Dr. Harding could never come back.

Landon nodded. He looked at Aggie for approval but Aggie wouldn't look back. Her gaze was fixed on Edgar.

"Do you think the story is true?" she asked hesitantly.

Edgar looked at all three of them. The green team. How quickly he had come to admire and love them. They were so much stronger and more full of courage than he was. They'd lost everything and been left for dead, but they still hoped for the best.

"You're not going to believe me when I tell you this," said Edgar. "You really won't, but I promise from the bottom of my heart that Atherton is real. And the story gets a lot better."

And then Edgar told them everything. He told them about the making of Atherton, about Dr. Kincaid and Vincent, about Cleaners and a collapsing world. He told them all about

Dr. Harding and what had really happened to him, how he had transformed into Lord Phineus and back again, how all that he had made was part of a grand and wonderful story that had led Edgar back to the Dark Planet. He told them who he was — made by Max Harding and hidden away in the grove on Atherton. He told them everything and they hung on every word.

"After I landed here in the Raven I didn't know what to do. I only wanted to find the Silo, to see where my father — well, my maker, I suppose — to see where he had grown up. And now I've found you all and I couldn't possibly leave you here in a million years."

"Wow!" said Landon. "Wow! Wow! Wow! This is, like, the best day ever!"

"Calm down, Landon," said Teagan. But she was just as excited on the inside as he was. And Aggie was, too. Something good was happening to her and her friends, and her heart felt alive with excitement as it never had before.

"What about Gossamer? Did you see the black dragon on Atherton?" asked Landon, wide-eyed.

"I don't know about any black dragon," said Edgar. He wasn't even sure what a dragon looked like. "But one thing you said makes me wonder if there really is a dragon. Dr. Harding didn't like anything that could fly, so if he were to make a dragon, I'm not sure it would fly like you say."

Landon beamed. "Well, sure, he'd fly! Every dragon flies. He's there, I know he is. We need to get to Atherton so I can find him. I'm going to find the black dragon!"

Aggie started to cry, then she started to laugh. Pretty soon she was doing both at once and she couldn't for the life of her get any words out. Before long the laughter was gone and it was only tears and quiet sobbing. She slouched along the green leaves.

"What is it, Aggie?" said Teagan. "Why so sad?"

Aggie wiped the last of her tears away. "I wish you could have come sooner."

Aggie wouldn't say why, but it was obvious to everyone that she had lost her family along the way and it had left her filled with grief, until now.

"I'm sorry," said Edgar, feeling the weight of the world on his small shoulders. "But I'm here now — and Aggie, the story is true. It's not a fairy tale after all. Max was real and he really cared. The story's not over yet," Edgar concluded. "It couldn't have come to the end without you three in it."

Aggie smiled weakly. Teagan wrapped an arm around her.

"Aggie, we can do this," she said. "I really think we can. You just have to believe."

Aggie took a deep breath of dusty air and let out a small but meaningful cough. She looked very tired to Edgar and he thought they should get her to bed. But she smiled despite her fatigue.

"We have to make sure Red Eye and Socket don't find out about this," she said. "And there's not much time. We only have tomorrow and . . ." She paused and glanced at her friends. Everyone knew what awaited Edgar and Vasher — the passageway of lies.

"Do you have some sort of plan, Edgar?" Aggie asked.

"I didn't until I found this," he said, taking the folded piece of paper from Vasher's bunk out of his pocket. "It's from Max. He left it for us a long time ago so we'd find it."

"No way!" said Landon. "I found that!"

Landon's energy cleared all the sadness out of the air, and the four of them gathered in a circle as Edgar unfolded the paper. It was a remarkably intricate drawing of certain parts of the Silo and Station Seven with a dense clutter of numbers, symbols, and words. Edgar couldn't read the words, but he didn't tell anyone as Aggie turned the paper and read.

"I can't believe he wrote this when he was — what do you think? *Our* age?"

She exchanged a glance with Teagan, her constant companion.

"All I know is this means we might be able to leave the Silo together," said Teagan, who was a hundred and seventy days younger than Aggie, which meant Aggie was supposed to leave the Silo first. "And that makes me very happy."

The two girls held a lingering smile while Edgar and Landon continued to examine the elaborate map and all the symbols.

"What do you suppose this is?" asked Edgar. He was pointing to a cryptic diagram that showed a square-shaped object surrounded by tiny dots exploding in every direction. There were two words inside the square no one had ever heard. "Hugin" and "Munin." Below the box was a long line of dots in a row that led to a small drawing of a boy's face. Could it be young Max Harding? Edgar didn't know. Below the boy's face were the words "Hugin will come if you call him."

"That's some weird stuff," said Landon.

Aggie was focused on the intricate drawing of passageways and chambers in the Silo and Station Seven.

"One thing is for sure," she said. "We need to follow this map."

Soon a plan was formed, one more vine game was played in which the girls won again, and everyone returned to their beds for a few hours of much-needed rest.

CHAPTER
19
THE WIDEST RIVER

Gossamer was a surprisingly agreeable companion for the many hours that Isabel and Samuel traveled down the winding path of the yards during the night. Now and then Gossamer would reach one of his great claws into a hole and pull out a squirming Pythid, burn it until crispy, and then drop it in his mouth and continue on.

The two children made a startling discovery about Gossamer when, after several more hours of trudging along, Samuel began to tire of the long journey.

"How long have we been at this?" he asked. Samuel's feet were aching and he'd more than once bumped up against sharp ledges and outcroppings of stone. He didn't want to be the first to complain, but it was becoming difficult to hold out against Isabel's dogged determination.

"What does it matter?" said Isabel. "We've got a ways to go and no one's going to carry us to the end."

"Are you sure about that?" asked Samuel. He'd been wondering for a while if there might be a way to ride atop Gossamer, but the many inhospitable black spikes that covered the beast from head to toe made it seem completely out of the question.

But then the dragon had fluttered its small wings. They were webbed like bat wings and smooth like a hammock between thin bones, and certainly too small to ever lift Gossamer's weight. At the ends were more spikes, wide at the base and curved to a point.

"Look there," said Samuel, watching Gossamer spreading out and shaking his wings again. Samuel felt a little sorry for the creature and wondered why Dr. Harding had made it so, but Gossamer didn't seem to mind. He sniffed and licked at the wings, as if they were a cherished oddity he couldn't quite understand.

"What if we sat on his wings? Then he could carry us."

Isabel looked long and hard at Samuel. "I should have expected this."

"Expected what?" said Samuel, but he already knew by the tone of her voice that he was in trouble.

"That you'd start complaining."

"But I'm not complaining! I'm just saying it might work, that's all. It would be easier than walking."

"Face it, Samuel," said Isabel, off and moving again when she saw that Gossamer, looking curious, was about to come back and join them. "You're from the Highlands. People from up there grow tired pretty fast."

It was times like these that Samuel wished he had been raised in the grove with Isabel and Edgar. They both had a certain kind of stamina and mind-set that eluded him. He'd never spent a long day in the clutches of manual labor, tired by noon with six or seven hours to go whether he liked it or not.

He chased after Isabel and, catching up, made his decision. "Walk if you want, but I'm giving it a try."

Isabel shook her head in disbelief.

"Could you stop a moment?" Samuel called out to Gossamer. "I want to ask you something."

Gossamer swung his tail to one side and its spiky surface crashed against rocks where it sparked blue and red. His head turned to Samuel and the awe-inspiring face stared him down. Gossamer's expressive eyes opened wide, and the sea of blackness surrounding them — the eyelids, the nose, the teeth and tongue — made the brilliant blue eyes sparkle all the more.

"Could I ride on one of your wings?" said Samuel.

Isabel tried to hide her amusement, but let a peal of her infectious laughter slip out. Even Gossamer couldn't resist it. He first smiled with his smooth black lips, then opened his mouth and made a sound that came from somewhere way down deep in his throat.

Samuel felt Gossamer's hot breath and feared for his life. *What if he blows fire all over me?* But he needn't have worried. Gossamer's laugh came from a different place than his raging plumes of fire.

Samuel pointed to one of Gossamer's wings. He flapped his arms and then held them out. Gossamer so loved children he would do anything they commanded. And he was a smart dragon, made by a very smart man. He could understand a great deal without much prompting.

Gossamer turned his body away from Samuel and Isabel and leaned back, letting his leathery wings unfurl on the ground in front of them.

"You've got to be kidding me," said Isabel. "He understands you."

"More importantly, he's going to let us ride! Come on, Isabel. Why not ride if he wants us to?"

Isabel shrugged. The idea of riding Gossamer had gotten under her skin and now she wanted to try it.

"I'll take the left one," she suggested. "You take the right."

Samuel made a little hooting sound of excitement and started for the assigned wing, careful to avoid touching any of the spikes at the bottom or the top. When he stepped on, Gossamer made a chirping noise as though happy to have someone aboard.

Samuel got down on his knees and then lay down and rolled over, facing the ceiling of the wide-open passageway. "This is great!" he cried. "You're going to love it. It's better than your bed back home!"

Isabel had to agree as she crept onto the wing and lay down. It was soft and warm, cradling her protectively. She couldn't see Samuel on the other side of Gossamer's hulking frame, but she heard him just fine.

"Carry on, Gossamer!" he commanded. "Straight down the path of the yards until we reach the end."

Gossamer knew the way. There were side channels that led

into the open expanse inside of Atherton, but the way of the yards was straight and true.

Riding Gossamer's wings felt like lying on the bottom of a small boat adrift on a rolling sea. The dragon's chest heaved slowly in and out, rumbling like a softly snoring giant of the woods. The effect was calming and soon the chatter between Isabel and Samuel became thin and wispy. And then both were fast asleep on Gossamer's wings as he made his way down, down, down into the deepest part of Atherton.

When the two awoke neither of them could figure out where they were or what was happening to them, enveloped as they were in the wings of the black dragon.

"Samuel?" said Isabel, half whispering as she tested the sound of her voice in the air. She'd awoken when Gossamer had stopped without warning. Samuel didn't have time to respond, for Gossamer reared up slowly and planted the back sides of his wings on the ground. Both Samuel and Isabel glided down, coming to rest on their own wobbly feet.

"Did we just . . . ?" started Samuel.

Isabel jumped and finished his thought. "Ride a dragon? I think we did!"

With Samuel and Isabel safely set aground, Gossamer shook his wings and folded them in tight. He stretched his long spiked neck and wandered several paces off in search of food. He seemed to know this place as he went down a side tunnel that required lowering his head to lumber through. A moment later the tunnel was filled with glowing light, the sound of wind and fire, and finally the crunching of teeth.

"He probably hasn't stopped to eat for a long time," said Samuel, stretching his hands toward the ceiling. Another burst of flame and wind arose from deeper down the side tunnel.

"He could be a while," said Isabel. "Let's see the tablet."

As Samuel pulled it out the pen and the firebugs came to life, the bottom half of the device glowing bright blue. He held it over the tablet so it was easier to see in the dim light.

"We could be anywhere," said Isabel, seeing that the yards kept going, circling this way and that, until finally at some point the way on the map abruptly ended.

"The chill of winter," said Samuel, running his fingers over the four words. He stood and held the pen up high, suddenly feeling certain that Gossamer had stopped not for hunger, but for finding the end of something.

"He knew the way and the way has ended," said Samuel.

"What do you mean?" asked Isabel, but in the next moment she could see the answer all around her as light poured from the round opening of the side tunnel, where Gossamer was torching another Pythid.

"Snowflakes," whispered Samuel. "Lots of snowflakes."

Images of snowflakes were carved deeply into the stone ceiling and down the sides of the walls, the edges set in cold black relief.

"What do you suppose is down there?" asked Isabel, glancing toward the end of their way.

Gossamer had returned from his feast and gazed down at them tiredly. He had walked for many hours with a heavy load and eaten a big meal.

"We can wait while you rest," said Isabel. The dragon

seemed to understand what Isabel was saying. Gossamer sat back on his enormous legs and his eyes fell half shut as Isabel crept up to him.

"Thank you for protecting us," she whispered, kneeling and touching the side of his massive black head. It was rough and hard like chiseled stone. Gossamer sighed deeply and drifted off to sleep.

"Let's take a look down the way while he rests," whispered Samuel. "Maybe we can find the end on our own."

Samuel put the tablet and the pen back in his pack and removed the small stash of water that remained. He handed it first to Isabel, who gulped down half, then took the leather pouch himself and finished it off. He shrugged at Isabel, put the empty pouch in his pack, and wondered where his next drink would come from.

"Come on," said Isabel. "He's fast asleep. I get the feeling it won't be very far to the end."

Samuel felt the same way as the two set off down the last part of the yards. It was wilder here, more jagged rocks and sharp beams of light shooting every which way.

Up ahead, the way came to a wall. A hard turn to the left was the only direction they could go, and it didn't look big enough to allow Gossamer to pass through.

"We can't go on without him," said Isabel. "I don't want to."

"Let's just have a look," said Samuel. "We've come all this way. Don't you want to see what the chill of winter is?"

Isabel looked back in the direction from which they'd come and wished Gossamer would wake up. When she turned back, Samuel had already gone.

"Samuel! Wait for me." She took out her sling and filled it with a dried fig, holding it like a pendulum as the fig swayed near the ground.

"I'm here," said Samuel from somewhere ahead in the shadows. "Come quick and see what I've found."

Isabel marched forward into a widening space, and in the growing light of orange and yellow she finally came to Samuel's side and gasped.

"It doesn't look like winter to me," said Samuel.

The two children stood, mouths agape, staring down at a perilous cliff that dropped off in front of them. It was hundreds of feet to the bottom, and what lay there was about as far from being cold and wintry as they could have imagined.

A river of fire, a hundred feet across, boiled and teemed along a twisting path as far as they could see in both directions. Beyond the hundred feet of molten rock, there was nothing but a rising wall of stone.

"This is the Inferno, only worse," said Isabel, horrified. It was the Inferno on a grand scale, billions of firebugs hovering like a fog over billions of pounds of liquefied rock infested with thousands of cave eels greedily chomping on everything their glowing jaws could reach.

"This is a disaster," said Isabel, sweat beginning to trickle down her temple. The passage was hotter here, fueled by steam rising through the air.

"We'll go back," said Samuel, finally concluding that he was ready to give up the adventure and let the adults decide what they would about this place. "We can hand in the tablets and the pen and show them the way."

"At least they're not up here," said Isabel, her mind fixated on the firebugs as she crawled closer to the edge. "They stay way down there, don't they?" It seemed to put her at ease to know she wouldn't have to endure an outright attack.

Samuel knelt and crept to Isabel's side and together they looked all around.

"There," Isabel pointed across the river. Near the far wall, a thin pillar of stone capped with a round platform rose about a hundred feet, and a bridge of stone led from the platform to a dark opening. It was hard to see for sure in the mottled light, but the soft shadows that danced on the wall behind the pillar looked for all the world like the shadows of falling snow.

"The chill of winter is there," said Isabel, suddenly curious beyond all reason.

"I think you're right," said Samuel. He couldn't see how they would ever get across the river of fire, but didn't want to discourage Isabel. "There must be a way — a bridge or a tunnel. We just haven't figured it out yet." He took the tablet and the pen from his pack and began scanning the burned lines, numbers, words, and symbols.

Isabel felt a terrible chill run through her as she thought of falling over the edge. She imagined she would be shocked with electricity over and over again until she hit the river and melted away in a puff of smoke. Her parents would be left to wonder what had happened to her, but there would be nothing of her left to find.

And yet, even in the face of this insurmountable obstacle, Isabel could not let go. She thought of Edgar and tried to imagine what he would think if he saw her there. He would tell her to turn back, and for reasons she couldn't quite explain, this more than anything else made her want to find a way across the wide river of fire.

From behind Samuel and Isabel an unexpected noise cut through the roar of boiling and hissing and snapping teeth. It sounded like the loud crash of rocks being torn asunder.

"What is that?" asked Samuel, looking up from the tablet and feeling the stones beneath him start to shake.

Gossamer had awoken and found them missing. He had never had a reason to go beyond the way of the yards before, so he'd never attempted to widen the narrow way. But it wouldn't take long for the great black dragon to pummel the walls into oblivion to come stand at the edge with Samuel and Isabel.

CHAPTER

20

THE PASSAGEWAY OF LIES

Morning at the Silo brought Red Eye and Socket's usual bad temper down upon the boys in the barracks.

"Get your lazy bones out of those bunks!" cackled Socket. He had already pulled out his bender and was walking along the row of beds, banging the frames loudly. Edgar leaped from his bed like everyone else and pulled on his sandals, hopping on one foot and then the other as he headed for the door.

"Hold up, you," said Red Eye. He took two clanging steps toward Edgar and tossed a pair of metal-soled boots into the air. The boots flew straight at Edgar's head and would have knocked him to the ground, but Edgar ducked as they whipped past and crashed into the wall behind his bed.

"What's wrong with you, boy? Can't you catch?" said Socket, laughing maniacally as he slapped the bender against the side of his boot. Edgar picked up the heavy boots and found they were badly scuffed and way too big for his feet.

"Put them on," said Red Eye. "You'll be taking a little walk later today. Only boots allowed where you're going."

From somewhere down the line of beds Edgar heard a howling cry of pain. Vasher had been whacked by another flying pair of boots.

"You two better start paying more attention," said Socket. "You're expected to be men out there, not toddlers!"

Socket always seemed to be the only one who ever laughed at his barbs and jabs.

"Enjoy your breakfast," said Red Eye as Edgar passed through the door. "It'll be the last meal you have under my watch. Who knows when you'll eat again?"

Edgar saw Hope when he reached the kitchen. She was telling the younger children silly stories while they drank their breakfast. All of the children had enormous, chalky white mustaches and giggled at one another. Hope knew Edgar would be leaving. She had a hard time looking at him. When she finally did look up they locked eyes.

"I'm sorry you couldn't stay longer," she said.

"Me, too."

Edgar wanted to tell her who he was, but there was so little time.

"What was he like?" Edgar asked. He stirred white powder into a metal cup of water.

"You mean Dr. Harding?"

Edgar nodded and began drinking his breakfast.

"He was a little like Landon, actually. He had a lot of energy. I think he only slept a couple of hours every night, because I tell you what, that boy had a new invention every morning. Did you know the Silo used to just be a place for orphans to live? There were no vines or powder or any of that. Later on, after he had been at Station Seven, he invented all these processes. Said it was good for kids to work, good for their spirits, gave them a sense of purpose."

"What else did he say?" asked Edgar.

"He said he would come back," said Hope. She grew sad then, and seemed older than before. How old was she? Sixty? Seventy? Older?

"Is there something you want to tell me?" she asked.

"Let's go! Let's go!" Red Eye yelled from the echoing hallway.

He wanted to tell her all about Dr. Harding. She deserved to know the truth. He heard Red Eye's boots coming toward the kitchen.

"Don't give up hope," said Edgar. "There's still a chance things might work out as he imagined."

Hope didn't say anything as Edgar raced out of the kitchen and into the hall wearing his clumsy new boots. She turned back to the youngest children and began telling them the story of young Dr. Max Harding.

Red Eye took the green and orange teams down the center of the Silo in one group, dropping orange in the vine room. If not for the oversize boots on his feet Edgar might have jumped off the descending platform so he could swing through the vines, the memory of the night before playing in his imagination.

When they finally reached the drying room Red Eye pushed them off the platform. "Socket will be down before long to check on you. He better find at least four blocks or it's going to be a very long day for green."

Red Eye focused his attention on Edgar and Vasher. "And don't you go getting lazy on me. You're still mine for a few more hours. I expect them to be productive ones."

He tapped his bender on the rail of the platform, then pushed a button and was gone through the opening in the ceiling.

"Finally, we can talk!" said Teagan. "It's like having a muzzle on in this place. Sometimes I think it's going to drive me crazy."

"Socket won't be long and he'll be looking for a reason to get mad," said Aggie. She was all business as she held her hand out. "Let's see it."

Edgar pulled the piece of paper out of his pocket, and like everyone else, seemed to forget that there was one member of the green team who had been left out of the loop. As the crumpled piece of paper passed from Edgar's hand to Aggie's, they glanced nervously at Vasher, who had already begun working.

"What's with you guys?" he said, both curious and irritated. He had thrown off the big boots the moment Red Eye was gone, and he walked in bare feet to a tamping station. "We've got four blocks to make, didn't you hear him? I've already been hit in the head with a pair of boots today. The last thing I need is a lashing."

He seemed particularly irritated by Edgar in his ridiculous boots.

"Take those off if they're going to slow you down," Vasher commanded. "Like Red Eye said, you need to keep working."

Vasher glared as Edgar untucked his soft sandals from the back of his shorts and wriggled out of his boots. In truth, Vasher wasn't angry at Edgar; he was terrified of being sent away. His frustration voiced itself as bitterness toward the only friends he had in the world.

Landon's quiet voice broke the silence. "We're not working today, Vash. We're going with Edgar."

"What do you mean, *going with Edgar*?"

Vash was so mad he wanted to punch Edgar as hard as he could. He pulled the tamper out of the chalk box and held it firmly in his fist.

"It's a lot to explain and we don't have time," said Aggie. "We planned this while you were sleeping last night. You should have come to the vine room like the rest of us."

"Nobody woke me!" insisted Vasher. He wanted to be included despite the fact that he had no intention of going anywhere with them, especially if Edgar was leading the way.

"We did try. You said you were too tired and didn't want to go," said Landon.

"This is crazy! You can't *go* anywhere around here. There's only one thing we need to do, and that's get the work done before Socket gets here."

Teagan drew in a big breath and exhaled. She didn't like confrontations and wanted it to be over.

235

"I'm going to say this as quickly and simply as I can," said Edgar, giving Vasher the benefit of the doubt and risking being caught before they'd even left. "I think I can get us out of here. I mean *really* out of here. But I can't do it from here."

Edgar pointed at Aggie, who held up the piece of paper with impatient exasperation.

"That paper shows me the way," he continued. "You don't have to go with me. None of you have to go, but you can if you want to."

Vasher glanced at each face in front of him and couldn't believe what he was hearing.

"So you're like Dr. Harding from the story, is that it? Came to rescue the world, did you?"

Edgar knew it sounded ridiculous. He shrugged and turned to Aggie. "We need to get going."

Vasher shook his head angrily. "Come on, Landon, we've got to get this done fast if they're going to stand around doing nothing."

But Landon didn't budge, and this hurt Vasher more than anything. He had felt less and less alive as day 4000 came and went, knowing he would soon be banished to the outside world on some duty he could only guess would take his life. He had shut down almost all the way, feeling nothing but cold and empty as he waited for the end.

But there had always been the one thing that had kept the dim light of emotion alive: Landon. He was like a little brother. If he let Landon go, the Dark Planet would win — Vasher would be dead inside just like Commander Judix or Red Eye or

Socket. Vasher simply couldn't imagine the loneliness of the Silo without Landon.

"You're not going out there without me," he said. "What if you get lost?"

Landon ran straight to Vasher and wrapped his arms around the older boy, sending a plume of white dust into the air around them.

"Trust me, okay?" said Landon, looking up into Vasher's eyes. "I know it sounds crazy, but I think this is for real."

Vasher hesitated, but only for a moment, then he nodded and dropped the tamper into the bin. With his arm around Landon, they walked back to the circle of friends and everyone huddled around the map as Aggie unfolded it.

"I've never been into Station Seven before, but one thing that's good is this," said Aggie, pointing to a group of words Edgar couldn't read. Aggie read them to everyone: "'Pipes and grates throughout. Use these to make your way.'"

"This will mean we can move through the station without having to walk on the floor where we'd be seen."

"We'll have to be really quiet," said Teagan.

"But we're all good climbers, right?" said Vasher, surprising everyone with his enthusiasm. He was secretly feeling more like leaving with every passing second. "I mean, if there's one thing we've learned how to do in the Silo, it's climb through ducts and over grates and swing from vines."

"It's like Dr. Harding knew the skills we'd need from the very start," said Landon.

"How do we get out of here?" asked Teagan.

"That will be the easiest part, I think," said Aggie. She walked to the door and found the dial that Red Eye had turned the day before. She read from the paper as she spun it back and forth.

"Twelve . . . nineteen . . . two . . ."

"Aggie?" said Vasher.

"I'm in the middle of this, can't you see?"

"The platform is moving."

Aggie stopped cold and looked over her shoulder.

"Socket's coming already!"

She went back to work — four numbers to go and her fingers wouldn't stop shaking.

"Forty-four . . . twenty-four . . . eight . . ."

"Hurry, Aggie! Hurry!"

They all stood close behind her, readying themselves to rush through to the other side.

"Thirty-one," said Aggie, and then there was a click and a *whoosh* as the metal door unlocked and opened. Everyone darted through behind Aggie. Edgar looked back as the door was closing and saw Socket's boots come into view. *Whoosh! Click!* The door was shut and locked behind them.

As the five children of the green team stood staring at one another in the faint light of the corridor, they felt certain that they would never return to the world of the Silo. There had only ever been one child who'd crossed over and went back again, and that was Dr. Maximus Harding himself. It seemed to them more than ever that Dr. Harding was guiding them to places they'd never been, cheering them on from the watery grave of the fallen House of Power.

If only they'd understood Dr. Harding's message a little better, they would have realized they'd left something terribly important behind.

●

"What's this nonsense?" said Socket as the platform reached the bottom and he found the drying room empty of children working. If they were hiding, they'd given him a perfect excuse to punish them. And yet if they were at some mischief elsewhere, his brother might slap him hard enough to dislodge his goggles.

"Where the devil are they?" he said aloud, holding his bender out as he inspected behind each of the large bins. He found Edgar's boots and then Vasher's and kicked both pairs across the room.

"Wait until I get my hands on them," he said, already imagining them hiding in the vines upstairs.

The communication box on the wall flashed and buzzed, startling Socket enough that he let go of his bender and it fell into one of the bins. He struggled momentarily with whether to retrieve his beloved weapon or go to the blinking red light and answer it.

"Socket! Where are you?"

It was his brother's voice screaming out of the device. Socket didn't want to answer it. He was sure that the green team had been found making trouble on one of the other levels, and he'd never hear the end of it.

"Socket! Pick up, you fool!"

Socket could tell this was no ordinary call. Red Eye's piercing voice was being broadcast throughout every level of the Silo.

"Yes, brother, what is it?" he answered.

"What took you so long?" Red Eye howled.

Socket was not a very fast thinker, and he could not come up with a very good lie on the spot.

"Just in the drying room checking on things."

"Pick up the receiver," said Red Eye. Socket wondered what his brother wanted to say that he didn't want the green team to hear. He picked up the receiver and placed it to his ear, lowering his voice clandestinely for effect even though he was alone in the room.

"What is it, Red Eye? What's going on?"

There was a sound of a pushed button and Socket knew from experience that this meant his brother had secured the line and it was only the two of them now.

"That idiot, Shelton, is going out in the transporter again. Commander Judix wants him to go beyond the wood, and the crew deserted. Word is Captain Grammel showed up early and they went to work for him. Commander Judix is furious."

"What's that got to do with us? We don't —"

"Stop your yakking and listen!" cried Red Eye. "Shelton's at the door and expects me to go out with him. I'm going to try Judix again — she won't answer me — but you might be running the Silo alone today."

Socket was overjoyed. He could already imagine it, taking

EQUIPMENT

- Silent
* MAXIMUM ENERGY EXPELLER

LEVELER
STANDARD MILITARY ISSUE
XO - FLEET BOOT

SMOG VISOR
V3-M100

GOGGLES -
STANDARD ISSUE

- light protection
- circuits
- scouting gear

COPPER SHIN GUARD

R.H.S. v.3
RUBBERIZED HEAD STRAP

TITANIUM SOLE
HEAT RESISTANT TO
2.500°

AIR SCRUBBERS

TRANSPORT

- TITANIUM ARMOR

all the credit for the food production, whipping the workers into shape the way he wanted to.

"That sounds dangerous," Socket commented with a false show of concern. "There's word of a war between the Spikers and the Cleaners. Not too much food left out there."

He bit his knuckle the moment he'd said the words, wondering if he'd scare his brother off his new duty.

"You think I don't know about the Spikers? I'm the one *told* you about the Spikers!"

Socket hated his brother. He was always right about everything.

"Give that new boy, Edgar, a swift kick for me," said Red Eye. "And keep them working down there. Judix is expecting a full pallet tonight with Grammel on the dock."

Socket looked about the room and saw how empty and void of activity it was. He seethed with anger as he thought of how far behind they were. *You'll be sorry when I find you,* he thought.

"I'll keep them working, brother," said Socket. "Don't you worry about a thing."

The line went dead and Socket hung up. He fished his powdery bender out of the bin, then began his search for children he would never find.

●

"What is it, Red Eye?" asked Commander Judix.

"Shelton is here at the door, ma'am, and he says you wa —"

"He needs a crew and you're all I've got. Socket can run the Silo for a while. I need you and Shelton to find more children."

Red Eye was speechless. His blood ran cold at the thought of being outside among the beasts in the forsaken wood.

"Is that all, Red Eye?"

Red Eye didn't answer, so Commander Judix continued.

"Have Socket bring a full pallet of blocks to Grammel's ship by end of day."

She only heard raspy breathing on the other end. Just to be sure he was paying attention she asked him a question.

"What's the new boy's name?"

Still nothing.

"RED EYE!" she screamed, and this produced a grunt on the other end. He was paying attention again.

"I asked you a question. What's the new boy's name?"

Commander Judix heard Shelton in the background goading Red Eye to get moving. And then, to her absolute amazement, Red Eye said the name. *That* name.

"The boy's name is Edgar."

He slammed the phone down and was out the very door through which Edgar had entered the Silo.

The communication box rang and rang until Hope walked past and answered it.

The voice on the other end of the line was frantic. "Did you say Edgar? Are you sure?"

Hope had never heard Commander Judix in such a state of panic.

"DID YOU SAY EDGAR?" she cried again. It was the secret of all secrets. Dr. Kincaid had told her and her alone of this abomination of Dr. Harding's. She had long assumed the boy was either dead or had never really existed at all.

"Commander, this is Hope. If you're looking for Red Eye, he's gone. Maybe you can reach him in the transport — I don't know. Are you okay?"

The line went dead and Hope was left to wonder about the name that had so upset Commander Judix. Things were beginning to feel out of control. Hope had known this feeling once before, decades ago when the Dark Planet had begun to fail. There were warning signs, some small and some not so small, but then there had come a point when everything unraveled at once. And something right now signaled to her that whatever had begun to change once more on the Dark Planet could not be stopped. . . . And that something was caused by what?

"Edgar," she whispered. "Who are you and where did you come from?"

She wanted to go and find him, but she couldn't leave the younger children alone for too long. She resolved to speak with him the moment his workday was over and get to the bottom of whatever bedevilment had entered the Silo.

Across the passageway of lies in Station Seven, Commander Judix was shaking uncontrollably in her chair. Edgar? *The* Edgar? The secret boy, hidden on Atherton by Dr. Kincaid. She'd never met Edgar, only been told of him after he was gone, but the connection was fraught with meaning. The little monster made by a mad scientist had been the beginning of the end. But he was here now, and that could only mean one thing.

"I must go to the laboratory first, and then I'll retrieve that horrible boy," she said.

When she turned to go, she was startled by a man standing in front of her, and she cried out. The man didn't wear metal-soled boots like everyone else, so she hadn't heard him sneak up on her.

"Boo!" he said, then his sandpapery, booming laugh echoed down the empty corridors.

Captain Grammel had arrived at Station Seven.

21

DR. HARDING'S LABORATORY

"Sorry to startle you, Commander," said Captain Grammel. "A long time at sea and all that — leaves me dying for some entertainment."

Commander Judix thought Captain Grammel was looking a little worse for the wear, and crazier than ever. As a sea captain one would expect him to have deeply tanned skin and wisps of windblown hair, but he had neither. In fact, he was completely bald save for a little white tuft on his chin that might be called a beard. It made his already thin face seem longer still. A small tube ran from his nose to a tank hitched to his back. And he wore the most outrageous goggles with enormous lenses, far too big for his face, for he was extremely poor of sight.

He made a sound that, once heard, could never be forgotten. It was a clearing of the throat that started down in his chest and repeated over and over, like something was caught and he couldn't quite get it out but refused to stop trying. It was a sharp, honking sound that echoed dreadfully down the halls and drove Shelton near mad when he had to hear it. Grammel was making the sound just then, the sharp *honk! honk! honk!* as Commander Judix tried to roll her chair past on her way to the laboratory. He stepped in front of her, let out two more awful honks, and wiped his nose with the back of his grimy hand.

"Sorry. Been holding that in a while," he said with one last *honk!* for good measure. "Where are you off to?" When he talked it was raspy and full of air, giving the impression that the tank on his back was probably forcing too much oxygen past his nose and down his throat.

"I have something to do that can't wait," said Commander Judix. "We'll have to conduct our business when I return."

"I'm on a tight schedule." He tapped his watch annoyingly. "Lots of demand out there on the shores, more than ever, and opportunity calls. Am I right?"

He leaned in close to the Commander's face. His eyes, huge and bleary behind thick lenses, seemed to wobble in his head as he let out yet another sharp series of honks.

"Get out of my way, you fool!" Commander Judix screamed in Grammel's face, and the man backed away, surprised. Usually it was he who held the upper hand in these meetings. He thought it might be a new strategy of hers to throw him off balance.

"I see how it is," he said, both hands on the arms of the chair and holding her back. "You want more fuel, do you? Well, you might not get *any* fuel if you don't start acting a little more hospitable. Where's the food and the drinks like I always get? What's happened to your manners?"

He paused a moment, let out a long and slithery *ahhhhhhhh* sound and wagged a dirty finger in her face. "You're angry because I've stolen your transport crew, is that it? Well, I'll tell you this — I didn't go looking. They begged me to take them in. You should be mad at yourself, not me. They can't stand you."

He flashed a row of surprisingly white teeth rimmed with gold and pushed up against the arms of the chair triumphantly.

"You will get out of my way," said Commander Judix. And now she spoke with the old Commander Judix majesty and cunning that had been such an important part in her rise to power. She could not be denied.

She had pushed a button on her chair and already Grammel could hear the sound of metal boots approaching from different directions. He stepped aside, astounded at the reception he'd been given, and two men arrived.

"Give him whatever he wants," said Commander Judix. "I'll only be a moment."

"That's more like it!" said Captain Grammel. He wouldn't be pushed around by anyone, especially not a desperate woman on a forgotten outpost in the middle of nowhere. There were plenty of 4000's along the shore, and he could — and did — throw them away when they became more trouble than they were worth.

He ordered the two men to bring him something strong to drink and whatever they had to eat that was fresh off the kill from the forsaken wood. It was the one thing he loved about this place that kept him coming back. It was the only place with fresh Cleaner, a delicacy hardly anyone in the world knew about, and he aimed to keep it his secret for as long as he could. All those bizarre creatures in the forsaken wood were dangerous, for sure, but my, they tasted so good!

As Commander Judix rolled toward the laboratory she began to feel a migraine rising up the back of her neck. It was a dangerous move, leaving Grammel to fume while she chased an unthinkable dream. Could Atherton be back within her grasp? Was that even possible? She turned down a side hall that would take her to a communication box. She would get Red Eye on the line again, just to be sure he'd gotten the name right.

●

"You're getting heavy!" said Vasher. Teagan was standing on his shoulders and Landon had climbed up the side of them both to the ceiling, as if they were a human ladder.

"Hold on! I almost have it," said Landon. He was so excited to be out of the Silo his hands wouldn't stop shaking.

"What's going on up there?" asked Edgar from the hall. He and Aggie stood by nervously, wondering if the door to the Silo was going to open. The hallway ran a good eighty feet long before there were any turns to speak of. If someone found them, there would no place to hide.

"Have you ever been in here before?" whispered Aggie. It had been years since she'd been out of the Silo at all, and she had never set foot in Station Seven.

"I've only been in the woods and the Silo. This place seems big."

"And empty. Like it's haunted or something."

They both looked down the long hall and wondered how far it went. At some point it became too dark to see where it ended.

"I got it!" said Landon. "Push me higher."

"Not so loud up there," said Edgar.

When Aggie and Edgar looked again they saw Vasher lifting Teagan up on his hands, which sent Landon right through the grate he'd opened in the ceiling.

"He's in," said Edgar, marveling at Vasher's strength. Years of working in the Silo had made him wiry and strong.

"You next," said Edgar, pulling Aggie gently toward Vasher.

Aggie began climbing up at the same moment Edgar heard a noise he didn't like the sound of.

"Hurry! I think someone's trying to open the door!"

Socket was on the other side, spinning the dial and trying to remember the code. Because the door was almost a foot thick, he couldn't hear the green team scrambling.

"Curse this thing!" howled Socket. "What are those numbers?"

He kept spinning and stopping until the door finally clicked and swung open.

The hallway was empty and still as he crept through.

"Anyone there?" he said softly. Socket hadn't had a lot of experience in Station Seven and it seemed deserted since the last time he'd been there. "Hello?"

Landon, Aggie, and Teagan had made it up into the space above the ceiling. They'd secured the grate in place just in the nick of time. Teagan looked at Aggie, both of them thinking the same thing. *Where are Edgar and Vasher?*

Socket kept walking nervously, becoming anxious from the loud sound of his own boots. He didn't want to meet anyone and have to explain himself.

Socket didn't really think they'd come this way — how could they have without the combination? — but he kept going just to be sure. He was approaching the place where the passageway split off into three directions. He paused, wiping the grime from his eyes. Here it was dark enough not to need his goggles, but his eyes were forever leaking watery goo that had to be wiped away. As he stood clearing his eyes he heard something, soft at first but growing louder.

Clang, clang, clang.

Boots, thought Socket. *Someone is coming!*

Socket backpedaled toward the door.

The green team's not in here. This was stupid! They're up to some mischief in the Silo, and time's wasting!

He dashed back through the passageway of lies and slammed the door shut behind him.

Vasher and Edgar breathed a sigh of relief where they stood hidden around the corner, barely out of view.

"What now?" said Vasher. Their little adventure was off to a frightening start and he was breathing at twice his normal speed.

"Up!" said Edgar, running back down the hall toward the door. They both heard the steps getting closer and closer.

"Hurry!" whispered Edgar. By the time they reached the door the grate was already out of the way again and Aggie held both arms down out of the ceiling.

"Come on!"

The footsteps were getting frightfully close. They were down to seconds or they'd be caught. Edgar and Vasher scrambled up the wall, and soon they were hidden in the ceiling like the rest.

A lone guard, brandishing a weapon in one hand, came into view down the hall. He slowed, seeing that the door to the Silo was shut. The guard crept toward the door and touched it as Aggie and Teagan slowly lowered the metal ceiling grate back into position.

The guard examined the unlock mechanism.

"What are those fools doing over there?" he said, and then for good measure he yelled uselessly at the door. "Stop banging the door!"

Everyone on the green team stayed perfectly still. It was harrowingly difficult, especially for Vasher. He wanted to move so badly that a nervous twitch began to form in his wrist. They listened for a long time until the sound of footsteps disappeared in the distance.

"That was double close," whispered Teagan. "It feels like everyone is looking for us. Maybe we should go back."

"No way!" said Landon. "Socket'll beat us senseless. We can do this. I know we can."

"No one's going to find us up here. Let's go as far as we can and see where it leads."

They all nodded, at once excited to be out of the Silo and scared speechless by two close calls in a row.

It was a maze of pipes and ducts hidden in the ceiling, and all the while they could see out of the tiny square holes in the grate. Once they stopped short, hearing someone moving, and watched as a black head of hair passed beneath them and moved on. But finally, with everyone's nerves frayed to the point of breaking, they arrived at a place where they were forced to stop.

"This looks right," said Edgar, seeing the concrete wall in front of them. It was an impasse but for a round hole above their heads.

"It's a retaining wall," said Aggie. Everyone looked at her inquisitively. "It holds the building up," she explained. She had never told anyone at the Silo, but her father had once been a craftsman. She knew a little bit about how things were constructed.

"Once we pass through the hole we need to drop back down," said Aggie, holding out her hand so that Edgar would give her the piece of paper. "That will put us on the other side of one door and leave us only one more to go through."

Edgar tingled at the idea of entering the room behind that door, because he knew what was there. The door was marked on the map with an MH for Maximus Harding.

"You first," said Edgar.

Aggie handed back the piece of paper and wriggled through the opening to the other side. She stood and looked back at everyone.

"Looks good over here," she said, but Vasher wasn't so sure. Every step away from the Silo had been a little bit more difficult for the oldest and most anxious of the bunch.

"Are we sure about this?" he asked. His twitching wrist betrayed how nervous he was.

Teagan touched Vasher's arm. "It's going to be okay, Vash. Just hang in there a little longer."

They were all afraid of being so far away from home. The Silo was all most of them could remember in any great detail, and even though it was a dreadful place to live, it had its comforts. They were fed, clothed, and given a bed. Life on the outside felt wide open and dangerous in a way none of them wanted to think about.

Vasher looked back toward the Silo, wiped his brow, and shook his hand as if it had fallen asleep.

"You ready, Landon?"

"You bet I'm ready!"

Landon passed through the hole feeling as free as a bird out of the Silo. He could imagine living among the hidden pipes and beams, sleeping up there and sneaking food. Teagan was next, then Vasher, and finally, Edgar.

"What's wrong?" asked Aggie, seeing that Edgar had a troubled look on his face.

"It feels like we're forgetting something. I keep thinking of that diagram with the exploding dots and those words — Hugin and Munin. What if it means something important?"

"We'll have to cross that bridge if we come to it," said Aggie. "But right now I think we're standing in front of your dad's laboratory. Don't you want to look inside?"

No one had ever said it quite that way before. *Your dad.* Edgar nodded almost imperceptibly. How had he ever managed to get here, standing in front of the dial that would open Dr. Harding's laboratory on the Dark Planet?

"Fourteen . . . twenty-seven . . . twenty-one . . ."

Edgar reeled off five more numbers and then the door clicked and popped open, much like the door to the passageway of lies. He pushed and the heavy door moved, silent and fluid, as if it sat on a layer of water.

"It looks deserted in there," said Aggie. Dr. Harding's laboratory hadn't been used for over a decade. It had barely even been entered. Murky shadows hung heavy over every part of the enormous room.

Everyone filed inside cautiously and the door was shut behind them with a soft click. The lab was lit from the outside by a giant windowpane that hung out over the water. The window was tinted in such a way that they could see out, but the light coming in was soft and dim.

"No need for goggles here," said Teagan, glad she didn't need to pull them down off her forehead.

The window rose high overhead in a wide half circle. Outside smog lay low on the waves of the ocean where Edgar spotted the long jetty of piled rocks and the shadow of Captain Grammel's ship.

The view of the outside world took everyone's breath away. No one besides Edgar had seen anything other than metal and machines and buzzing fluorescent light in a very long time. There were the vines in the vine room, but this was completely different. This was *outside*!

"I think that's where the passageway of lies leads to," said Vasher, mesmerized by the vision beyond the glass. "Socket told me once. *Down the path of rocks and into the ship. That's where you're going. And you're never coming back.* He laughed and laughed. I thought he was just being mean, but it looks like he was telling the truth."

Edgar was overwhelmed by the room. So much about it reminded him of home and of his father. Models of Atherton at different stages were everywhere. A glass-encased chamber was filled with dead fig trees like the ones in the grove back home. Baskets and pulleys and ropes hung from the towering ceiling. Though he'd never been here before, he knew this place better than anyone else on the green team.

"Your father was amazing," said Aggie, examining all the tables filled with scientific tools and gadgets, the rows and rows of books with sliding ladders rising to the high ceiling, the giant chalkboards covered in scribblings beyond anyone's comprehension.

Everyone else had scattered in different directions, picking up strange objects and peering around corners.

"Look at this!" said Landon from somewhere deeper in the laboratory. He'd found a wide table filled with skeletons and bones and drawings.

"You guys?" Vasher stammered nervously from deep inside the chamber. He was staring at something behind a soaring shelf of teetering books.

"What is it, Vash?" asked Landon. Everyone gathered around Vasher. Behind the giant shelf of books stood Gossamer, huge and menacing and all in black, staring down at them.

Teagan felt sure it would spring to life and shred them to pieces with its great black horn. She screamed and ran for the door.

22

HOPE

Teagan's voice bounced off the high walls, but Gossamer didn't move.

"It's not real," said Aggie. She inched up next to it and touched the leg. It *felt* real, but it didn't move. The model before them stood twenty feet high but Gossamer was much bigger than this — four or five times larger, in fact.

"It's from the story!" said Landon. After getting over his shock he was elated to find that this creature might really exist. Could it be possible?

"It's Gossamer!" he said. "He's on our side. He's here to help us. Wake up! Wake up!"

Landon waved his arms even though he knew it was only a model of something Dr. Harding might have made.

"Even if it's not real it means Dr. Harding *wanted* to make it," said Teagan. "This whole story is real, and everything Edgar is saying — it's all true. He really did make a place for us, after all."

"Where does the piece of paper say we should go now?" asked Vasher uneasily. To him, Dr. Harding's laboratory felt like a madhouse.

Edgar pulled out the map and they all gathered around Gossamer's feet. All but Aggie. Without anyone noticing she had drifted back behind a rising shelf of books. She had seen something there on a pedestal that had made her curious.

"Um, Edgar?" she said. "Remember when we were in the vine room and you told us your story? What did you call the thing you flew here inside of? The spiky black ball?"

Edgar crept over to Aggie and followed her gaze.

"The Raven."

"That's what I thought."

Suddenly, everyone was gathered around Aggie and they were all looking at the same thing. A model of two black ravens perched on a dead tree limb, their eyes locked on the green team.

"They're spooky-looking birds," said Landon, a shiver running down his back. "There were a lot of them on the beach where Captain Grammel picked me up. I hate the sound they make."

"Do you see what I see?" asked Aggie. Her voice was shaking, almost angry.

"Oh, no," said Vasher.

"What? What is it?" asked Edgar.

The base of the pedestal on which the sculpture of the ravens sat was carved with words Edgar could not read. Teagan read them aloud, growing more concerned with every word.

"'Hugin and Munin from the fallen age of Norse, who fly the world over and question the living and the dead.'"

Edgar scanned the piece of paper frantically until his eyes fell on the diagram.

"Hugin and Munin are ravens!" declared Landon. "But that means —"

"How could I be so stupid!" Edgar cried. "This diagram shows a block of something with the words 'Hugin' and 'Munin' in the middle. The block explodes into little particles. If Hugin and Munin are ravens, then the Raven I came in on needs whatever that block is."

"You need a powder block from the Silo," said Aggie, surer than she'd ever been about anything in her life.

"Dr. Harding, you're a genius!" said Landon, not fully understanding what a bad piece of news this was.

Teagan rolled her eyes.

"He might be a genius but he's not making this easy for us."

"Don't you see?" said Landon. "He had to keep it all separate so people wouldn't know what he was really working on. We've been making something super important all along, we just didn't know it until now."

"Well, now that we know, we're going to have to go back and get a powder block." Teagan sighed.

Edgar thought of how heavy and awkward the blocks were. Getting back into the Silo would be a trick of its own, but carrying a powder block all the way back to the lab? It wouldn't be easy. And that was only the half of it.

"The Raven is in the forsaken wood," said Edgar. "I thought I'd be able to go back there alone and meet you all somewhere or — I don't know. I hadn't thought that far ahead. But I don't think I can wander out there carrying a heavy block of powder with me. I barely made it into the Silo to begin with. And since we're on the subject of the Silo, can we really risk going back there?"

"Wait!" said Aggie. "Let me see that map."

Edgar handed it over and Aggie scanned it.

"There! Right there!" she said, trying to keep her voice down but having a hard time doing it. She read the words they'd all seen before and already forgotten, the tiny sentence under the box.

"'Hugin will come if you call him.' So we can call the Raven — we just have to figure out how."

"I think you're right!" said Teagan.

Aggie beamed. She loved how it felt to contribute something important.

"Now all we have to do is get a powder block all the way from the Silo to here so we can keep going," said Edgar, thinking it sounded like a near impossibility.

"What was that?" said Vasher. There was a slight sound from the door as it opened quietly, but there were no footsteps. Edgar put his finger to his lips. Everyone stayed perfectly still behind the wide, tall shelf of books. Commander Judix had entered the room, rolled smoothly across the metal floor, and sat before a black table in her chair.

Peering around the corner of the shelf, Edgar watched as Commander Judix, someone he'd never seen before, took something out of her vest pocket and placed it on the table. It was a black disk, like the one Edgar had in his own pocket, and he knew what the table would do.

The surface lit up, a blue glow reflecting on her face. She was so pale and cold looking, like she was more dead than alive, and the blue light only made her more frightening to look at. She hovered over the table, her hollow eyes watching as the fire-bugs moved, and then all the children heard an audible intake of breath.

"The way is open once more," she said, her voice full of wonder. If Edgar could have seen what she saw, he would've known there was a pulsing blue cluster where the Raven sat in the forsaken wood. She had found his way back to Atherton.

"The boy will have the key," said Commander Judix, her voice shaky with excitement. Her whole existence could change in a flash if only he didn't slip through her fingers. She turned in her chair, stopped short and went back for the black disk, grabbed it and was off. The table went dark again and Commander Judix rolled to the back wall by the door, touching buttons on a communication box. "Shelton? Shelton!" she cried, but there was no answer and she cursed the box.

Turning her chair around, she began rolling fast — straight toward Edgar and the others — and Edgar pushed everyone back. She parked before another communication box and reached as high as she could to touch the very top glowing button. This time there was a hissing as it came to life.

"Shelton! Answer me!" she frantically screamed into the speaker.

More static, and then his distant and crackling reply: "I'm here, Commander. What is it?"

"Go straight to the launch site! Go now! The Raven has returned."

A static-filled pause, then Shelton's bemused voice slowly resumed.

"That can't be. It's some kind of trick."

"It's not a trick! It's him!"

It struck her then that maybe Dr. Harding himself was back — could it be? It was impossible for her to imagine, but there it was. Maybe he had brought the boy back for some reason.

"Dr. Harding may be there, in the vessel. If he is, bring him to me straightaway. Now go! And be quick about it!"

"We're turning now," said Shelton, still sounding skeptical. "But it's a dangerous place. The instruments show it crawling with Cleaners. I'll have to take it slow."

"Go!" yelled Commander Judix. She was so agitated it made all of the green team back away in fear until they were as far away from Commander Judix as they could get. She pushed the second button down and screamed again.

"Socket! Answer me!"

Commander Judix had pushed the button that made her voice heard everywhere in the Silo, but Socket wasn't about to reply to the angry voice.

Commander Judix slammed the third button down, which rang the barracks where Hope spent all of her time.

"Hope! Pick up!"

A second later Commander Judix got the reply she was looking for.

"What seems to be the problem now?"

"Excellent! You're there. Now listen, Hope. I need you to hold the new boy until I get there. Do you understand? Don't let him out of your sight and just stay there. I'll be right over."

Hope had been right. The whole world was in chaos again. Things were spinning rapidly out of control.

"I'll try to find him. He's working with the green team, but Socket just came by here in a mad rage looking for them."

"What do you mean, looking for them? Where are they?" She was incredulous.

"I don't know, Commander," said Hope. "This is what you get when you put two fools in charge of your Silo. I'm sure they're somewhere."

"Find that boy!"

Commander Judix slammed her hand against the button and screamed in frustration. The green team watched as she wheeled her chair in a half circle and rolled away toward the door.

Edgar peered around the corner to be sure, and when he was positive Commander Judix had left the laboratory, he stepped out from behind the shelf.

"She's really horrible," said Landon. "Even worse than I imagined. No wonder this place is so terrible."

"And she knows who you are," said Teagan as she looked at Edgar. "She knows Dr. Harding made you, so she must also know there's a chance Atherton is really out there. She wants to go there, I'm sure of it. That's why she's so crazy.

She wants off the Dark Planet and she'll do anything to get her way."

Aggie agreed, but she had something else on her mind. She walked right up to the communication box and pushed the third button down.

"Hope? Are you there, Hope?"

Edgar almost tried to stop her, but then he realized the time had come to trust an adult. They were out of options. The search was on for Edgar in the Silo. Hope was probably their only chance.

"Aggie? Is that you?" came the reply. Hope sounded completely flabbergasted.

"It's me and the rest of the green team. We need your help."

"Child, you better get back here. You're in a world of trouble. I'm not sure I can cover for you this time."

"You won't need to, because we're never coming back to the Silo."

"Where are you?"

"We're in Dr. Harding's old laboratory. We need you to bring us a powder block. Can you do that?"

Hope couldn't believe her ears.

"What on earth do you want with a powder block? And how did you get all the way over there?"

"It's Edgar — the new boy — he needs it. Trust me, Hope. If you bring me a powder block it will help us get out of here. Everything about Dr. Harding is true. It's all happening right now."

Hope's throat went narrow and she began to feel like she was going to cry. The very last thing Dr. Harding had told

264

her before he'd left the Dark Planet rang in her ears. *You know how I can't trust any adult but you. I doubt that's ever going to change. So if I ever do figure this whole thing out, you can be sure I won't tell anyone old like me. Trust the children; they'll know the way.*

Hope's voice was like a whisper and she could hardly get the words out.

"Unlock the door," she said. "I'll be right there."

The line went dead and the green team stood in a circle smiling at one another.

"We're not done yet," said Vasher. "But at least we have a chance."

Edgar took the black disk out of his pocket and held it up so they could all see it.

"What is it?"

"It's the key to the Raven. The *only* key."

"We need to find the yards," said Vasher, who had been scanning the map. His head twitched with excitement. Everyone but Edgar could tell the stress had finally gotten to Vasher. He could control himself, but it was hard. As the day wore on what he really wanted to do was run around the room, yelling and knocking things over.

"The moment Hope gets here we need to go," said Aggie. "When Commander Judix finds Edgar gone she'll go crazy. She won't rest until she finds him."

They nodded and followed as Vasher led them along the glass wall of Dr. Harding's laboratory. Someone was outside.

"Who is that?" asked Aggie, looking out at the long rock jetty that ran from the beach. They could see a small figure in the distance with some kind of cylinder on his back, heading for the docked ship. It was Captain Grammel.

"I don't know who it is, and I don't care," said Vasher, who banged his hand against the glass nervously as he moved.

A little farther on he came to another metal door. This one didn't have a combination lock and was, in fact, rather ancient in its design. It had a regular knob along with a long row of bolt locks that could be turned. There was a gold plate on the door with black letters: THE YARDS.

"Now all we have to do is wait for Hope," said Edgar.

They all looked back at the open door to Dr. Harding's laboratory and Teagan said what they were all thinking.

"She'd better get here soon."

CHAPTER

23

ON GOSSAMER'S WINGS

"We'd better move to the side," said Samuel. "We don't want to get clobbered when Gossamer comes through."

But Isabel felt differently about how to respond as the dragon approached, and she started back in the direction from which they'd come.

"Isabel! Get back here!" Samuel called as she disappeared up the narrow way toward the sound of breaking rocks. "He'll smash you to bits if you're not careful."

Gossamer had already broken through the better part of the way to the ledge. Isabel was close enough that she was at risk of being hit by a flying boulder.

"Gossamer! Stop!" she shouted.

The pounding abated and rocks tumbled to the ground until all was still, like a storm coming quickly to its end. Gossamer's head and long neck emerged through the opening. On seeing

Isabel he bellowed warmly and Isabel felt his hot breath push her hair back.

"Isabel? Are you all right?" asked Samuel, who had come up close behind her. The light in the narrow way glowed orange from behind them, dancing on Gossamer's black horn and scales. He was the most powerful thing they'd ever seen. Was there anything that could stop him?

Gossamer shook his head and growled, pulling one front claw forward and ripping stones back. He was careful not to blast through and send a shower of boulders over Isabel or Samuel. Gossamer's other front claw came next, and soon he was back at it, pounding his huge claws into the rock walls and blowing them apart behind him.

"Take it easy," said Isabel, backing up toward the edge. Gossamer stopped once more and seemed to listen, tilting his head to the side and raising one pointed ear. "There's an edge here. You don't want to fall off."

Gossamer couldn't have understood them — or could he? His head went up and down and he breathed little bolts of fire from his nose.

"I love this creature," said Samuel, smiling at the thought of a beast this big he could call his friend.

Gossamer cut his way through what remained of the tunnel. When he emerged into the open and stood on the ledge with Isabel and Samuel, they were struck by how large he was. They now realized that he'd been crouching all the while, never really standing at full size. And he had been muted in shadows until they were able to see him in the full light.

"He's huge," said Isabel, her voice shaking as she took in the view of the magnificent and frightening creature standing at full height in front of her.

"Let's make sure to keep him on our side," said Samuel. "I don't want him turning on us."

"He would never do that," said Isabel. Something about the way his neck craned low and his face came near, sniffing and carefully nudging her with the side of his nose, told her that Gossamer would never stop trying to protect them.

"What do we do now?" asked Samuel, looking across the steaming river of fire.

"I wonder . . ." said Isabel. She held out a shiny black fig and Gossamer took an immediate interest in it. He sniffed it, almost sucking the dried fig right into his nose, then tentatively put his tongue out and touched it. It was a tiny treat, but a treat nonetheless, and he rolled it around on his tongue as if it were a candy. The hard, dry fig dissolved as if burned by acid until it was gone.

Gossamer raised his head and turned away. It was a good thing he did, because the next moment he sneezed. It was a fire-filled roar of air that shot down through the open space. He coughed briefly, wisps of black smoke exiting his nose.

"I think he liked that," said Samuel, for Gossamer appeared to be smiling as he turned to Isabel and sniffed for more.

Isabel took out her sling and loaded a second dried fig from her pouch.

"Back up a little," said Isabel, and Gossamer obeyed.

Isabel put the dried fig into her sling and began twirling it over her head. Gossamer's black eyes watched carefully as the fig went round and round.

"You're not going to do what I think you are?" asked Samuel. He'd sat on the wings and knew they were small and frail. He knew Dr. Harding hated flying things. Samuel had assumed . . . "I don't think he can fly," said Samuel. "What if he jumps out over the ledge and we lose him?"

"He can fly," said Isabel, swinging the fig faster and faster.

"But how do you know? Dr. Harding hated flying things. What if he made Gossamer so he couldn't fly?"

"He made the Nubian. They can fly."

Samuel had to admit this was true, but he was afraid for Gossamer. He could imagine the black dragon jumping for the fig and falling, clawing his way along the rocks as he fell to his death.

"I don't think you should do it, Isabel," said Samuel. "I have a bad feeling about it."

But Isabel was completely convinced. She imagined Dr. Harding making this glorious creature and how he would have *wanted* to make it flightless. But he would see how it was made to fly and wouldn't be able to stop himself. The temptation of seeing it floating on air would have been too much.

"He can fly," said Isabel, and she let the fig go.

SNAP! FOOSH!

The fig sailed through the open air. Gossamer leaped after it, but no wings emerged from his sides. The wings Isabel and Samuel had ridden on didn't appear at all. Instead, the great black beast dropped like a rock, pointing its horned head down into the wide river of fire.

"You've killed him!" he cried. "I told you not to do it, but you wouldn't listen!"

Isabel and Samuel dashed to the edge. The fig sailed fast and true toward the other side where the raised stone platform sat waiting. They both watched Gossamer. He kept falling, and Isabel began to doubt. Could she have been wrong? A panic rose in her throat as she thought of what she'd done. She would never forgive herself.

But then, the wings unfurled like a fan and the children saw that there was more to these wings than they'd originally thought. They had only seen one of the many folds in Gossamer's hidden wings back in the yards. Now they snapped all the way open.

"He's beautiful," said Isabel, so pleased that she had been right.

Gossamer sailed through a foggy layer of firebugs — which didn't affect him in the least — and then gracefully turned and started back up the ravine. He rose even faster than he'd fallen, flapping his long wings and crying into the open air.

"I can't see the fig, can you?" said Samuel, searching for any sign of movement.

"That's because he just ate it," said Isabel. Gossamer had turned and was now coming toward them. Samuel couldn't help backing up toward the tunnel.

"Come on, Isabel. Let him land without having to worry about knocking us down."

Isabel agreed this was probably a good idea. The wind alone might sweep her off her feet. She darted back into the tunnel as Gossamer landed. He appeared to be very pleased with himself as he spread his black lips. The fig rolled on his tongue, where it sizzled and steamed.

"Well done!" said Isabel. Gossamer responded by rocking his head up and down happily, bumping it on the ceiling of the tunnel without seeming to notice.

"Better wait here while he sneezes," said Samuel. And sure enough, a moment later, Gossamer leaned out over the edge and sneezed even more powerfully than the previous time.

"How many more of those do you have?" asked Samuel. "He really likes them."

Isabel fished around in her pouch and pulled out a dried fig. "This is the last one."

Gossamer was back, sniffing at Isabel's hand as she looked at Samuel.

"Do you want to finish what we started?" asked Isabel.

"Are you asking me to ride a black dragon across a river of fire?"

Isabel nodded and smiled. It sounded ridiculous when he said it that way, but it was precisely what she was thinking. Samuel didn't answer so much as give her a look that said, *If you're crazy enough to do it, so am I.* He half expected her to lose her nerve, but if she didn't, how could he give up the chance to finish such a marvelous adventure?

"I need you to wait this time," Isabel said as she brushed past Gossamer's head on her way back to the ledge. "Can you do that for me?" She hoped he would let the fig sail all the way across this time before trying to retrieve it. "And there's something else," she continued, pulling the sling from her belt and placing the fig inside. "Can you take us with you?"

Gossamer turned his head as if he was trying to understand.

Samuel stepped closer and pointed to Gossamer's folded wing, then to himself and Isabel.

"Can we ride across with you?" he asked.

Gossamer seemed to weigh what had been asked of him. He looked out over the flaming river and the distance across, sniffing instinctively. As he did this Isabel started swinging the sling until it was humming in a fast, wide circle. She watched the stone platform on the other side with great intensity as Samuel motioned Gossamer to wait.

"Stay, Gossamer. Don't go anywhere yet."

SNAP! FOOSH!

The fig was gone and Gossamer almost couldn't stop himself. If not for Isabel's cry of "Wait!" the black dragon might have gone without them, but as it was he watched intently until the fig reached its target, bounced along the surface of the pillar of stone, and disappeared on the other side.

"You really are an amazing shot with that thing," said Samuel.

"Thank you," said Isabel. She liked the way it felt to impress him as she stood in front of Gossamer's shaking legs. He was so eager to go it was all he could do to stay put. Gossamer took one last look back into the tunnel and down at Isabel.

"I don't want to go that way," she said. Then she pointed toward the pillar on the other side. "I want to go over there."

Gossamer crouched on the ledge and laid out the first fold of his wings as he'd done for them before. Samuel climbed on one side and Isabel on the other, each lying on the soft, leathery fold of a wing.

"What do we hold on to?" asked Samuel, groping for a hold.

Isabel called back: "The top edge doesn't have any thorns. Can you shimmy up and grab hold?"

Samuel got up on his knees and crawled forward until he reached the top edge of the wing. He found it was sticky and sandpapery, thick like the growing limb of a tree.

"I've got it!" he said, lying flat and feeling more secure.

Gossamer glanced over each shoulder to be sure they were holding on tight. If he was going to have riders, they would need to be on tight or risk being thrown off as he flapped and flew. Looking out over the deep chasm, Gossamer roared and blew a stream of red fire and black smoke.

"Here we go!" said Isabel.

Gossamer jumped, but this time he didn't wait to unfold the rest of his wings. The moment he was away from the ledge the full length of his wings were out and they glided smoothly through the air.

"Woooooohooooooo!" yelled Samuel as he heard Isabel's uncontained laughter.

They sailed through warm air and, halfway there, Gossamer turned down enough for both of them to see the mist of blue firebugs and the raging red river below. As they gained speed Samuel began to wonder if he could hold on, but then Gossamer leveled off and turned to the right. Samuel and Isabel slid along the wings until they leveled off once more.

Riding on Gossamer's wings was the most exhilarating thing either of them had ever done and they wished it would never end. But when the wings tipped back they both realized at once that they would soon be landing. This would be the most dangerous part, because Gossamer couldn't avoid a certain amount of flapping as he tried to slow down. The wings tipped even more and the quick flapping began. One of Isabel's hands lost its grip and she let go, spinning wildly on Gossamer's wing as he touched down and came to an abrupt stop.

"You did it, Gossamer! You did it!" said Samuel. He couldn't bring himself to climb out of the cozy space. Neither could Isabel. The memory of flying was so near it made them both want to hold on to the moment forever.

Seeing they were in good shape, Gossamer started to fold his long wings and gazed into the opening at the end of the platform.

"I think he wants his treat," said Isabel. "We'd better get off."

And so they did, but not before closing their eyes, smiling broadly, and remembering what it was like to ride on Gossamer's wings.

"Go on," said Isabel. "Go get the fig."

Gossamer bent low and passed through the opening, which seemed oddly just the right size for him to fit through.

"At least he didn't have to make the opening any bigger," said Samuel. "I imagine that's a lot of work."

The two followed Gossamer until they reached the opening and realized this was the end of their journey. Where there had been orange and red light before, there was a new, more brilliant white creeping out from behind many of the rocks.

"What do you think we'll find?" asked Samuel.

Isabel shrugged. "Whatever it is has captured Gossamer's attention. He should be back by now."

Samuel and Isabel walked through the opening, where they

found the dried fig sitting on the ground. Samuel bent down and picked it up, handing it to Isabel.

"That's odd," he said as he watched her examine it and put it back in her pouch. "He didn't seem to have any trouble finding the last one."

"Let's keep going," she said. "He's fast, but he can't be that much farther ahead of us."

As they curved downward their way drifted from side to side in a long zigzag. It brightened as they went, and all of the new, whiter light came from the ceiling, which had taken on a sharp, glassy appearance far above. When they finally came to the end of the passageway they found Gossamer standing at the opening, looking out.

Samuel and Isabel walked up next to Gossamer, who also seemed to be mesmerized by the unexpected view. They now realized that they must have reached the bottom of Atherton. A gaping hole opened to reveal the Dark Planet way off in the distance.

"Do you think Edgar is still there?" asked Samuel.

"I do," said Isabel, feeling something inside that told her he wasn't home yet.

"Gossamer seems . . . I don't know, different," said Samuel. The dragon regarded this new surrounding with a sense of understanding, as if a distant memory had filled his mind.

"Maybe he knows something," said Isabel.

"What's this?" asked Samuel. He was the first to see a massive wall rising to their right. There were thousands of moving shadows shining through it, like large fish dancing in an underground sea.

"Those look like . . ." started Samuel, and Isabel finished his sentence: "Cleaners."

"I think that's the bottom of the lake in the middle of Atherton," said Samuel. "Or some hidden chamber of water we can't see from up top. There are thousands of Cleaners behind there."

The shadows moved fluidly and seemed to touch the translucent wall and move away again, over and over, as the Cleaners danced and swayed.

The wall was covered with thousands upon thousands of gigantic egg-shaped impressions. Within each wide impression were millions of sharp spears of light.

"They're filled with crystals," said Samuel. "I've read about them before. It's like glass, only it isn't. It grows."

They moved closer still and both seemed to realize at once that this wall was more dangerous than it had appeared at first. At closer look, the crystals were like spikes, hard and deadly and filling the wall.

Isabel's eyes followed the wall up and over her head. The ceiling was covered with white spikes, too. If she hadn't known what she was looking for she might have mistaken it for a ceiling that was merely glistening. But seeing the wall up close, she knew better.

"I'm not sure we should stay here," she said. It would only take one to fall from the ceiling to pierce her right through.

"I think you're right," said Samuel, looking back and wondering how quickly they could escape.

"Gossamer," said Isabel, looking back and seeing he was

still gazing out at the Dark Planet. He turned to her and looked sad. "Something's wrong with him."

"You're right, he does look different," Samuel agreed. "Let's get him out of here. That might improve his mood."

"Come on, Gossamer. Time to go," Isabel coaxed.

He followed at first, though it was with some reluctance — but when they came to the way out, he made a strange noise.

"What is it?" said Isabel.

Gossamer edged forward and brushed her aside.

"He wants to go first," said Samuel. "Better let him."

As Isabel stepped aside she noticed a kind of sadness in Gossamer's expression, but also anticipation for something the children could not understand. "What is it, Gossamer? What's wrong?"

But he didn't answer. Instead, he drew in a breath and blew fire all along the ceiling. Then he lay down before the opening as if guarding it from their entry.

A few seconds later the ceiling began to rain down all through the passageway in pure white shards that shattered like glass when they hit the ground. The fragments were about a foot long, four or five inches across at the base, and sharp as needles at the tips.

"He's trapped us," said Samuel in disbelief.

Isabel couldn't believe Gossamer had betrayed them. She wouldn't believe it.

"Let us through, Gossamer," she said, sure the beast would stand, unfurl its wings, and cover them as they went. But Gossamer only drew a breath and set his enormous head on the ground to rest.

"Maybe we misjudged him," said Samuel. "Who knows what he's really thinking?"

But Isabel was unmoved.

"He blocked the way for a reason. He's waiting for something to happen."

Gossamer lifted his head, craned his neck away from them, and blew fire on the ceiling of the passageway again. The shower of white needles looked as if it might go on forever.

"So what do we do?" asked Samuel.

"We do the only thing we can do." Isabel went to Gossamer as he laid his head back down. She touched his nose gently and wondered what he was thinking behind those dark eyes, so much like her own.

"We wait with him."

CHAPTER

24

THE YARDS

No one on the green team could be a hundred percent certain who would come into Dr. Harding's unlocked laboratory next. Maybe Commander Judix had sent Red Eye or Socket to search the station and it would be one of them who stumbled in. The green team was hiding by the door to the yards when the door to the lab slipped quietly open.

Everyone waited, barely breathing.

"Anybody home?" said a soft voice they all knew.

"Hope!"

Everyone said her name at once and ran through the laboratory as Hope entered and pushed the door gently shut with her shoulder.

"You came!" said Aggie. "I knew you'd help us!"

Teagan, Landon, Aggie, Vasher, and Edgar all gathered around the tall slender caretaker of the Silo and beamed. She wanted to hold each one of them, but her hands were already occupied with the item they'd asked for.

"This thing is really heavy," said Hope. "I hope you're not going far."

"We're not sure how far we're going," said Vasher.

"But we think we're getting close," said Aggie. She didn't want Hope to try and stop them or worry too much.

Hope set the powder block down with a thud on one of the many tables strewn with junk. If a person hadn't known it was from the Silo they'd probably think it belonged here. It fit right in with all the other puzzling objects.

"I can't stay here for long. Commander Judix will be looking for me. It's going to look awfully suspicious if I'm not there."

"You don't have to go back to the Silo, you can come with us," said Landon, expectation rising in his voice. He liked the idea of having Hope along to keep him safe. "We're going to find Gossamer."

"I can't go with you, Landon."

"Why, sure you can!"

Hope turned her gaze on Edgar and spoke volumes without saying a single word.

Who are you? Please tell me you're not deceiving these kids.

Edgar was blunt, not because he wanted to be, but because he had to be. Time was running out.

"Dr. Harding created me a long time ago. Probably right here in this laboratory where no one could see. I was his biggest secret. He's gone, Hope — I mean he's *dead*. But he sent me back here, I think to finish what he started."

The words stunned Hope, but looking at the boy, it all added up. It was why he was so different, and it was just the sort of thing Dr. Harding would do.

"He never said anything about you. He must not have trusted me as much as I thought."

"Actually, that's not true," said Edgar. He held out the piece of paper they'd been using all along and pointed to a set of words. The old woman whispered them aloud.

"'Hope you can trust.'"

Her eyes filled with tears and she began to wonder about something Edgar had said. Could it *really* be true?

"You said Dr. Harding sent you back. Back from where?"

"From Atherton, of course!" said Landon. "He came in this thing called the Raven. The Raven needs a powder block for some reason, at least that's what we think —"

"Landon, please," said Vasher. Sometimes the rapid-fire sound of Landon's voice made Vasher tremble.

"We really need to go," he said. "Every second we stay here makes it more likely we'll get caught."

Hope knelt down and put one hand on Aggie's shoulder and another on Landon's. All of the green team was pulled in close.

"I've been asked to leave the Silo before. I couldn't go then for the same reason I can't go now."

"All those kids," said Landon, suddenly realizing why Hope had to stay. "You can't leave them alone with Red Eye and Socket. You're all they've got."

Hope smiled at the youngest boy and worried for his safety. But she knew the truth of the matter. The Silo wasn't safe, and eventually Captain Grammel's ship wouldn't be safe, either. In fact, nothing about the Dark Planet was safe. She was only a stopgap for these kids on the way to something far worse. Wasn't it worth it to let them at least try?

"You seem to have a plan," she said, trying to put on a good face and encourage them. "If you get sent back to the Silo I'll be there to make certain they don't punish you too badly. But if by some miracle you get off the Dark Planet, don't come back here unless you're sure it's safe."

"We really have to go," said Edgar. The whole group was feeling a huge weight of anxiety as the minutes slipped passed.

Hope looked at each member of the green team as she went for the door.

"I'll be waiting at the Silo if you get in trouble."

When the door shut behind her there was a frenzy of activity. Edgar grabbed the powder block and cradled it in both hands. Aggie and Teagan had the map out again, scanning it to be sure where they were going. Vasher and Landon were already racing across the lab, past the statue of the ravens and the model of Gossamer until they arrived at the door to the yards.

Vasher turned all seven of the locks on the old door. Each snap calmed him, as if he'd been overfilled with energy and the twisting motion had let out a bit of steam.

The door was thick and wooden, but it was tightly sealed on every side. When it opened they were all immediately aware that they were now exposed to something from the outside. It smelled of smog and filth that stung their nostrils. Beyond the door lay a staircase that went down a few steps and turned hard under the laboratory to places they could not see. A row of ten or twelve masks and goggles hung along the inside wall.

"Should we put these on?" asked Edgar. The air outside seemed thicker and more poisonous here at the water than it had in the forsaken wood.

"I think that would be a really good idea," said Aggie, pulling on a filter mask and goggles and helping Edgar with his. Edgar let everyone go down the stairs before him and was just about to close the door behind them when he pulled his goggles up on his forehead and took one last look out the window.

Captain Grammel had made it down the jetty and fired the great boilers on his ship. Clouds of black smoke billowed from wide pipes as the boat moved off without leaving a load of fuel for Station Seven.

"Stay low along the rail," said Vasher. His voice sounded muffled from inside the mask.

Edgar's lungs still burned even with the mask on, and the haze seemed to envelop them in a deadly fog.

The map led them outside into the smog, along the wall where there was a hard right turn. The line of companions sped up, but as they neared the turn they piled up in a jumble and froze in their footsteps. A noise, big and monstrous, erupted from somewhere they couldn't see. The haze grew thinner as it rose, but down where they were standing they could only guess at what the sound was.

"That's really close," said Teagan, her voice shaking behind the mask. They all knew about Cleaners and Spikers, the most terrifying things on the Dark Planet — they'd heard them at night through the walls of the Silo. "They must have moved right up to the edge of the forsaken wood."

Edgar could tell there was a fight on and he remembered the screaming monsters he'd seen not so long before.

"Cleaners," he whispered, barely audible outside his mask. The powder block was getting really heavy and he was afraid he might drop it. He wished they could just keep moving.

"And Spikers, too," said Landon. "They're fighting close to Station Seven."

"Do you know what that means?" asked Vasher, glancing around nervously in his goggles. "It means we're losing power. I heard Red Eye and Socket talking when we were low on fuel once before. There are two lines of electrical defense, like lines they can't cross over. Back then — this was five or six hundred days ago — the outer line went down for a few hours."

"Because Grammel was late with the fuel," said Aggie, stunned at the idea of monsters so close. "I remember that."

"I saw the ship leave, right before we came outside," said Edgar, wondering if it had been the man they spoke of.

This seemed to calm everyone a little, and Vasher said: "Then they've got the fuel and they're just setting up is all."

The air around them filled with a crackling and snapping sound mixed with the cries of creatures at war with one another.

"One's hit the inner line!" said Vasher, wishing for all the world to be inside where it was safer.

"Let's keep going," said Aggie breathlessly. "We can't do anything about the lines, and these masks aren't filtering out everything." Her arm itched as if the smog was eating through her skin, then she took the lead and went around the corner.

They walked a few more steps and bumped into a gate, which squeaked open. They'd arrived at the entrance to the yards.

It was smaller than they'd thought it would be, surrounded by ten-foot walls of concrete block on all sides. No one spoke, but they all would have agreed the yards was a sad and haunted little place. There were broken benches and boxes of dirt, a chipped stone pathway and blocks that had fallen from the walls scattered about. A low fog of filthy air hung over a slide that had been tipped on its side and lay next to a rusted merry-go-round.

Landon edged over to the merry-go-round and pushed on one of the metal bars made for children to hold on to. It turned, squeaking as it went, and stopped the moment he let go.

"This is the place where he played," said Landon, his voice soft and full of awe. "When he was just a boy, like me. This is where he had all his best ideas, don't you think?"

He looked back at the others hopefully but no one answered him. All they heard was the sound of beasts getting closer as they frantically searched the map for what to do next.

"I can't carry this thing much longer," said Edgar, struggling to hold the powder block. Vasher held out his shaking hands.

"Don't drop it. I think it needs to stay in one piece."

Edgar placed the heavy powder block into Vasher's trembling hands.

"There should be a statue in here somewhere," said Edgar, shaking out his tired arms. "It might be newer than some of this old stuff, because he would have put it here himself long after the yards had stopped being used. He must have come back here. I've seen this trick of his before."

Aggie looked at him, but Edgar wouldn't go into any detail. He was thinking of Mead's Head in the Highlands and how it was used to unlock the way into Mead's Hollow.

"I found it!" said Teagan. She had moved off to one of the corners where the haze was thickest. Everyone gathered around, and Landon was the first to guess what it was.

"It's him, isn't it?"

In front of him stood a sculpture of a boy sitting on the stump of a tree. The face seemed to be pondering some great invention. And to everyone's surprise, the face was the same as the one they'd all seen on the piece of paper.

"Yes," said Aggie, holding out the paper so everyone could see. "It looks just the same!"

"You see! I told you!" said Landon. "He loved being a kid the most. He wanted to stay that way."

"I think maybe you're right," said Edgar.

The sound of pounding and screeching was closer than ever and it made everyone jumpy. Cleaners and Spikers had figured out they could get nearer to Station Seven. They were wasting no time trying to lay claim to newly found territory.

"They'll keep coming until the line goes back up," said Aggie. "It's all-out war."

Edgar knelt down at the statue and felt around the base until he came up with a way in which to hug the sculpture and try to turn it. It didn't move at all no matter how hard Edgar tried.

"It says to turn it to the left," said Edgar, pulling the paper out and handing it to Aggie. "That's correct, isn't it?"

Edgar thought maybe he'd misread, but Aggie nodded that he'd been right.

"You try it, Vash — you're stronger than I am."

Edgar took the powder block again and Vasher was down on his knees in a flash, trying to turn the sculpture with all his might.

"You've got it, Vash! You've got it!" cried Landon as he heard a clicking sound. Vasher regained his balance and cleared his head.

"All we have to do now is tip it over," said Aggie. Vasher grabbed it by the head and pulled away from the corner of the yards. Young Dr. Harding tipped over, revealing a dark hole with a narrow set of stairs leading down. Somehow it was troubling to see Dr. Harding's statue toppled in such a pitiful way, his face in the dirt.

"He's got a twisted sense of humor," said Aggie, shaking her head.

"You have no idea," added Edgar, thinking of all the strange and wonderful things his father had done on Atherton.

The sound of warring Cleaners and Spikers was growing steadily louder, and another monster was hurled into the line of electricity amid shrieks and cries.

"Why don't they turn it back on?" said Vasher. "It doesn't make any sense!"

They quickly started the descent into a secret place they knew nothing about, fearing an attack from any side at any moment.

No one spoke until they reached the bottom, a long way down, where the air felt cold.

"I think we can take off our goggles and masks," said Edgar. He set the powder block carefully on the hard floor and removed both pieces of protective gear, breathing a sigh of relief as he blinked and rubbed his sore eyes. He found himself standing in a room bathed in faint light, full of wonderments he hadn't expected.

●

"Don't you dare come back here!" yelled Commander Judix.

"But we have to come back!" cried Shelton. He and Red Eye had been guarding the Raven in the forsaken wood, but so many creatures were on the move the two men were growing more nervous by the second. "We can't keep these monsters off the transport forever. What's happening over there?"

"Is the door to the vessel open or closed?" asked Commander Judix, ignoring Shelton's request for information.

Shelton couldn't believe her question. What was wrong with her?

"It's open," he said, exasperated as he rolled his eyes in Red Eye's direction. "What does it matter?"

"Then you can't leave! The boy must have the key. Without it the vessel's not going anywhere."

"You don't actually think this thing has someplace to go?" said Shelton, bewildered that his commander thought the arrival of an old relic could mean anything more than some malfunction of a long abandoned system.

"Commander," he tried again, "you don't believe someone on Atherton *sent* this thing?"

"Of course they did!" cried Commander Judix. "I'm going for the boy. Don't move! And don't let any of those filthy creatures near my ship!"

The line went dead and Shelton glanced at Red Eye.

"She's finally gone crazy. I mean *really* crazy."

There had long been two kinds of people at Station Seven: those who had never really believed in Atherton's viability to begin with and those who still believed Atherton was a thriving world just barely out of their reach. Shelton was the first kind, Red Eye the second. Red Eye had long lain awake at night wishing he could get to Atherton — all that clean air and water, no more children to take care of, no more Commander Judix or monsters to deal with. He could walk outside if he wanted. Maybe he could take off his goggles in the light of day!

"She's crazy, just as you say," agreed Red Eye. "And it appears she's let the fuel go almost dry. Maybe you're right. Maybe we should go back before things get out of hand. She might lose the entire station."

The sound of monsters moving all around them outside continued, but they seemed uninterested in attacking the tank-like transport. The fight was on, and each side was racing for the new ground that had opened up in front of Station Seven. A giant Cleaner grazed at the side of the transport, and it tossed Red Eye and Shelton to and fro inside.

"You're right," Shelton declared as he gathered himself. "We're getting out of here."

But Red Eye had used the moment to put his hand over his shoulder and retrieve his bender. He held it out toward Shelton and smiled menacingly.

"I never liked you much," said Red Eye.

"You're as mad as she is!" said Shelton. It was no real weapon, not like the military issue Leveler at Shelton's side, which he reached for just then. But he had underestimated both the power of the bender and Red Eye's skill at using it. In a flash, Red Eye whipped it down hard on Shelton's hand, cutting it open across the back. The Leveler dropped to the metal floor with a clang and Shelton shrieked.

"Oh, you've no idea what I can do with this superb weapon," Red Eye said, kicking the gun out of Shelton's reach as he stepped closer to the injured man in front of him. "Have to be careful with the kids. It's a welt you want with them. But I do so like the chance to really let it loose once in a great while."

Snap! Red Eye swung the bender again, this time across Shelton's legs, just above the knees. He howled in pain as the ripped fabric began to stain red.

"They do like the smell of blood. It's sure to slow at least one of them down, don't you think?"

Red Eye pushed the button that opened the transport door and it swished to life. In the misty fog of the forsaken wood he watched the long legs of a passing Spiker stop and bend down, sniffing the rancid air.

"Time for you to go," said Red Eye.

"No! You can't!" yelled Shelton. The Spiker heard the cries and leaned down closer still, where its lolling head could be seen outside the door. Red Eye mercilessly whipped at Shelton's feet until the man had no choice but to tumble out of the transport and run for his life. As the door closed the Spiker chased after Shelton, but Red Eye never saw the end result. He was too busy looking into the monitor at the open door of the vessel that would take him to the place of his dreams.

●

"Where is he?" demanded Commander Judix, and then again, much louder before Socket could answer. "WHERE IS HE?"

She had rolled frantically down the passageway of lies, collecting two of her remaining guards along the way to escort her. She'd unlocked the door to the Silo and passed into a world that she had tried desperately to avoid at all cost. Commander Judix rolled right onto the platform and was lifted up to the barracks level in search of Edgar. A moment later, Hope had secretly left the Silo without Commander Judix suspecting a thing.

"I asked you a question," said Commander Judix, her face contorted with rage. She had found Socket in the kitchen, foraging for food. "What have you done with him?"

"He's working in the vine room, ma'am," Socket lied, wiping the chalky remains of a hastily consumed cup of powdery water. "But they're very busy today. Trying to stay on schedule for Grammel."

"Grammel's *gone,* you worthless —" In her rage she'd said more than she intended, but what did it really matter? "Just lead me to the boy!"

"I tell you he's working," said Socket. "In the vine room, with the others. If you stay here I'll fetch him for you."

Commander Judix breathed a grave sigh of exasperation as

Socket stood blinking furiously behind his goggles. "Get on with it!"

Socket bolted from the room and in a flash was quickly riding down the platform in the middle of the Silo. He didn't stop until he reached the drying room at the very bottom. Picking up the receiver on the communication box, Socket pressed the code for the transport vehicle.

"Red Eye? Are you there? I need help!"

There was no answer on the other end, only the fizzing and popping of dead air.

"Red Eye!" Socket yelled again. "Where are you?"

Still no answer.

Socket didn't know what to do. The entire green team was missing. How could he have lost an entire team? It was outrageous! His brother would be furious, not to mention Commander Judix. What might she do if he didn't return with this new recruit in hand?

"What is it? What do you want now?"

"Red Eye!" Socket began. "I've made a terrible mistake. You have to help me! I can't find the green team. They're hiding from me! I hate them, hate them, hate them! But they won't come out. The Commander is here and she wants the new one. I don't know what to do!"

A long pause of crackling static ensued. Socket knew better than to rush his brother. It only made him impatient when he was already worked up. But as the seconds ticked away, Socket couldn't stand it any longer.

"Brother? Are you there? Help me!"

There was a shred of compassion left in Red Eye and he knew his brother wouldn't survive two days without him. He'd left him for a few hours and look what had happened! He'd lost an entire team.

"Better get him," mumbled Red Eye. "He'll never make it here without me."

"Get outside by the lower door," said Red Eye, his voice was tinny and distant. "Use the drying room door — the one that we never open. Hang on."

The line went silent again and Socket glanced at a small door in the far wall that led to the outside. The combination for its lock was known only by a few, and Socket was not among them.

"Twenty-one, Two, Seven, Nine," said Red Eye. "Give me twenty minutes to race across and I'll get you."

"Can you come any faster?" said Socket.

And so Red Eye raced across the forsaken wood, watching the monitors carefully in order to avoid the red dots that indicated moving Cleaners and Spikers. There were surprisingly few of them about, but there was a huge cluster of red dots moving along the lines of defense near Station Seven.

"I have a bad feeling about this," he said, pressing his big metal boot heavier on the accelerator.

Socket was already at the door, trying the combination. He had the numbers mixed up in his head and couldn't get them straight. Fumbling at the dial and pulling on the handle for the third time, he heard the sound of the platform rising on its hydraulic metal pole.

"Oh, no," he whispered. "She's coming for me!"

Socket turned back to the dials and tried again and again. He had the right numbers but couldn't seem to place their order. And it was hard to see through his goggles as sweat began to pour down his face. He blinked feverishly as the platform came to a quick stop and began its descent.

"She's coming! And the two goons with her!"

He tried again with the four numbers, yelling over and over, "Come on! Come on!"

Click!

"Yes!" he cried, for he'd finally gotten the order right and the door had come open. He had no mask, no protection, and he knew it would damage him to go outside. But he didn't care. He simply had to get away from the coming fury of this woman and her henchmen. He had to find his brother.

Socket passed through the opening and as he closed the door behind him Commander Judix and her two guards arrived in the drying room.

"He's not here," one of them said.

"Do I look like a blind fool?" yelled Commander Judix. "Search every corner of this facility. If anyone gets in your way, kill them. Find that boy and bring him to me!"

One of the two guards, a slightly older man who'd been her ally for years and years through a great many bad decisions, was brave enough to ask her a question.

"Commander, we don't know what boy you're talking about. What will he look like?"

"You'll know him when you see him. He'll be healthier than all the rest, like he doesn't belong here. Have Hope help you, she knows what he looks like."

The men were a little too slow in their departure and heard one last command.

"If you see Socket, throw him outside. He's lied to me for the last time."

Commander Judix went straight to the laboratory and let herself in, rolled in front of the console, and dropped the black disk onto the screen. She stared unblinking at the dot of light. As long as it was there she knew the way to Atherton remained. If only she could find Edgar, take the key, and get inside the vessel. It was so simple! She would be free at last of all the bad memories, the awful mess in which she'd had to live.

She heard the sound of giant monsters crashing into the line of electricity. She hadn't anticipated such uncontained violence from the forsaken wood. These creatures wanted more space and would fight to the death for it, and that would mean trouble for Station Seven. It wouldn't be long before one of them crashed into the only remaining line of power and broke through to the other side.

Then she'd be face-to-face with them once again — and they'd finish the job.

"Where are you, Edgar? Where are you hiding my key?"

The Commander of Station Seven hunched like a cat over a mouse, unable to take her eyes off the pulsing blue dot against the black surface.

Little did she know the dot was about to move.

CHAPTER
25

DR. HARDING RETURNS

The green team was standing in a round room with a shiny black floor and five statues placed around its rim, each about Edgar's height.

"The legend says he was an amazing artist," said Teagan. "I guess the legend is true."

"Let's get a look at each one, can we?" asked Landon. Everyone had calmed down a bit now that the sound of warring creatures outside was muted from underground, and they nodded, unable to resist the temptation to explore. A few seconds later they had gathered around the first statue.

"There's a carving here, in the stone," Aggie noticed. "It says 'The Birth of the Nubian.' What does that mean?"

The statue was of a bird that looked much like an arrow. It had a mean face that bore down on them as they stared at it.

"That's a flying creature that lives inside Atherton," said Edgar. "It can't get to the surface."

Aggie had already moved on and found that the next statue looked like a languid creature bursting out of a river, trying to clamp down on something with its razor-sharp teeth.

"This one says 'The Making of the Inferno,'" said Aggie. "I don't like it."

Edgar quickly explained what he knew of the Inferno by the details he'd heard from Isabel and Samuel. When they stepped in front of the third statue Edgar recognized it right away.

"'The Fall of Atherton,'" said Teagan, who had jostled ahead of Aggie so she could be the one to read this time. "What is it?"

"It's Atherton, after it changed," said Edgar, ever amazed by the bizarre world he'd known his whole life.

Everyone in the group had a picture in their mind of what they thought Atherton looked like. Stories had been handed down about how Dr. Harding loved towers and levels and things that were round, probably because his earliest memories were of the Silo. He had made many models of Atherton, all of them with different levels, wider at the bottom and thinner at the top. But this thing, this fallen Atherton, looked nothing like what any of them had expected.

"Atherton used to be shaped differently, but then it collapsed in on itself," said Edgar, thinking back to the catastrophic events of only a year before. "After that it filled with water and all the Cleaners were trapped."

"So there are no Cleaners on Atherton?" asked Landon.

"We have lots of Cleaners, but they're harmless now," Edgar

said. "I think these statues represent a series of events, probably in the order they occurred."

"Why do you say that?" asked Vasher, who had been quiet up until then, captivated by the intricate carvings of each image.

"This fourth one is a Cleaner," said Edgar.

"That's no Cleaner," argued Aggie. "I've seen them and they have lots of legs. This one looks more like it swims in the water."

"What's it say?" asked Edgar, seeing words etched in the base of the statue.

"It says 'Transformation of the Cleaner.' But that doesn't make sense. It's *not* a Cleaner."

"But it is," said Edgar. "This is a Cleaner on Atherton, after it's been dumped in the water and left there. They lose their legs and most of their teeth. They become a harmless fish."

"I love Dr. Harding!" said Landon.

Edgar smiled and continued. "And this happened because of the fall of Atherton. So it's in order, you see?"

Aggie had moved on to the last statue and was looking at it, puzzled by what she saw. It was a round ball, completely white, with oceans and land marked out in relief.

"It's the Dark Planet," said Vasher. "Only it's not."

"What do you mean?" asked Teagan, touching the statue against her better judgment.

"I mean it's not dirty. It's clean," answered Vasher. "*Really* clean."

"'The Chill of Winter,'" said Aggie, reading the inscription on the statue. "I don't think it's white because it's clean. I think it's white because it's covered in snow."

"What's snow?" asked Edgar, who came from a world where there was no such thing — nor rain or wind.

"You really *aren't* from around here, are you?" said Vasher. He had remained unconvinced at some level that Edgar could really be from this mythical place called Atherton. Edgar's genuineness was starting to win him over.

"We haven't seen anything like snow or winter in a long time, at least not since I've been at the Silo," said Teagan. She tried to remember — had she ever seen snow? She'd read about it, seen pictures, and maybe even seen videos when she was much younger. Everyone else seemed to have the same experience of trying to remember what winter felt like.

"I think we must be seeing these statues in the wrong order," said Edgar, looking back at the gray and black depictions around him, then noticing the floor beneath him. "This wintry Dark Planet must be first in line, then the rest."

Edgar fished around for the black disk that controlled the Raven and pulled it out. "This floor looks familiar," he said. "I wonder . . ."

Edgar gently set the disk on the black surface of the floor, and by the time he stood back up the floor was already filling with firebugs. They poured forth from under the statues, merging as a giant ball of blue light under the floor at the center of the room.

"What's happening?" asked Aggie. Everyone backed away from the middle of the room.

"What have you done?" said Teagan, petrified by what was appearing through the black fog.

"It's a face!" said Aggie.

"Not just any face," said Edgar.

Aggie and the rest didn't know what to make of the dazzling blue light. The bugs danced and moved, and there was no doubt about it.

"It's *his* face," said Edgar. There on the floor, surrounded by thick black, was the glowing blue face of Dr. Harding in full relief. All the tiny dots moved and pulsated in perfect harmony in order to make the mouth begin to move. And not only that — they heard a voice, too.

"Hello, Edgar! If this floor has been activated it means I have succeeded in my long and complicated plan. Bravo!" said the glowing blue head of Dr. Harding.

"Wow," Aggie whispered in awe. "This is the craziest thing I've ever seen."

The head of Dr. Harding ignored her.

"As I'm recording these words I still haven't told you all of what I planned, but I must have succeeded for you to be standing here among my things. I'll be brief and to the point, as the firebugs do tire after a few minutes of such rigorous thinking."

Edgar couldn't believe his ears. It was like his father was right there in the room with him.

"I used to love the yards, the place where Dr. Kincaid found me," the voice went on. "I was sad for weeks and weeks when I couldn't come here any longer. I made this secret place much later, or I should say the firebugs made it for me. Amazing little creatures when you put them to work on something. They work harder than honeybees and do precisely what I tell them. It's a very good thing I invented them, or we wouldn't be having this last moment together. It's too bad they have to be kept in such close quarters so no one gets hurt, but then all my inventions seem to have at least one broken part. When I'm gone they'll say it was my signature, won't they?

"A few important details for you now. Once Atherton has been a year in its final resting position, it will have completed the . . . what shall I call it? The birthing process, I suppose. Yes, that will do. You have only to take the Raven back now. But don't forget to bring a big block of powder! You've followed my clues well, no doubt, so I'm certain you have it with you."

The whole green team edged in closer to Dr. Harding, glancing at one another knowingly for having figured things out as he'd hoped they would.

"Without the powder block I'm afraid things are going to go from bad to worse, so you really must have it with you. You need only set the block on the black table inside the Raven.

"I've kept an eye on the forsaken wood and feel just terrible about all the things I abandoned there. It was easy at first, but it certainly did get out of hand. A lot of bad inventions roaming around that need cleaning up. You may trust that I have this problem well in hand. And I've taken the necessary precaution to keep you out of the wood unless absolutely necessary. Your transportation will be arriving in the yards shortly, so you won't need to go find it."

Everyone smiled at this news, especially Edgar. The Raven would be waiting right outside! It was beginning to feel like this was all going to work.

"Don't be alarmed when you arrive back on Atherton in a place you've never been. It's awkward talking this way — because I haven't told you everything yet — but I must assume

I've revealed enough since you stand before my glowing blue head. As long as you have Gossamer in place, everything will be fine when you get back."

"He's talking about the black dragon!" Landon exclaimed, looking at Edgar. "Hey, wait a minute. You said you'd never heard of Gossamer."

"I haven't," said Edgar. He was suddenly very worried that he had failed. If Gossamer was part of the plan it must have been spelled out somewhere, but he'd missed it.

"Gossamer has been patient a long time and will surely be excited to get on with things. Do as I have told you and he won't harm you. He's especially fond of children and will do anything to protect them. My apologies if this gets you into a pinch, but Gossamer began, like so many of my creations, as a glimmer in my childhood mind. I have it all planned out so that you will have written instructions, which you clearly found. Bravo!"

"We might be okay," said Edgar. "I have two friends on Atherton. Hopefully, they've met Gossamer even if I haven't."

Edgar couldn't believe he'd sent Isabel and Samuel to deal with a dragon when he had given them that tablet. It was the only place he could think of where the message could have been hidden.

"Gossamer will listen and he is surprisingly intelligent," Dr. Harding went on. "That's what you get when you start with a human brain. Oh, my. Did I say that? I think it's best we pretend I didn't bring it up, don't you?"

Everyone in the room was entranced by Dr. Harding's voice. He was in so many ways still a child himself. There was a sense of wonder and good humor in everything he said. This was the man Edgar wanted to remember, not the one gone mad in the Highlands, transformed into a terrible ruler, and finally redeemed in the end. As he listened to the last of what Dr. Harding would say, Edgar noticed the man's voice become happy in a different sort of way, as if he was coming to the end of something big and tiring and was looking forward to a good long nap.

"I love you more than anything else, Edgar. There is nothing else I made that comes close, nothing I loved half as much. You were fearfully and wonderfully made in a world gone mad.

"I have come to accept the reality of my situation. I am a scientist and proud of it. Some of what I've done has not turned out as I expected, but my aim was always true, and I aimed awfully high, didn't I? It would never have been enough to make a new world. I aimed for so much more than that. It was a story I wanted to tell, one that would captivate the minds of children everywhere, with monsters and dragons and wars aplenty. If they wanted a boring time of it, they shouldn't have chosen a child to get the job done.

"Make sure everyone in the Silo is taken care of as I mentioned — or will mention, I should say. I really must get my timing down or risk forgetting to tell you altogether. These are the faulty ways of my mind lately. No matter. You're here now, Atherton needs you back, and the time of winter has come. I suspect your ride has already arrived above you in the yards. Best you be on your way.

"The story has come to its final chapter. It began in the mind of a child, and it will end with a Raven, a dragon, and a storm like no other. How stupendous!

"I am signing off for the last time. Your faithful servant, Max Harding."

The firebugs fell away slowly and Dr. Harding's face began to melt. Edgar leaned over and tried to touch the face with his hands. The floor was warm where it had been. He could feel the humming bugs under black glass as they moved off and disappeared beneath the ring of statues.

"I love you, too," said Edgar, for those were the words that truly rang in his head, the words his heart would always remember. "You haven't been the father I expected, but I'll never forget you. And neither will anyone else."

There was a rising resolve in Edgar's voice as he said the words, and when he stood, everyone in the room could see that he was different now. There had always been a sadness about Edgar, a loneliness and a questioning that wouldn't go away. The feeling was gone, like an outer shell cracked and thrown to the ground. Edgar felt free as he never had before. His preoccupation with the past had vanished and all at once he realized how much energy his long search for answers had taken.

"The Raven is waiting for us up there," said Edgar. He looked at all the faces around him and saw the expectancy in their eyes. "Are you all ready to see Atherton for yourselves?"

26

A SPIKER ON THE BEACH

Commander Judix was beside herself with dismay as she watched the cluster of dots on the screen in Dr. Harding's laboratory.

The Raven was moving.

"But this can't be!" she shouted.

Commander Judix touched the screen and followed along with her hand, agitated beyond all reason, wishing she could leap from her chair and run to catch the vessel. How could it be moving? Edgar must have escaped from the Silo, gone through the forsaken wood, and snuck past Shelton and Red Eye. But that was all impossible! There was only one way past the barrier of electricity, where the transport vehicles passed through, and even that way only opened if it was prompted by the transport itself.

"This is madness!" said Commander Judix, her mind racing. She had let the first line of defense slip. Cleaners and Spikers were warring at the edge of the last line of electricity, crashing into it. And all those impacts were draining fuel at an alarming rate.

Commander Judix had thought she would have several days, maybe even a week to find the boy, get the key, and make her escape, but it was looking like it might only be hours before monsters were crawling all over the beach. And now even that didn't matter, because the vessel was unexpectedly on the move — and she wasn't in it.

"I *won't* let it leave without me," she repeated over and over.

The communication box on the wall crackled to life. It was chaos in the engine room, where fuel was converted to electricity.

"Commander! Where are you? We're into our final reserve! We need Grammel with that fuel! Where is he?"

"We've got a breech at nine o'clock!" It was a second voice from a different part of Station Seven. "It's alive! It's alive! I repeat, we have a live breech at nine o'clock!"

She couldn't stand the idea of leaving the dot behind, but tearing herself away, she rolled quickly to the pillar of books and pushed the communication button that would have her voice heard in both places at once.

"How long will the fuel last?" she asked. There was a moment of static-filled silence before her answer came in which she thought of rolling back to the screen.

"A day, maybe less. It depends on how many touches we get. It takes a lot of fuel to absorb those hits."

"It's a Spiker that's broken through!" said the second voice. "It's on the move!"

"Commander Judix, what are your orders?"

The Commander felt physically ill and began to shiver. She didn't care about anyone else. Not those who had stayed on at Station Seven, not Hope, not the children. There was only her and her goal of leaving forever.

"Assume lockdown positions," she said. "And kill that thing before it attacks the station."

Commander Judix turned off the receiver. Lockdown meant the windows would be covered in shields of metal. Metal, metal, metal! She *hated* metal. And she didn't want to hear anything more about Cleaners or Spikers or lack of fuel. Commander Judix wanted to be left alone as she watched the glowing blue dots foretell her doom.

To her great surprise, when she returned to the screen, the cluster of glowing blue dots had stopped. And what was more, they appeared to have stopped almost directly on top of the laboratory where she sat.

"What trickery is this?" she said, confounded by this new turn of events. And then it crossed her mind that maybe, just maybe, this thing had come looking for Dr. Harding. Maybe it had come on its own by some forgotten program in an endless loop. It could have landed in its usual place, then moved on in search of its master.

"Where are you hiding?" she said. "You're outside, on the roof, aren't you?"

She rolled away from the screen and crossed the laboratory, pressing a button on a panel. A door *swish*ed open and she entered a small elevator with masks and goggles hanging here and there.

"The way to Atherton will be there! And the door will be open, as it was in the forsaken wood."

Commander Judix put on a set of goggles and a mask as the elevator rose to the roof. When the door swung open again the elevator room filled quickly with caustic smog. Looking this way and that, she desperately hoped to see the vessel awaiting her arrival. But it was nowhere. There were only glass rooms filled with rows of dead plants and trees.

She rolled down the long rows as she listened to the awful sound of beasts fighting in the distance. Being outside was terrifying, all the more so because she hadn't been outside in so long. She arrived at the roof's edge and couldn't see over the ledge. It was too high from where she sat, and she cursed her chair, hitting the wheels and the handles over and over with her clenched fists. Then she rolled away, toward the distant side of the roof, just to be sure the vessel wasn't hidden somewhere else.

Could she have seen over the rail, Commander Judix would have caught site of Edgar and his friends emerging from the yards and standing in front of the Raven. If anything, the million-spiked object seemed even more frightening than when Edgar had left it in the forsaken wood. There was no person or beast he could imagine getting within ten feet of its pulsating, needle-sharp tips. And yet Edgar knew he must find a way to open the door, get everyone inside, and set the powder block onto the black table.

"Don't go anywhere near it," whispered Aggie through her

mask, which she had put back on. She'd never seen anything quite so threatening.

"It's okay," said Edgar. "I think the Raven is like Gossamer. It's on our side."

"How do you know that?" It was Teagan in doubt this time. "What if it starts firing arrows at you?"

Edgar had to admit he'd be cut right through if even one of the long black spikes fired in his direction. He wouldn't stand a chance. They heard a crashing sound from the yards and realized something very big and dangerous was practically on top of them.

"It's a Spiker!" Vasher struggled to hold the powder block as his face twitched nervously.

"Open!" Edgar yelled at the Raven, but it just sat there, the long spikes pulsing horrifically. He turned back to his friends with searching eyes. The masks were beginning to fail and everyone was starting to cough. Soon they'd be forced back inside or risk serious harm. The thought of Aggie and the others becoming any sicker bothered Edgar tremendously.

"Edgar," said Landon.

"What?"

"The door," Landon continued as he pointed past Edgar. "It's opening."

Edgar spun around and couldn't believe his eyes. "This is going to work! We're getting out of here," he cried, grinning ear to ear.

But things weren't exactly as he'd hoped when the door slid all the way open.

"What the devil!" said Red Eye.

"You got me in a lot of trouble!" said Socket. Then, thinking a tiny bit more, he added: "How did you get all the way out here?"

Socket and Red Eye both wore their usual thick goggles, and both had their benders out, swishing them from side to side in the pale light. Every single member of the green team felt a crushing sense of defeat. They had almost made it, only to find their tormentors standing in the very place they wanted to be.

"You don't know how to operate it," said Edgar. He wasn't about to give up that easily.

"Shut your mouth!" said Socket. "You're in enough trouble as it is."

Red Eye rolled his eyes at his brother. They were so far beyond ever being able to go back to the Silo and life the way it had been. He was only interested in one thing: getting to Atherton.

"You know how to run it?" asked Red Eye, who had been utterly confounded by the inner workings of the Raven and its vast black, blank surfaces. It had moved of its own will to arrive near the yards.

"I know exactly how to operate that thing," said Edgar. "And what's more, I know how to take it to Atherton."

"Atherton?" said Socket. "You're kidding?"

Edgar shook his head. "If you don't know what you're doing you'll never make it. It's complicated."

Red Eye weighed his options before answering with a growl.

"You can come, but the rest stay."

"No!" yelled Landon. He couldn't imagine being left behind on the Dark Planet.

Socket moved forward and swung his bender with a *swish! swish!*

"Shut up! You're staying here and that's the last of it."

Above the Raven, Commander Judix had heard the voices growing in volume and had made her way back to the rail. She grabbed it and hauled herself out of her chair.

And there it was. Outlined in the murky light of afternoon sat the jet-black vessel that had come to take her away. She was, unfortunately, incapable of climbing down to the ground to reach it.

Commander Judix watched in disbelief as Red Eye and Socket stood in front of a group of children from the Silo. When she saw Edgar, even through the haze, she knew it was him. Her anger flared and she screamed.

"Red Eye!"

Red Eye, Socket, and all the children looked up and couldn't believe their eyes.

"Commander?" said Red Eye. "Is that you?"

"Of course it's me! Get up here and carry me down!"

Socket wanted nothing at all to do with Commander Judix. He retreated into the Raven and stood in the shadows as his brother approached the Commander.

"You don't really think I'm taking you with me?" said Red Eye. He had longed for a moment like this. Never in his wildest dreams did he think it would come true, and with such perfection! He was leaving the wretched Dark Planet for a waiting paradise and she — this monster of a woman who had treated him like dirt for far too long — she was trapped on the roof of Station Seven.

"You will come here this instant," said Commander Judix in her most authoritative tone. But for once the voice failed her. Not only did Red Eye refuse to bring her to the Raven, he laughed at her. He snorted and wheezed until the dirty air burned so badly in his lungs he had to stop.

And that was when he heard it, the presence of a Spiker. It was closer than anyone had thought, and just then, its enormous clawed foot came down next to the Raven. The Raven wasted no time in response. A series of at least thirty black spikes shot out at lightning speed and sliced right through the Spiker, piercing through the other side of its leg. The monster shrieked and hobbled a few paces off to lick its wounds.

In all the commotion Edgar waved his friends through the door and into the Raven. Vasher clutched the powder block close to his chest.

Socket stood in the corner, shivering with fright and staring at the black ceiling, which had begun to glow. Two cave eels stared him down as if they might jump out from behind the glass and chomp off his head with their sharp teeth at any second.

"Don't move," said Edgar, tricking Socket into believing he might actually be in danger. "If you do, they'll tear your limbs off."

Red Eye came briskly into the Raven and Edgar kept the ruse going.

"He better stay still, and so should you," said Edgar, acting as if the slightest movement might trigger an unexpected attack. "We all need to be slow and careful now. You won't like what happens if they get angry."

Red Eye's breathing slowed and he stayed very still.

"You better not be trying to trick me."

From outside they heard Commander Judix screaming for them to come get her. Edgar felt a pang of guilt at leaving her behind, but if she returned to Station Seven, there was yet a chance she could be saved.

Edgar slowly placed the disk on the black table in the middle of the Raven, and the door began to shut.

"At least we won't have to listen to her howling any longer," said Red Eye.

Aggie thought this was one of the meanest things she'd ever heard anyone say. With a Spiker so close by, she could imagine the poor woman's panic. She had known the feeling of being left behind to fend for herself on her long walk through the wood on her way to the Silo. She wouldn't wish it on anyone, no matter how cruel they'd been.

The table burst to life and Edgar saw the images of everything he'd seen before.

"When I do this, you're probably going to see a lot more creatures than you see right now," said Edgar. "After everyone is settled in I'll start things moving. You're going to feel as if the chair you're sitting in is trying to pull your pants off."

"What?" said Red Eye.

"Shhhhh!" whispered Edgar. "They hate loud noises."

As if to prove his point an eel emerged behind the glass near Red Eye's head and stared down at him. Edgar turned and winked again at the green team and they took some reassurance that everything would be fine. "Slowly now," said Edgar. Red

Eye was wary of moving while the cave eel watched him, but he gathered his courage and slid down into one of the chairs.

"Nice to see you brought something for me to eat," said Red Eye, seeing the powder block sitting on Vasher's lap. Vasher's twitching had calmed and he actually glared at Red Eye. There was no way he was giving up this treasure so it could be eaten for lunch.

"I'm not moving," whined Socket from where he'd slumped down on the floor. A glowing cave eel was trained on Socket's head from behind the black glass.

"I don't recommend that," said Edgar. "The Raven gets moving pretty fast. It will be nothing like what you experienced getting from the forsaken wood to here."

But Socket wouldn't move.

Edgar shrugged his shoulders, actually feeling a little bit guilty at what was about to happen.

"Stay in your seats," he said, placing his hand over the twirling snowflake. He thought twice about it and looked at Vasher.

"Why don't you set that down on the table here? You're not going to want to carry it all the way to Atherton."

"Yeah," said Red Eye, leaning forward menacingly. "Set it down so we can all have some."

Vasher held his arms out and gently set the heavy powder block on the table. The moment he did all the firebugs dispersed at once. They formed a column below the surface of the table and the powder block began to melt away, like it was sitting on a bed of acid. It hissed and smoked while the firebugs grew brighter and brighter until everyone but Edgar had to look away. He alone saw as they changed from blue to a brilliant shade of red.

"You can look now," said Edgar, and everyone turned back to the table. All the images were back in place as before, but now everything was a soft glowing shade of red. And there was one new item that hadn't been there before. It was the only thing Edgar had ever seen made of white firebugs: a shimmering snowflake pulsing from the bottom of the image of Atherton.

Edgar tapped it, and the inside of the Raven came to life.

Eels swam everywhere and firebugs multiplied until it looked like a star-filled night all around them. The two eels that had watched Socket darted off with the rest, gobbling up red firebugs by the hundreds as the Raven began to move. Edgar felt the seat hug him close, pulling him down and holding him steady. Everyone gasped at the feeling except Socket, who wasn't seated in a chair and seemed not to understand what was about to happen.

The Raven shot into the air, spinning as it gained speed on its way to break out of the Dark Planet's atmosphere. Socket tumbled end over end and found himself pinned to the glass. His goggles flew off and smashed into one of the chairs. He was a man in a tumbler, spinning circles at the back end of the vessel while everyone watched from the safety of their seats.

"I tried to warn him," said Edgar.

Red Eye scowled deeply at Edgar. He couldn't wait until his seat let him go so he could beat the boy senseless. The last thing he'd done was to slowly put his bender away, so at least his favorite weapon hadn't been lost. "When we get to Atherton, you better run," said Red Eye. "All of you better run!"

"I don't think it will be us doing the running," said Landon. "Just you wait until you meet Gossamer. He doesn't like adults, especially mean ones like you."

"I never met anyone as dumb as you, Lanny," said Red Eye. "Let me spell it out for you. There's no such thing as dragons. Got it?"

Landon didn't say anything else. In fact, everyone seemed perfectly happy to stay quiet as the Raven started its journey across the sky. Even Socket had settled into a comfortable spot, curled up like a baby at the bottom of the ship.

●

Commander Judix slumped down in her chair and watched the Raven leave the Dark Planet. It was, in her view, the final insult. She had long been a cold and calculating person, and yet she had never given in to the darkness entirely. She would remember her mother's touch or the voice of a lost friend, and the tiniest bit of hope would return. But in that moment of watching the Raven fly away, the Dark Planet had finally won. She felt nothing. When the Spiker leaned down and caught sight of her, she was unmoved at its arrival. There would be pain, but at least she would feel something in the end.

She felt the Spiker's huge nose sniffing at her hair, and then, to her great surprise, she began to cry.

27

THE CHILL OF WINTER

"Wake up," said Samuel. "Isabel, wake up!"

He prodded her shoulder and felt Gossamer's warm breath on his neck. The black dragon had awoken first, nudging Samuel where he lay curled up next to Isabel, nestled safely in one of Gossamer's warm wings.

For two days they'd been stranded with the great dragon, the sound of falling crystals a constant reminder of how completely trapped they were. They feared being stuck inside Atherton until they starved to death, and tried without much success not to dwell on how worried their parents must be. One thing was for sure: If they ever did make it out alive, they were in big trouble.

"He wants us to move," Samuel said as Isabel rubbed her eyes and woke up.

"Do you hear that?" asked Samuel. Isabel was slower to wake than Samuel was and she wasn't sure what he was talking about. "It's *quiet*."

Isabel and Samuel carefully crept down the wing and stepped aside. They heard the faraway sound of two or three crystals falling from the ceiling.

"He's stopped trying to keep us here," said Samuel. "Maybe he's thinking about taking us back the way we came. We might actually get out of here alive!"

When they were clear of Gossamer's spiked head and neck he stood and lumbered heavily away from them. The space they were in was vast and brightly lit. On one end was the wide opening to the outside of Atherton, on the other was the vast wall of pulsing white light. Samuel and Isabel had watched it for hours and wondered what its purpose could be. The more they looked the more they were sure that Cleaners were swimming behind the white wall in the deepest part of the waters of Atherton. It was a thick, foggy sort of glass that hid them in shadow, a glass that was covered with billions of sharp spires.

"What's he looking at?" asked Samuel. Gossamer wasn't one to leave their side, but something had caught his attention at the opening.

"What is it, Gossamer? Do you hear something?" asked Isabel.

Everything had turned unnervingly silent, and Samuel was left with the distinct feeling he and Isabel should hide. "I have a feeling something's about to happen," he said.

"Maybe we should step back a little," said Isabel, fear rising in her voice. They looked in every direction. There was the towering wall of icy glass crystals, the small passageway to the side where they'd come in, and the vast opening to the outside. They had stayed well away from the opening for all of the two days they'd been there, because they knew the closer they got the harder gravity would try to pull them out into open air.

Samuel and Isabel were both shuffling back slowly when Gossamer roared into the open space outside. It was hard to imagine anyone on the surface of Atherton not hearing the crushing volume of the black dragon's voice.

"Why's he screaming so loud?" yelled Samuel, but Isabel couldn't hear him.

Gossamer flapped his leathery wings and dove for the opening.

"Where's he going?" yelled Isabel. She had been afraid before, but now she was terrified. "Don't leave! Please, Gossamer. Come back!"

She ran from the safety of the passageway with Samuel chasing her.

"NO, Isabel!" Samuel sprinted after her. Both of them realized the mistake they'd made and tried to stop, but momentum was on gravity's side. They slid closer to the opening on loose rocks and dirt until they finally skidded to a halt ten feet from the edge.

"Step back, Isabel!"

But Isabel couldn't stand the idea of being left behind by her protector inside Atherton. Without Gossamer, she didn't see how they could survive. She took one more step toward the edge, where gravity's pull was like a fast-moving river that was getting deeper and deeper.

Samuel held on to Isabel's arm. "Isabel, please! I can't hold you if you won't help!"

"I'm trying!" she said, finally coming to her senses as she felt the force of gravity growing. "I can't back up!"

And just then, right when they were both more afraid than they'd ever been, the Raven rose from somewhere beneath their line of sight, its million black spikes sliding in and out threateningly. It crept up slowly, as if it were studying the two, trying to decide if they should be destroyed or not. The shocking sight of the mysterious vessel sent Isabel and Samuel into a panic.

"I'm sliding, Samuel!" screamed Isabel. As Samuel reached unsuccessfully for her hand, she rolled head over heels toward the Raven, which hovered directly above the edge of the hole and seemed to watch the scene unfold without emotion.

Isabel's legs went over the edge first and then her body followed until all Samuel could see was her head and her hands, which held on for dear life. Her eyes were white with fear as she slid, clawing the dirt with her fingers and then — *flit!* — she was gone.

"Isabel!"

The Raven hovered closer to Samuel, leaving him speechless as its enormous weight glided overhead. Samuel looked back to the edge and thought about jumping after Isabel, though he knew he would be jumping to his death. Was there any chance he could save her?

He heard Gossamer before he saw him, the monstrous black wings flapping somewhere out of view. But a second later the miraculous presence of the black dragon filled the cave once more.

"This is all your fault!" cried Samuel, choking back tears. "She trusted you! You're nothing but a monster!"

Gossamer flew up and in, pushing Samuel away from the edge with the power of his wings. The wind nearly bowled Samuel over as he ran back toward the passageway, angry and afraid. When Samuel was safely back from the pull of the opening, Gossamer landed. He blew a puff of black smoke from his nose and laid his soft wing along the floor. Isabel slid down, battered but alive.

"Isabel!" shouted Samuel, overcome with gratitude that his friend wasn't lost forever. "Are you all right?"

Isabel stood, feeling her arms and head. Her hair was a crazy mess on top of her head, and there were small cuts and bruises everywhere, but nothing appeared to be broken.

"I think I'm all in one piece."

When they looked back at Gossamer he began to move, quickly making sure Isabel and Samuel were okay and then going straight to the Raven. Two of Dr. Harding's most imposing creations sat nose to nose with each other, and Gossamer seemed oddly pleased at the arrival of the spiked object.

"What are they doing?" asked Samuel, completely bedazzled by this new mystery. The Raven landed on the ground on thousands of black shards. As imposing as the Raven was, it was still dwarfed by the size of Gossamer, who stood over it, craning his neck in every direction as he examined the new arrival. It was, Samuel thought, like a mother inspecting an egg for the first time.

Isabel and Samuel crept forward until they stood about twenty feet away from the Raven. They didn't dare get any closer. When the door began to open they jumped back, and Gossamer moved behind the door, where those coming out wouldn't be able to see him. If anyone turned around, though, there would be no hiding the crouching giant.

Light from the white wall filled the inside of the Raven as Red Eye and Socket emerged, swishing their benders back and forth. Socket had found his goggles, but the dark lenses were spidery with cracks and the world of Atherton was harder to see than he'd hoped.

Edgar called out from inside the Raven. "I can show you where to go," he said. "You should let me come out."

"*Edgar?*" said Isabel. She couldn't believe her ears, and it showed in her voice. "Is that you?"

"Edgar!" yelled Samuel.

Isabel and Samuel wanted to bolt forward to look for their friend, but neither of them felt they could safely go anywhere near the Raven.

Red Eye and Socket had no intention of letting their prisoners go. "Stay right where you are," commanded Red Eye, staring down Samuel and Isabel. He returned his bender to his back, but he had found Shelton's Leveler, a very powerful handheld pistol of sorts, which he pointed in their general direction.

323

"Bring me Edgar, and one of the others — the small one," said Red Eye. Socket reached back and stored his bender, then disappeared inside. When he returned a moment later he had a firm grip on Edgar in one hand and Landon in the other. Landon had pulled his small goggles down over his face and looked around in wonder.

"It's really you!" Isabel cried, her arms outstretched as she impulsively moved toward him.

"That's far enough!" said Red Eye. He grabbed Edgar roughly with his free hand and yanked him close.

"You shouldn't do that," warned Samuel.

"And who's going to stop me?" said Red Eye. Seeing no adults to confront him, he slipped easily into his typical arrogant behavior. "I've got the boy *and* the Leveler."

Samuel and Isabel shook their heads. They had an idea of what was coming.

"Don't shake your heads at us!" demanded Socket. He raised his hand to strike Landon and show who was in charge. It was then that he felt the hot breath on the back of his head. Socket looked over his shoulder. His brother followed suit.

"You better let them go," said Isabel. "Gossamer doesn't seem to like you very much."

Gossamer's head was frighteningly close to Red Eye and Socket. The dragon opened its growling mouth and revealed rows of black teeth.

"Gossamer, it's really you," said Landon slowly, mesmerized. Socket's grip had slackened and Landon pulled himself free, stepping farther back to get a good look at the monstrous black dragon. He broke into a great smile and looked at Socket. "Oh, he's mad! You really made him angry!"

In a flash Gossamer had one huge claw around Socket and lifted him off the ground, but his fiery blue eyes never left Red Eye. Socket squirmed and screamed as Red Eye pushed Edgar to the ground. His plan was to dive back inside the Raven and return to the Dark Planet as fast as he could; Atherton was not what he had expected.

But his leap to safety ended in midair in the claw of the black dragon.

Gossamer held both men close to his face and inspected them. He had a mind to throw them both into the air and shower them with flames, reducing them to bones and ashes before everyone's eyes. Red Eye and Socket screamed in terror as Gossamer held them tightly, gazing with those terrible, piercing eyes. The Leveler fell out of Red Eye's hand and Gossamer pulverized it with one foot.

"Does he listen to what you say?" Edgar asked Samuel and Isabel. He wanted to go to them, embrace them, and hear all about how they'd come to be here with such a commanding beast. But he couldn't do that until Red Eye and Socket were taken care of.

"He usually listens to us," said Isabel. She looked to Edgar a little worse for the wear, as if she'd been beaten up or rolled down a steep hill, and it made him wonder about the adventure she'd had

"Tell him to set them down," said Edgar.

"Put them down, Gossamer," yelled Isabel.

A burst of dark smoke drifted from Gossamer's nose. He put Red Eye and Socket down reluctantly but kept a close eye on them. They were fairly near the edge and they felt the pull of gravity.

"Can't we go back to the Silo?" asked Socket, who'd already had quite enough of the monsters and bright lights, and now had this bizarre feeling that he was going to be pulled off the edge.

Edgar pointed toward the wall opposite the passageway, which seemed as good a place as any to make them wait until he could figure out what to do with them. The rest of the green team already had their goggles on as they streamed out of the Raven and blinked rapidly in the light. Gossamer sniffed the door to the Raven, pronounced it empty, and set his gaze on Red Eye and Socket.

"Throw the benders off the edge," said Edgar. "Then sit over there and don't make a sound."

"We'll do no such thing!" shouted Red Eye. "Send us back to the Dark Planet. That's all we want."

"Give them a good roar, Gossamer," Samuel ordered. "Everyone cover your ears!"

Gossamer took in a colossal breath. It felt like all the air was being sucked out of the chamber. All the children covered their ears, and then Gossamer roared at Red Eye and Socket, his massive teeth only inches from their faces. For Red Eye and Socket it was the kind of noise that felt like it had the power to kill them both where they stood. Forever after they would have an annoying ringing in their ears that would make it nearly impossible to hear what anyone was saying.

When the roar was over the two men pulled out their benders without hesitation and threw them toward the vast opening to the outside. Gossamer blew a mighty red flame at the benders and the horrible weapons were vaporized for good.

"What's that you say?" said Socket, looking at his brother and hearing only the ringing.

"What?" said Red Eye, banging his head with the palm of his hand.

The rest of the green team looked around, stunned and confused, as Edgar, Isabel, and Samuel hugged one another. The time of their reunion had finally come and the questions flew. Soon Edgar understood how his two friends had used the tablet to find Gossamer, and Isabel and Samuel understood that Edgar had brought the Raven. None of them had any idea what was supposed to happen after that.

"These are my new friends," said Edgar, "Vasher, Teagan, Landon, and Aggie."

All four of the children from the Silo looked apprehensively at Samuel and Isabel. They were self-conscious of the way they looked, because even from inside their goggles Samuel and Isabel seemed as healthy as Edgar did. Teagan wondered for a brief moment if she fit in better on the Dark Planet than here.

"They have to wear the goggles, because of the light," said Edgar.

Samuel was already talking to Vasher and bending down to shake hands with Landon. Isabel knew immediately what she had to do.

"I'm very happy to meet you," she said, drawing near Aggie and Teagan. "Thank you for bringing Edgar back and for coming here. We're going to be great friends, we three, I'm sure of it."

Aggie and Teagan felt better then. Maybe things would be all right.

"I think we're about to see what Dr. Harding meant by the chill of winter," said Edgar. "Maybe we saw the statues in the yards in the right order, after all."

Gossamer had been watching the Raven, nudging it gently with his snout as the group gathered together. They watched as the black dragon blew soft flames on the black surface of spikes.

"I think he's cooking the Raven," said Landon.

"Be quiet," said Vasher. "Let's not distract him."

The Raven's door slid shut and it rose into the air and drifted slowly toward the wall of white crystals. "They're the same," said Samuel out of the blue, noticing that the Raven was shaped the same as the many oval shapes of glowing white light on the vast wall.

"What do you mean?" asked Vasher, who was keenly interested in all that was happening.

Before Samuel could say anything more Gossamer walked behind the Raven, fanning it with flames. The spikes began to glow red and orange, though the center stayed black as night. Seeing the spikes turn red seemed to spur Gossamer on, and he blew thicker, darker flames as they moved closer to the vast wall of white crystals. When they came within fifty feet of the wall, Gossamer stopped blowing. As the Raven spun in a slow circle, its spikes appeared to have been lit like a million long candles.

"I get the feeling we should be in the passageway," said Samuel.

"So do I," said Isabel.

She and Samuel led everyone out of the chamber and stood a few feet back inside the tunnel. Edgar spotted Red Eye and Socket huddled against the far wall. He yelled for them come near, but they couldn't hear him. He wasn't at all sure it would be a good idea to let them come too close, anyway. He hadn't wanted to see them burned to death by a dragon, but he surely didn't trust them.

Gossamer turned and blew fire on the Raven again. A few seconds later a sound like firing arrows filled the air. Everyone marveled as the once black spikes that surrounded the Raven became flaming spears flying into the white wall by the tens of thousands. The Raven moved up and down, firing glowing orange arrows into every part of the wall. Soon the wall was trembling and Gossamer was howling magically, flapping his wings eagerly as if preparing for a task he'd waited his whole life to begin.

"He's not leaving, is he?" asked Landon, suddenly aware that his dream of being with Gossamer might come to a quick end. He ran out into the open yelling Gossamer's name until he stood at the foot of the black dragon. "You can't leave! I only just found you."

Gossamer leaned down close and seemed to smile at Landon. His big tongue rolled out and Landon touched it. It was hot, but not so much that he couldn't put his fingers on it, and Gossamer licked all the way up Landon's arm.

"Are you ever coming back?" asked Landon.

Gossamer couldn't respond, but his big eyes stared down at Landon and nudged the boy toward the passageway with the soft part of his nose.

"He licked me! I bet he's never done that to anyone else, *ever!*"

The wall of white began to change. It moved like it was alive, bulging in a thousand different places, until a section crumbled loose and drifted in the air. It was a mirror image of the Raven, only it was white, not black. It was the same size and oval shape and covered on every side by white shards. A few seconds later a second white Raven broke free, and then, as if by magic, there were hundreds of white Ravens floating in the chamber.

"I've seen something that looks like this before," whispered Aggie. "My dad had a picture of it. This is winter."

"It wouldn't have worked without you," said Edgar, looking at all his new friends from the Silo. "I don't think white Ravens are possible without powder blocks. It's the secret ingredient."

Gossamer flapped his wings and ran for the opening of the chamber before any part of the storm could escape. The black dragon took flight, zooming down and out of sight, then charging back up again and holding steady as he roared into the chamber. A steady stream of white Ravens fell in line behind Gossamer and he flew away, his dark outline disappearing fast as he raced for the Dark Planet.

"He was saying goodbye," said Isabel, putting her arm

around Landon. The two of them would miss Gossamer more than anyone else.

"I think he's coming back again someday," said Landon. "In fact, I'm sure of it."

Vasher watched in awe as the sky fill with white.

"There must be ten thousand of them."

"More than that," said Samuel, seeing that the wall was anything but finished producing them. A steady blizzard of white Ravens blew through the chamber, all of them following the black dragon. The making of winter lasted an hour. Red Eye and Socket stayed pinned to the wall the entire time as white Ravens raced by.

At last winter was over, and the black Raven came to rest on the floor of the chamber, its door wide open.

"All of its spikes are gone," Edgar pointed out. What remained looked like a gigantic egg filled with liquid.

"Are those cave eels?' asked Isabel. "And firebugs — do I see *red* firebugs?"

"It's okay, Isabel," said Edgar. "They're contained inside their own space. There's a layer of glass, then a few feet of liquid, then another layer of glass, then the inside of the Raven — understand? They're trapped."

He glanced across the way at Red Eye and Socket.

"Let's get inside fast," said Edgar. "I think I'd rather send someone else down here to get those two."

Edgar entered first so that he could show Isabel how safe it was, and everyone else followed quickly behind. Edgar poked his head out the door and saw Red Eye and Socket running for the Raven. He set the black disk on the table and the door closed.

"I think a good long wait will do them some good," said Edgar.

He looked at Isabel, Samuel, and everyone from the green team and his heart swelled. Six close friends were more than he could have hoped for. He wanted nothing more than to bring them all safely back to the grove.

"Come on," said Edgar. "It's time we were getting back home."

"You mean it gets better?" said Landon, smiling from ear to ear.

"Wait until you try Black and Green," assured Isabel. "There's nothing quite like it."

Vasher looked at Teagan. "What's Black and Green?"

"Who cares!" she laughed, drawing in a huge breath of air and letting it out with a sigh. Vasher did the same. He could feel the pristine air that surrounded Atherton healing him by the minute. Everyone else on the green team was feeling better, too. Their eyes didn't sting so much and their lungs were tingling with energy.

As everyone chose their seats Aggie explained what it would feel like to Samuel and Isabel. Edgar set the black disk on the table between them and red firebugs emerged.

"Are you ready to see your new home?" asked Edgar, gazing at each of his new friends and settling on Aggie. He could imagine walking along the lake with her at night, maybe even holding her hand.

"We've been ready for a while," said Vasher.

Edgar nodded, set course for the grove, and sat back in his chair. He closed his eyes and Hope's face flashed before him and he was sad, thinking of her and all the children stuck in the Silo. He tried to imagine what would happen to the Dark Planet, but he could not put the pieces together.

In time he would learn the truth.

CHAPTER
28

THE STORY OF ATHERTON
FINDS ITS END

Edgar had only a few hours to gather everyone. He woke early, nudged Landon awake, and crossed over to the table in Dr. Kincaid's cave. A pitcher of water awaited him along with fig butter and bread from the night before. Bread! It was one of the things he had so appreciated about having Samuel as one of his best friends. His mother had been the baker in the House of Power, and there was never a shortage of leftover buns or biscuits or loaves at the Inn.

"Better wake him up," said Edgar, his mouth already full so that Landon could hardly understand him. Landon jumped out of bed and gobbled down some bread, then guzzled water right from the pitcher.

"Get up Vash! It's *the* day — the day we've all been waiting for," said Landon.

Vasher didn't move. He and Edgar and Landon had become

like three brothers living under the same roof. Vasher treated Landon like a little brother, but never Edgar. And the feeling of being brothers was somehow perfect, because it left an opening for Samuel to be best friend to all three.

"He's not going to wake up," said Landon, taking a second bite of bread slathered with fig butter. "It's way too early."

Edgar put his hand in the pitcher and cupped a small amount of water, then he stood over Vasher and let it *drip, drip, drip* onto his face.

"That should do it," said Landon, and sure enough Vasher was up out of his bed in a flash.

"Grab some breakfast," said Edgar. "We're going to be late."

Though Vasher had calmed down noticeably since his arrival on Atherton, he still loved to sleep. Sometimes Vasher thought about the passageway of lies. A few more days on the Dark Planet and he would have been in the service of Captain Grammel. He might even be dead.

Neither Vasher nor Landon put on their goggles when they left the dim light of the cave and stepped into the light of Atherton. Something about the clean air and cobalt blue sky had healed them over a period of weeks during which Dr. Kincaid had been giving them a home brew of herbs and spices. It was almost impossible to choke down. According to the old scientist, the concoction was designed to "clean every bit of gunk out of your system."

Everyone missed Dr. Kincaid and his ever-present companion, Vincent. The two men hadn't been seen on Atherton for almost a month, but the day had come when they were scheduled to appear once more.

Soon the three boys arrived at the Inn, which had become the center of the community on Atherton. The Inn sat near the water at the edge of the biggest grove, where hundreds of people gathered regularly. Briney, who had long prepared all the rabbit and mutton at the old inn had remained the head cook. Samuel's mother was the baker. A cook who had managed to escape the House of Power made all the soups and stews.

But it was Briney's wife, Maude, the very woman who'd gotten the tablet from Edgar and given it to Samuel and Isabel, who managed the Inn and kept everything organized. With the arrival of Aggie and Teagan, Maude had decided to leave her days of herding sheep. Her season of silence had come to an end, but she would forever remember it as a time when she was preparing to become a mother for two girls from the Dark Planet.

"Aggie!" said Landon impatiently, seeing her and Teagan at Maude's side as they talked with Samuel's mother in the kitchen. "Come on! We have to go!"

Aggie and Teagan were both apprentice bakers and they were, at this moment, covered with flour from head to toe. Maude nodded her approval. She and everyone else on Atherton had known this day was coming and had already agreed to let them go.

"Be careful," Maude said as both girls removed their aprons and stood in front of their new caretaker. Their hair had grown an inch or more already, and Maude whisked the flour from both their heads.

"Don't get too close to the edge."

"Samuel will be waiting for you out front," said Samuel's mother, nodding toward the door. "You know how he hates to come in here while I'm working. Always nervous I'm going to give him something to do."

Landon was eyeing a freshly baked row of loaves as the two girls dashed toward the door.

"Already got a bag packed for you," said Briney, coming in from the back room with two cloth sacks, one in each hand.

"Dr. Harding and Vincent will want a feast, I'm sure." He lifted one of the heavy bags. "This one's got your bag of fresh water, your sticks for roasting, lighting flint, and your dried figs for making a nice fire to cook over." He lifted the other bag. "Two loaves and two wrapped and ready rabbits. They're good for the morning, but cook 'em up by noon."

"No Black and Green?" asked Landon, who had stepped into the Inn to take the bags. He'd had Cleaner many times since his arrival and absolutely loved the sweet and salty taste.

"Too messy," said Briney. "We'll save it for tonight at the big celebration."

Briney handed off the bags and Landon scurried for the door. An early morning crowd was starting to gather, looking for the Inn's famous morning fig biscuits and sticky fig buns.

Samuel and Isabel had arrived with the crowd, and the moment Landon stepped outside Samuel waved all of the green team along with Edgar and Isabel away from the Inn. "We better get out of here before my mom puts us to work. If we stand around she'll have us delivering sticky buns all over the grove."

The group of seven started off, talking and laughing as they went. They were like a collection of oddly shaped magnets, able to pull apart for a while, but always drawn back together where they felt most comfortable. They walked past a poorly built shack sitting at the end of a long pier and saw two men sitting out front gutting Cleaners. It was a truly disgusting and slimy job, the one job no one on Atherton wanted to do. But someone had to do it.

"Hi, Red Eye," yelled Aggie, though she knew he couldn't hear her.

"What's that you say?" said Socket, his ears buzzing. They worked for Mr. Crane, who was a very demanding boss, and they lived in the little shack at the end of the pier. Red Eye and Socket kept to themselves mostly, but they seemed to find some sort of peace there by the lake.

Sometimes Edgar would walk by at night and see them staring out at the water, neither of them saying a word, and he wondered what they were thinking. Edgar imagined they probably had some regrets. Maybe Red Eye and Socket wished they could go back to the Silo and do things differently, or maybe they'd do it all the same if they were given the chance. One thing was certain — there were enough Cleaners to be gutted to last them a lifetime, so they were going to have a lot of time to think about what they'd done.

It took the group a while to walk to the very place where Edgar's trip to the Dark Planet had begun. They went straight to the rim of Atherton, crawling on all fours so they could peek out and see what they could see. But it was daytime so they couldn't make out much of anything; only blue sky in every direction. But at night everything would change. Then, just like on the Dark Planet, they would be able to see the whole universe laid out before them. The night stars were there for both worlds to see.

"Do you think it looks any different?" asked Aggie, unable to see her old home but thinking of little else. "I wonder how the other teams at the Silo are doing. And Hope — I wonder if she's okay."

They had all wondered the same things. They'd made a solemn promise not to go near the edge for two months — sixty days! — and even Edgar had kept his word. For whatever reason, Dr. Kincaid wanted them to stay away until the Raven returned. So they had kept the promise, though it had been very tempting to sneak away at night and peer out over the flat edge of Atherton.

It was midmorning as they backed away and opened the bags.

"Let's start the fire and cook the rabbits," said Landon. "They'll be here soon and we can have it all ready."

Everyone thought this sounded like a good idea. It would keep them busy while they waited, and besides, they had grown hungry on the long walk. They set to work starting the fire, skewering the whole rabbits, laying out the bread and leather bag of water.

They became so involved in setting up the feast that none of them saw the Raven come silently into view. It made a distinct sound of many sharp points hitting a hard surface when it landed and everyone jumped up.

"It's got its spikes back!" Vasher said. The Raven looked as scary as ever.

The door opened and Dr. Kincaid emerged with Vincent. Edgar thought Dr. Kincaid looked a little less ancient on his return, like a long sadness had been lifted and it had given him a new lease on life. They hugged and laughed and the questions flew, all of them deflected until they sat together around the fire and the crackling rabbits.

"They smell marvelous!" said Vincent. Landon watched as Dr. Kincaid peeked curiously inside one of the empty bags. He had only known Dr. Kincaid a short time, but already Landon knew the old man's great love of a certain kind of food.

"Briney said if I bring you to the party there'll be plenty of Black and Green," said Landon.

"A clever one, that Briney," said Dr. Kincaid. "He knows how I hate parties."

The doctor smiled at the amazing new eight-year-old who had arrived on Atherton. "I suppose we'll have to go, won't we?"

"I suppose we will," said Landon.

Dr. Kincaid glanced at Vincent with a knowing look, and then turned his gaze on everyone.

And this is what he said.

"You can interrupt me if you must, but I think it will be better if you don't. Try to let me tell it all at once, then you can ask your questions."

He had been thinking of how he would tell them on the whole journey home. Dr. Maximus Harding had always loved a good story told well, and Dr. Kincaid aimed to honor the maker of Atherton.

"It took me a while to piece everything together, but after studying the items in his laboratory more carefully, visiting the secret room under the yards, and talking with a lot of people, including Hope, I believe I have the whole of what Dr. Harding has done in hand."

Everyone's eyes lit up at the sound of Hope's name and they all opened their mouths, desperate to ask about their friend. The firm look on Dr. Kincaid's face stopped them all.

"We will get to Hope soon enough," he said. "You have my word. But first to the matter of the chill of winter."

Vincent settled in by the fire and began turning one of the neglected rabbits over the coals. He was content to let Dr. Kincaid tell the whole tale.

"The migration of white Ravens — as you so kindly named them — numbered in the hundreds of thousands. So the first thing we have figured out is this: It would appear Dr. Harding used Atherton not only as a new home for a very few, but far more significantly, as an incubator for something awfully important.

"He was smart enough to realize that telling others would only lead to problems. If Commander Judix had found out — which she almost certainly would have with her powers of persuasion — she might have corrupted everything. Too much meddling and Atherton probably would have never performed its task. Trust me as you go out in the world: Decisions by committee are almost always long in coming and dead wrong. A world-changing vision comes from one person, not five or twenty or a hundred, and more often than not, the best of plans are laid to waste by the many."

Teagan was fidgeting, trying not to ask about Commander Judix. What had happened to her? Was she still in control of Station Seven? Was she even alive? Teagan barely held her tongue as Dr. Kincaid went on with the story.

"The white Ravens could not have been formed by any

other method or in any other place besides Atherton. For reasons I can't fully understand, these incredible objects are the product of a changing Atherton. The swimming Cleaners are involved in the deepest part of the lake, the eels and firebugs and rivers of fire all play their part. I think even *we* play a part. The powder block was the final element, the trigger if you will, that turned the caterpillar into a butterfly."

Dr. Kincaid received some confused looks for this last comment, but he raced onward before anyone could ask a question.

"As I said, the white Ravens left Atherton by the hundreds of thousands, and many of them circle the globe still. They release crystals into the air by the trillions. Day and night, from high in the sky of the Dark Planet, the crystals seem to melt and break free, falling through the muck and filth of a broken world, and in so doing, change everything."

Dr. Kincaid poked his finger at one of the rabbits. "Those are done," he said, his mouth watering at the thought of such a tempting treat. Vincent pulled the spit off and slid the rabbits onto one of the cloth bags. The cooked meat steamed as Dr. Kincaid pulled off a leg and began eating. It was nearly impossible not to ask a question or two while he enjoyed the food, but everyone held firm as they'd been instructed, and after he finished the leg he was back to the story of what they'd found.

"Do you see how that cloth soaks up the grease from the cooked rabbit? The crystals are something like that. They fall, like an endless winter ice storm, and as they fall the smallest particles of the poison on the Dark Planet are collected. But the real magic happens after that, because the crystals aren't like the cloth. They don't hold the things they touch, they make them disappear. Not everything the crystals touch disappears, only the things that have sought to destroy the Dark Planet."

"But what happens —" Samuel started, but Isabel stopped him with a brush of her hand.

Dr. Kincaid, determined to tell the whole story at once, stopped and filled his mouth with a hunk of bread Samuel's mother had made. He followed with a gulp of water. Then, when he was sure they were going to stay quiet, he went on.

"The shards that don't get used up in the air fall to the ground as rain, and you should see what happens when they hit the oceans and land. You can almost feel the Dark Planet being scrubbed clean, getting healthier by the hour as the rain falls and falls and falls. Pollution of every kind sizzles and steams away. It's nothing short of spectacular.

"Ten days ago Vincent and I both noticed the rain getting heavier. But when we woke three mornings ago the rain had turned softer again. By the time we left there was almost no rain at all at Station Seven. And guess what? We weren't wearing masks outside when we left, and neither was anyone else."

Everyone circled around the fire smiled at once.

"It took Gossamer a little longer to clear out the wood than we thought it might. You've never heard anything quite like a dragon going to battle against an army of giant Cleaners and Spikers. Days and nights of fighting, until only the queen Spiker and a very tired black dragon remained. Gossamer is a warrior beyond anything I have ever seen. Vincent and I spent the better part of an entire day watching from Station Seven. The smog had cleared from the forsaken wood. Fallen trees and creatures lay everywhere, and we were able to watch as Gossamer destroyed the last and biggest of Dr. Harding's mistakes. It was the scariest, most awe-inspiring show I've ever seen or ever will see.

"But do you know what the best part was? Through it all, Gossamer never once breathed fire on anything. He was too afraid of burning down a single tree or accidentally setting the Silo on fire. He took one look at the Silo and somehow knew it was filled with children. He protected it above all else, and I don't think a Cleaner made it within a hundred yards of the Silo in all the days of clashing."

Dr. Kincaid paused a moment, pulling once more on one of those floppy ears of his. Then he shook his head with a smile of wonder on his face.

"Do you know, I don't think Dr. Harding ever really grew up? For him, saving the Dark Planet was a story that had to be told, not a problem that needed to be solved. I wonder if we thought more like he did, more magically, if we'd have figured things out on our own a long time ago. It's funny, but I remember he was always terrified of anything that flew. Even small bugs bothered him, but especially birds. And to think he made Gossamer to get rid of all the terrible things he made by accident. Sometimes our biggest fears must be overcome in order to find our way. I suppose Dr. Max Harding knew that better than anyone."

Dr. Kincaid stared at everyone. It appeared that he'd come to the end, and Edgar was the first to venture a question.

"Why didn't you bring anyone back with you?" He was thinking of Hope, but also of the other children in the Silo.

"We can't do that, Edgar." It was Vincent, who had been sitting silently next to Dr. Kincaid the whole time. "We can't start shuttling people back and forth between the two worlds. Atherton wasn't made to accommodate everyone on the Dark Planet. Now, thanks to Maximus Harding, we think the entire planet will survive — so long as they learn from their mistakes. We're sending the Raven back to the docking station, where it will stay."

Edgar wanted to protest, but he knew Vincent was right. Things could get very complicated if people from Atherton wanted to go back and others were constantly showing up from the Dark Planet. What if Atherton failed as the Dark Planet had? There was only one sure way for that to happen: invite a lot of people from the Dark Planet to bring their things and live here. Edgar could already imagine Atherton turned into a place of metal and machines. The best solution was to cut the cord for good now that the Dark Planet had been restored.

Vincent walked to the Raven, went inside, and returned with something in his hands. "Hope asked me to give this to you."

He held out a wooden box and no one knew who should take it. It was from someone they loved and were never going to see again. Edgar felt like he was part of the green team now, but he didn't think it right to take it himself, so he waited until Aggie reached out and gently took the box from Vincent. It was a lot heavier than she'd expected.

"Open it!" said Landon.

Aggie undid a string that held the box shut and took the lid off. Five more boxes were hidden inside.

"Are these what I think they are?" asked Aggie. She handed out the five small squares, each of them a perfect two-inch square.

"Those aren't really boxes you're holding. I mean, you can't open them. They're actually solid glass of a kind that's pretty hard to break. Otherwise we might have all of Atherton crawling with vines."

"But what's inside?" asked Isabel as she watched Teagan turn it in the light and peer inside. Everyone on the green team knew, just like Aggie knew.

"They're the flowers that never bloom, from the Silo," said Teagan. "Only these ones did bloom!"

Dr. Kincaid just nodded. He could see the wonder in their eyes at the sight of the flowers they held. They were shaped just like the Raven with pointy leaves fanning out in every imaginable color. A miniature raven of every color and hue.

There was a note inside the box. Aggie read it out loud, trying her best to imagine Hope saying the words to them.

"'For the green team, so you know you're gone but never forgotten. With love and affection, Hope.'"

Aggie turned the paper over and found a much longer note on the back.

"'I sat on the beach with all the children from the Silo and watched the waves come in last night. We breathed the clean air and roasted fresh fish from the sea. They begged and begged to hear about Dr. Harding, so I told them, only this time we all looked up and imagined you there, watching over us. The story is finally told to the very end, with a happy ending, after all.'"

No one spoke. It was as if everything that needed to be said had been said.

Dr. Kincaid had one more surprise and he pulled it out of his own pocket.

"Landon," he said, "one day soon Gossamer will return to Atherton and make his home here. He'll go back inside Atherton where he belongs. But I promise I'll take you to see him at least once. In the meantime, I found this in Dr. Harding's laboratory. I think it was the first of many models, because as I recall, he always started small and made things bigger until they were too big for his imagination to hold."

Dr. Kincaid held out a model of Gossamer about four inches tall. It was perfect in every detail, right down to the black spike on its nose and the claws on its feet.

"This is way better than a flower!" said Landon, taking Gossamer and smiling bigger than any of them had ever seen him smile before. "And I'm holding you to it, Dr. Kincaid. We'll go together and I'll protect you. He'll listen to me."

"That sounds perfect," said Dr. Kincaid.

After a while they packed up their things and started off, but not before Vincent put the black disk inside the Raven, set its course, and dashed out the closing door. They all watched it disappear over the edge on its way to its final resting spot. On the way back Edgar and his friends heard about what had become of Commander Judix, Station Seven, and Captain Grammel. None of them had fared well in the end, least of all

Grammel, who was thrown overboard by his crew and washed up on the shore near the yards.

When they arrived back at the grove the party at the Inn was in full swing. There were a few thousand people living on Atherton, but this was a private party of about fifty of Dr. Kincaid's closest friends. There was plenty of Black and Green, just as Briney had promised, and lots of laughing and dancing.

After a good deal of celebrating, the sky grew dark and the seven friends huddled together by the door of the Inn. Soon Dr. Kincaid emerged, then Vincent. The nine of them snuck away as they'd long planned to do. Twenty minutes later, the group was standing within a stone's throw of the edge of Atherton.

"Please be careful," said Dr. Kincaid. He'd said it many times, but there was something about a steep drop-off and seven kids that worried him. "Vasher, keep Landon at your side."

Vasher nodded, and then the nine were crawling the final distance, feeling the pull of gravity on their arms as they went. They all arrived at once, even Dr. Kincaid, who loathed crawling on his old knees. But he had to be there when they looked over the edge. He'd made them wait two long months, and now they would see for themselves.

Aggie, Teagan, Landon, and Vasher had seen the Dark Planet only once when they'd first arrived, but they could remember how dirty and dead it had looked.

Now, Aggie was able to believe that not only people could be transformed, but the whole world could be, too. "It's beautiful," she whispered.

"I can't believe how different it looks," said Isabel. "It's so blue and green."

"It's the way it's supposed to look," said Dr. Kincaid. "The way it was made to look before we got our hands on it. The blue is water — lots of clean water — and the green is land."

"What's the white?" asked Vasher.

"Snow and ice," said Dr. Kincaid.

"We'll have to change the name of the Dark Planet," said Vincent. "It's not dark anymore."

"Why not call it by its real name?" asked Dr. Kincaid, remembering what the Dark Planet had been called before.

"I don't know. It seems we could do better. New world, new name — don't you think?"

Dr. Kincaid mulled the idea, but it was Teagan who shouted out the name that stuck.

"It's the Blue Planet now," she said. "Blue is the best color of all, and our old home is bluer than anything I've ever seen."

They stayed there for a long time, looking down at a world once broken. Edgar couldn't help thinking of Dr. Harding. He was so proud of him and all that he'd done, proud enough to never call him his maker again.

"My father did this," said Edgar.

"Hopefully, they won't make the same mistake twice," said Dr. Kincaid, gazing at the Blue Planet. "Because we're not likely to see anyone like your father come along again. He was one of a kind."

They backed away from the edge of Atherton and began walking.

"We better get back to the party before they eat up all the Black and Green," said Dr. Kincaid, his arm around Landon. Landon broke into a run, holding the little model of Gossamer so it looked as if it was flying over his head. And then everyone but the old man was running, racing each other back to the Inn, laughing and dancing in the grey night of Atherton.

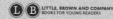